Absolute Responsibility, Strict Accountability

Absolute Responsibility, Strict Accountability

By

Thomas C. Fairley

Copyright © 1999, 2000 by Thomas C. Fairley
All rights reserved.
No part of this book may be reproduced, stored in a retrieval system, or transmitted by any means, electronic, mechanical, photocopying, recording, or otherwise, without written permission from the author.

Backcover Photo by: Denis Lemay
(Front cover used by permission)

ISBN: 1-58820-351-4

This book is printed on acid free paper

1stBooks - rev. 10/24/00

ACKNOWLEDGEMENTS

Books do not appear as a finished product either magically or mystically. Rarely do they spring fully formed from the writer's head as Athena sprang from the head of Zeus.

Instead, they go through a process not unlike the one sculptors use to create their peculiar form of art. It's called addition by subtraction. Maple syrup goes through the same mathematical formulation. Forty gallons of sap must be boiled away to result in a one gallon remainder.

The words in this book, added to blank pages of paper, were all subtracted and/or boiled down from elsewhere and from other people. Probably 90% of what appears in the book evolved from conscious memories and experiences, while at least 10% rose to consciousness from who knows where.

Without conversations and life experiences with John McMenamin, Tim Sullivan, Angus Watkins, Jim Wright, Andy Bahl, and John Reuben, to name but a few, I would have been impoverished for ideas and vocabulary.

Also, from the beginning, Kate Fairley has grasped what I wanted to say and has suggested ways to say it more clearly than I imagined. Her constant encouragement and support made each page possible.

A special thank you to Rob Clouse and Harvey Byrd who moved me through and rescued me from scores of computer quagmires.

My editor, Bob Noonan, has worked his wonders and has put the book into its final form.

At 1st Books, Rebecca Lake, George Karnes and Pat East have brought it to market. Without their labors and all the others, *Absolute Responsibility, Strict Accountability* might still be "out there," trying to subtract itself into print from my life of nearly 60 years.

DEDICATION

This book is dedicated to my wife, Kate. Morning coffee, music, conversation with Kate, and ideas are born.

AUTHOR'S NOTE

In 1958, I was a senior in high school. My father, a skilled tool and die maker, made top wage, $5 an hour, in the local Westinghouse plant. When his company began to ship washing machine parts to Puerto Rico, to be assembled there, I remember his telling me that something was very wrong in our country. It was cheaper, he told me, to pay the freight charges both ways and the Puerto Ricans' wages, than it was to assemble the parts here. This upset him terribly. I didn't understand: what did I know about anything, then?

When his union told him there was nothing it could do, my dad began to research his options. For him, final responsibility to do something, anything, to protect American jobs, rested with the United States Congress. Sadly, he told me that American jobs were "going down the toilet," and that no one seemed "to give a damn, not even Congress."

Today, more jobs than ever are being shipped overseas.

A life-long Democrat, my father voted in every election. He read newspapers, listened to radio and television speeches, and talked to me about the candidates. He thought Adlai Stevenson would have made a fine President. Perhaps he would have. I know my dad thought Mr. Stevenson put together a fine sentence, and that indeed was high praise. As I remember things now, I was impressed by Mr. Stevenson's tone of voice as well as his white suits and hat.

When Stevenson lost twice, my father seemed to lose all interest in politics. He still voted, but it was habit, not conviction. He said the candidates had begun to look and sound alike, and his choices seemed to be between which one wasn't so bad, and which one was worse.

For the last 25 years, I've had the same feeling about politicians that my father had some 40 years ago. I'll never forget the quip offered after the mayor of a town I lived in was sent to jail for embezzling city funds: "We ought to elect Mayor X to Congress, because he really knows how to do it now." Common today, but rarely heard of when I was a boy, are congressional resignations because of sexual misconduct. Today, jail sentences for numerous Congressional Representatives are passed out with regularity. Impeachment charges and censure dominate the lives of our elected officials to the extent that something must change politics as we know them. Clearly, our politicians will not voluntarily change themselves, regardless of their rhetoric. The following is offered in the spirit of helpful observations on the part of a reasonable, law abiding, never-arrested, tax paying citizen.

PREFACE

The following is not a blueprint, although some may see it as such. Instead, it is an outgrowth from an old legend.

Long ago, a certain ruler killed all receivers of stolen goods, and let the thieves go free. For this he received much criticism. To explain himself he used weasels. Servants placed food in front of the weasels, who then carried it back to their burrows. The next day more food was placed before the weasels, but unbeknownst to them their burrows had been filled in. Having no place to hide the food, they returned it.

No receivers: no thieves.

*"...take arms against a sea of troubles,
And by opposing end them....
...To die, to sleep;
...perchance to dream."*

Hamlet, III. i.

PART ONE

Chapter 1

As IRS Director Mildred Hartsfield opened the car door, her head exploded. Conrad Hartsfield's brain could not process what his eyes saw. Only moments ago he had kissed his wife-- something he'd done each morning for the last 23 years. He fainted.

The shooter, Deborah Saraf, did not linger. From her cover she moved deliberately back to the van, where she rapidly changed her clothes. The first part of her task was now complete. She felt no remorse.

Deborah's incursion team removed her sealed portable shooting cover and gun stand. Then they swept the small site for any possible droppings, shoe prints, or traces of anything human. The team also took care of her weapon, a SIG SG 550 Sniper model.

No one spoke as they drove her to a bus line for the next bus into D.C. She carried nothing but an old purse and a shopping bag from J.C. Penny. Williams, her chauffeur, would meet her just past the 18th Street bus stop.

It had begun.

Moments later, and in a far different neighborhood, Speaker of the House Karl Stilski met a similar fate as he opened his front door. Stilski was a large man whose equally large head made it possible to drop him from 600 yards. His decapitated body fell backwards into his home. A widower, Stilski had a housekeeper who found him at 7:30 a.m., when she arrived for work.

The shooter and trainer for all of today's assassinations was Jack Sparks, a man of average height, build, and features. "Sparky" had performed numerous operations like this, as a Special Forces/CIA operative. He left that service in disgust several years ago, honorably discharged after 29 years of selfless service to his beloved country.

Former Lt. Col. Sparks climbed down the ladder erected at the tree base, and walked away. The three members of his team swept the kill site for anything that might give the FBI anything resembling a clue. Satisfied that all was in order, they loaded the equipment into their old VW bus. It was so dirty and so ugly the team knew that nobody would ever remember seeing the old jalopy.

Within minutes of Mildred's death, sirens were screaming from the local EMS garage to the Hartsfield home. Mildred's neighbor and gardening buddy, Louise, from across the street, had seen the execution and called for help. First on the scene were the paramedics from Gallows Road. They thought they'd seen it all, but never before had they observed a human head blown to smithereens. When Sheriff Taylor Lee arrived he called for the coroner, and several detectives from his special crimes unit.

Minutes later Calvin Hunter, the Director of the FBI, was also notified of the crime. He in turn called Sheriff Lee.

"Yes, sir," Sheriff Lee said. "Yes, sir. Yes, sir. But our men...I understand sir." He punched his cell phone's off button and cursed the Feds for what he knew to be gross interference on his turf. Neither he nor any of his officers were to touch anything at the crime scene. As much as he hated obeying that order, he was still a team player, and since Ms. Hartsfield was the director of the Internal Revenue Service, he'd keep everybody away from the crime scene until the FBI got there.

Chief of Staff Joseph McNaughton didn't bother to hang up the phone when he got the call. He jumped from his huge chair and sprinted the corridor to the president's office. Mac never saw Mr. Abernethy, President Huber's secretary, wave him in.

President Huber was talking with two other officials, CIA Director Robert Benton and Head of the Secret Service Charles Newhouse, who were seated in front of him. "Sir," McNaughton shouted, "Mildred Hartsfield has just been shot! She's dead!"

"My God!" said the president. "That makes three, all before 8 a.m."

"What are you saying?" asked the stunned McNaughton.

"The Speaker of the House was killed this morning as he was leaving his house for the Capitol," answered Newhouse. "So was Martin Koyn, chairman of the House Ways and Means Committee."

"What the hell is going on, Charles?" demanded the president.

"It's too early to tell, sir," replied Newhouse. "But first reports indicate these were well-planned operations. We haven't a clue who's responsible yet."

"When will we know something?" asked McNaughton. The intercom buzzed, preventing an answer.

"Yes, A?" the president asked his secretary.

"Line one, sir. It's FBI Director Hunter."

Punching the speaker phone button, President Huber said, "Calvin, I hope you have something good to say to me."

"Well, sir, I wish I did. The fact is we've just had reports of three more shootings. House Ethics Chairman Ron Claxton, Foreign Relations Chair Jennifer St. Claire, and Thornton Quigley of Environmental Resources. They've all been killed."

With that it seemed all the air was sucked out of the room. Each man collapsed further into his chair. No one spoke. The enormity of the killings, the monstrous evil unleashed on these public servants, rendered them momentarily motionless.

Finally, President Huber asked very quietly, "Who's responsible?" No one answered.

National Security Advisor Gene Cummings entered the office and walked straight to the president. "Mr. President, I've just learned that NRA Executive Director Boyd Fuller was shot to death 25 minutes ago."

"That makes seven," said the President. "Turn on the television. Let's see if the media has it yet." Cummings reached for the clicker, and CNN came on immediately.

Correspondent Priscilla Pickering began speaking at once. "We're about one block below the home of IRS Director Mildred Hartsfield, where FBI agents and local Sheriff deputies have her home and several adjoining homes cordoned off. Sources tell CNN that Director Hartsfield has been murdered. We are unable to get any closer because of the heavy security surrounding the area. I've never seen so many deputies in battle gear holding a perimeter in such a lovely residential neighborhood."

The picture changed back to the studio, and CNN announcer Horst Kaufmann said, "This just in: In addition to IRS Director

Mildred Hartsfield, Speaker of the House Karl Stilski, and House Ways and Means Chairman Martin Koyn, three other members of Congress have also been brutally murdered. They are House Ethics Chairman Ron Claxton, Jennifer St. Claire of Foreign Relations, and Thornton Quigley, Environment Resources. Our reports indicate that all six victims were killed by exploding bullets to the head. We go live now to the White House, where CNN Senior Correspondent Travis Funk has this report. Travis, what have your heard?"

"Well, Horst, nothing seems available to the press corps just yet. White House Press Secretary Peter Hopkins has told sources close to CNN that he will have something for us in about 25 minutes. Until then, we know only that the reports you just read indicate five members of Congress, and the Director of the Internal Revenue Service, have all been murdered. No additional details have been released yet. Back to you, Horst."

"This story gets more and more incredible," reported Horst. "Boyd Fuller, Executive Director of the National Rifle Association, was added to the list while Travis filed that report. That makes seven prominent figures murdered this morning. Will that number grow? Stay tuned. We'll be right back."

Chapter 2

From the back seat of her limo, Deborah Saraf watched CNN and listened to the news. Everyone had performed perfectly. Tomorrow, seven others would die. It was time for the first fax to go to CNN headquarters in Atlanta. Last evening she had one of the office 'cleaning crew' program the computer of Ann Campbell, secretary to Boyd Fuller, to send the fax. Additionally, her 'cleaner' planted several small exploding and burning devices that melted Ms. Campbell's entire system when it finished transmitting.

Into the car phone she spoke one word, "Now," then hung up.

The fax from Boyd Fuller's office was transmitted to CNN in Atlanta. It read:

Question: What do you call today's seven assassinations? Answer: A good beginning.

*Wasn't it Mark Twain who said that he'd made an extensive investigation of the American people and could find no native criminal class..."**except Congress?**" I believe he was right. In 1998 Congress passed a $550 **billion** spending bill. That was criminal. This year 2006, the spending bills have gotten so large that they no longer fit on a standard line of print.*

Democrats blame Republicans; Republicans blame Democrats. Result: no one's responsible or accountable. Pretty neat.

An old adage from the pen of the great Irish thinker Edmund Burke is still true: Evil continues as long as good people do nothing. Until today, we were good people. We voted, paid our taxes, raised our families, belonged to churches and civic groups. What we did today makes us criminals. We have become the evil we opposed.

Congress knows how angry we commoners are. It just doesn't care. Nothing we tried before today much mattered. That's why we, a group of citizens, have taken this drastic action.

Neither the Executive Branch nor the Judiciary has anything to fear from us. We plan to rid the country of three problems: (1) present members of the House of Representatives who were not elected to a first term; (2) high officials in the IRS; and (3) officers and lobbyists for the NRA and the Managed Health Care industry. For the present, members of the U.S. Senate will not be executed, unlike the Romans, who assassinated their Senators. The Senate is small enough and smart enough to fix itself. If it does not, we'll deal with it next.

We're sorry it has come to this. But nothing from ordinary citizens gets through to Congress, or gets its attention. It has inured itself against protests, letter-writing campaigns, and e-mail assaults. We the people no longer matter. Phone calls from constituents are turned into comedy as soon as the irate caller hangs up. Staff laughter following the call is deafening. After today, however, Congress needs to remember the story of Pharaoh and the 10 plagues.

No matter what Moses did, nothing got Pharaoh's attention. Moses turned rivers into blood and destroyed farms with grasshoppers, and Pharaoh did not respond to his simple demand. The same thing can be said of our Congress. Our streets have turned into rivers of blood, and Congress gets back into bed with the NRA and approves more legislation favorable to their agenda. No school shooting horror, no-drive by shooting war, no obscene number of callous murders by gun, has gotten Congress to pass significant gun legislation.

We lose 500 family farms each month, and Congress passes more banking laws favoring foreclosure.

Liberals blame conservatives; conservatives blame liberals. Result: no one is accountable or responsible. Pretty neat.

Nothing from common citizens touches the place where a heart used to be in the Congress of the United States. Instead, lobbyists with money are the only ones who have real access to our Representatives. All one need do is watch the suitcases full of money walk into the Halls of Congress. Congressional Representatives keep their doors open and their money pouches ever at the ready for the managed care and gun lobbyist to fill them with cash. Lobbyists suck-off congressional votes favorable to their narrow interests. In that regard congress is the same as past presidents we've known. The form may be different but the results are the same. However, we citizens are the only ones who get soaked and stained.

Some of the thieving lobbyists will soon die, but all those elected Congresspersons who are the receivers of that tainted cash will die sooner.

The only thing that ever got Pharaoh's attention, and resulted in direct change, was death. We promise more of that tomorrow, and tomorrow, and tomorrow.

Chapter 3

White House Press Secretary Peter Hopkins stepped in front of the microphone. His face was pale and his expression quite sober. "Ladies and gentlemen, five members of Congress, the Director of the Internal Revenue Service, and the Executive Director of the National Rifle Association have all been shot and killed within the past three hours. IRS Director Mildred Hartsfield was the first to die. An exploding bullet decapitated her. Speaker of the House Karl Stilski was similarly decapitated. Representatives Martin Koyn, Ron Claxton, Jennifer St. Claire, and Thornton Quigley suffered the same fate. The last to die so far today was Boyd Fuller, Executive Director of the National Rifle Association. And yes, he, too, was killed by an exploding bullet.

"No group has yet claimed responsibility. The President, the Director of the FBI, and the Director of the ATF want to assure the country that they will do everything within their considerable powers to bring these killers to justice. It is too early to give you any details. We have not yet found all the places where the killers hid to do these cowardly deeds."

"But you have found some," interrupted Max Cooper of the UPI.

"We think so" responded Hopkins. "A logical position about 500 yards from Director Hartsfield's home seems to be a possibility."

"Can you tell us anything about that spot?" shouted Phillip Nelson of the *Washington Post*.

"No, I can't. That information is still being sifted for anything that might help the FBI identify the shooter."

Nelson again: "Are you saying the killers left some clues behind?"

Hopkins thought about his answer a bit too long, because in the silence Mitchell Gordon shouted, "What about the bullets? Were any fragments found?" With that, the room seemed unable to contain itself any longer. It began to roar, with everyone shouting at the same time.

Hopkins did not try to reclaim order. He simply stepped down and walked back into the White House, leaving the information-hungry corps to frenzy feed upon itself.

Chapter 4

When CNN news officials received Deborah Saraf's unsigned fax, they sat holding it incredulously. But their disbelief changed quickly when they realized how fortunate they were to be its recipient.

Their conference meeting rippled between euphoria and skepticism. Was it real? Who sent it? Where did it come from? The identifying header said, 'Office of Boyd Fuller, New York City.' Could that be right? Should they broadcast it, or should they turn it over to the FBI?

The decision didn't take long. The fax went straight to the newsroom. Veteran reporter Horst Kaufmann began, "CNN has just received this fax. It reads: 'Question: What do you call today's seven assassinations? Answer...'"

And so it was read publicly for the first time.

FBI Director Cal Hunter's jaw clenched tighter and tighter as he listened to each and every word CNN read from the anonymous fax. They should have sent it to him first. It should not have come out this way.

His phone's red light came on. "Yes, Mr. President. I saw it the same as you did. Yes sir, but what can we do? It's already been aired. Agents in Atlanta are already en route. We'll have it within minutes." With that the phone went dead. The president was already on to something else.

Court order in hand, Special Agent in Charge Gary Wamsley walked into the headquarters of CNN, Atlanta, and presented the paper to news director Francis James. Wamsley figured a scolding wouldn't further his cause. Besides, time was too important to clutter it with ego. All he wanted was the fax.

Director James was in no mood to play games, and clearly wanted to be rid of the FBI. The original fax and five copies were ready and waiting.

"Thank you," was all Agent Wamsley said as he took them. Immediately he exited CNN headquarters and headed straight to the airport, where a department jet carried him and the fax to the crime lab in D.C.

Chapter 5

Agents in New York were already in Ann Campbell's office, removing everything for analysis in the crime lab. Meticulously, Boyd Fuller's office was also searched for anything that might help to identify his killer. Other agents were on their way to Ann Campbell's apartment.

Ms. Campbell greeted them from her specially equipped motorized wheelchair. A car accident had left her paralyzed from the waist down when she was nine years old. She was getting ready to leave for work when the agents arrived. They gave her the few moments she needed to compose herself. Ms. Campbell was made of stern stuff. She had to be.

How could she help? she asked .

Standard questions: enemies, debts, women and/or men other than his wife, threats? Negatives all.

No surprises in the crime lab. Technicians had expected the meltdown they found in Ms. Campbell's computer. This was a first class operation. Every possible component that might contain something, anything, had burned and melted beyond redemption. Nevertheless, the technicians would try. Perhaps some scrap remained.

Nothing did.

Boyd Fuller's computer was a different story. He kept an enemy list. Each name on that list would be checked, and just maybe his killer would be printed out for them. For once they should be so lucky.

The remainder of his files held the standard financial campaign plans, membership rolls, advertising ideas, major supporters, future gun legislation, lobbyist strategies, names in Congress already on board, and names in Congress needing more grease. Lastly, the listing of each vote of each Congressperson on each bill the NRA wanted passed or defeated revealed nothing new to the agents.

Identical investigations were conducted in the offices and homes of the other six victims. Not one shred of evidence was harvested pointing them to the killers.

"Its some group, all right," FBI Deputy Director George Sprong told the assembled task force of special investigators. "They haven't told us their name yet, but as we all know, they will. The lab is bound to come up with some hard evidence to help nail these bastards. Special Agent in Charge of this investigation is Ellen Coaster. Task forces will report directly to Ellen, who in turn will communicate with Cal Hunter. We want them in 24 hours or less. No sleep for anyone until we have the killers in custody."

Ellen Coaster enjoyed her work. It was her life. Never married and never really involved with anyone, she had devoted her life to the Bureau. This was not her first national case, where she was Special Agent in Charge. Nevertheless, it still thrilled her.

After graduation from high school in Warren, Ohio, Ellen joined the Marines. She rose from grunt to Second Lieutenant in six years. By then the shine of the service had worn off, and she didn't see her career path opening much further in the years to come. She applied to George Washington University in D.C., as a pre-law student. After graduation Ellen went to Harvard for her law degree. The Bureau recruited her in her last year of law school, in 1991.

"I'm appointing six tasks forces to work this case," she told them. "Tony Manutti will head up physical evidence. Skyler Robinson's group will analyze communications. Banking and money transactions go to Herford and Hooks. Poisons, guns, bombs, ammunition, etc., Nick Eisenman. Finding their headquarters goes to the mole, Wes Joshua. And last but not least, Shirley Baxter is to head profiling. Director Hunter wants this group in 24 hours. I'll help any way I can, but I need as much detail from you as quickly as you can develop it. Skyler, any first impressions of the CNN fax?"

"Sorry El," Robinson said, " but we've yet to analyze the entire text. I will say this. Whoever they are, they make a strong case for what they've done."

Heads turned to stare at him. The room got so quiet several people forgot to breathe. "You know what I mean," Robinson recovered. "That bit about lobbyists and access. Stuff like that. What'd you think, that I agreed with them? Naw."

The Secret Service was relieved to learn that the president and vice-president were not targets. But could anyone believe killers? What if the executives were next? Different procedures to guard both men descended quietly, but noticeably. Neither official would ever again enter or exit a car, helicopter, or airplane out in the open. Each would board or exit while inside some building that was well guarded and thoroughly searched. Never again would any president be killed on their watch.

They would also do something never done in the entire history of the Secret Service. They would ask for help! It was not their job to guard members of Congress. But clearly, congressional members needed to be watched over.

Charles Newhouse called General Otto Dunlap, Chairman of the Joint Chiefs of Staff. "General, I want you to call up to active service a large number of your national guardsmen and women to help protect members of Congress." The lengthy silence coming from Dunlap unnerved Newhouse. Finally he asked, "Otto, did you hear me?"

"Oh, yes, I heard you," came the reply. "And believe me, there's nothing I wouldn't do to fill your request. But Charles, we both know this is impossible. We'd need an Act of Congress in the first place, and secondly, no member would accept such protection. Image and all, you know."

"I don't give a rat's ass about any of that," Newhouse responded. "Seven more are slated to die tomorrow, according to the fax. What if it happens and we've done nothing to prevent it? Can you live with that? I can't."

"You make a good point, Charles. Let me see what I can do. I'll call you back soon."

Newhouse moved quickly. He placed a conference call to Chief of Staff Joe McNaughton and to National Security Advisor Gene Cummings. Both men were available, and he informed them of his call to General Dunlap. Cummings agreed immediately, but McNaughton opposed the idea strenuously.

"For God's sake Charles," he said, "you'll turn the city into an armed camp. The political fallout will make the president look like he's giving credibility to this group. Cal Hunter has assured us that the FBI will nail them within 24 hours."

Unconvinced, and undaunted by Joe McNaughton's opposition, Newhouse began calling members of Congress to solicit their ideas and support. To his surprise, only one house member showed lukewarm interest in his plan. Most shared Joe McNaughton's view. The killers would be behind bars in 24 hours or less.

Was this just macho bravado, Newhouse wondered, or were members of Congress so far removed from the realities of life that they thought of themselves as immune to everything that effected mere mortals? He didn't know.

One last hope. He dialed the president's office. Mr. Abernethy said he'd make sure President Huber returned his call ASAP.

Five minutes later the president called back. "What's up, Chuck?"

Newhouse hated that appellation, but he let it slide. "Mr. President, I want you to activate National Guardsmen to protect members of Congress. I'm having a difficult time rounding up any support. Secret Service cannot give any personnel to the task. I believe an executive order for some temporary protection would be in order, and I'm hoping you'll do just that."

"Joe McNaughton told me you were moving along those lines," replied the president. "But I'm inclined to go along with Joe. These killers bit the wrong dog. We'll have them by noon tomorrow."

"But, sir...," Newhouse started to protest, but the line was dead.

Chapter 6

Deborah Saraf, the billionaire widow of aerospace magnate Isadore Saraf, Jr., was dying of cancer. After the day's exertion, it was with considerable effort that she showered and changed into a beautiful cream-colored silk pants suit that accentuated her dark, shoulder length hair. In the mirror she noticed that gradual weight loss due to her disease had emphasized her fine cheekbones and jaw line, making her appear more aristocratic than ever. A temporary look, she reflected grimly.

One hundred guests were invited to her home for an afternoon tea and fundraiser for the Washington Symphony Orchestra. Her check for $50,000 was already in the large fish bowl just inside the huge entrance tent leading to her spacious gardens. Of course, for this crowd such charity sums were not seen as a hardship, or even a duty. For them, such gift giving was a pleasure. Besides, the real reason for attending Deborah's tea was to be seen. Only Triple-A list people ever crossed her threshold for this fundraiser. It was a way of checking oneself in the financial reality mirror.

Deborah knew the shocking murders of that morning would have no effect on the afternoon festivities. The assassinations might be a topic for a few dreadful moments, but lighter, more important topics would soon replace them. Topics such as where one would spend one's summer.

The grounds, the gardens, the hostess, the company, the food and drink, were all elegant. Live music from quartets, trios, and quintets, made up of players from the WSO, was heard in various parts of the garden as well as inside the mansion. Guests dressed much the same for today's tea as they did for the Kentucky Derby. The women wore large hats and white gloves. The men tried to outdo each other with brighter and shinier ascots.

The money collected today would exceed $1 million. A pittance for this gathering.

Just as Deborah had expected, there were no cancellations, and zero no-shows. When Dr. and Mrs. Carlton Billings

Thompson arrived, Deborah made a beeline to the doctor's arm. Kisses, kisses. Mrs. T. was also known for her gardens, and she was whisked off by several other guests, who wanted to show her Deborah's newest species of roses. They were smaller and tighter than most. Their fragrance would attract, of all things, butterflies. Imagine that!

"How are you, Deborah?" Dr. Thompson asked. "Is the new medicine helping?"

"I think it's too soon to tell, but I seem to be noticeably stronger," she replied.

Enthusiastically, "Good, good. If you have any problems with it, or if you need to see me, just call. I'll be right over."

"Thank you Carlton. You are a dear."

"Now, now." He waived the compliment away and joined others, who had begun to pull at him for his opinion on one medical problem or another.

Deborah could hardly wait for the last guest to leave. Politeness required everyone to be gone by 5 p.m. sharp, and politeness was this crowd's mantra. She rushed upstairs and changed into beige travel clothes. The old raincoat and hat she wore made her even more invisible. A small and equally beige overnight carry-on bag was packed and waiting.

Williams drove her to the airport, where she avoided traveling in her private jet. Using an assumed name, she flew coach for the three-hour flight to St. Louis. The plane was crowded with businessmen and women. Most seemed preoccupied with tomorrow's presentations. Some listened to music on the headsets built into their seats. Others worked on their portable PCs. She sat by the window, pulled her collar up as high as possible, and covered her face with the old rain hat.

She slept for most of the trip. When she landed she took a taxi to the downtown Quality Inn, where she paid cash for the single room. The motel was crowded and noisy because the Missouri State Gun and Knife Show convention had drawn so many people into town. She'd had very minimal exposure.

Her rifle and bullet were elsewhere, with the team. Having more money than God had its advantages.

Deborah played tomorrow's events in her mind one last time before she turned on the television. The shootings were on every station. She would have turned it off, but the tone of a speaker's voice caught her ear. Senator Paul Young, of Louisiana, was on one of those talk shows.

"...if he thinks he can intimidate me, come on," he growled through clenched teeth. "I haven't forgotten anything the United States Marine Corps taught me." His distinctly Southern vocalizations seemed to intensify with each heavily accented word. Then he reached into his suit coat and pulled out a .45-caliber revolver. "An officer never surrenders his side-arm. And I'll shoot the [bleep] if he thinks he can kill me like he did my good friend Boyd Fuller and the..."

Deborah clicked off the TV. Using her secure cell phone, which was serviced by her own communications satellite, she called the Center.

First ring; "Yes?"

"It's me," said Deborah. "Did you see Senator Young just now?"

"Yes."

"Change one of the team assignments for tomorrow. I don't care which one. Substitute Senator Young, instead. I want him shot in the heart with his own .45, and I want his jaw blown off. Leave him in his back seat, and park the car three blocks from CNN's Washington studio. Also, I want you to add the following paragraph to tomorrow's message; 'Although our first message indicated that the United States Senate would receive a by, Senator Paul Young has made a serious error. Should there be any others like him in the Senate, let his example speak to y'all. It upsets us that Senator Young did not understand. All he really had to do was wait, watch, and change. The death of Senator Young should tell any doubters that we are capable of altering our schedules, should circumstances dictate.'"

T. L. Grimes III, U. S. Navy, retired, the group's communications specialist, sat looking at the wall for a few moments. How could he change an assignment just like that? Deborah knew how long it took to plan each hit. He called Williams.

"Williams, it's Atlas." Atlas was Grimes' AKA. "Deborah just called and wants us to hit Senator Paul Young of Louisiana instead of one of the congressmen on tomorrow's list."

"I'll be right over."

An hour later Williams rode the service elevator to the first floor below street level, and walked briskly to T. L's computer station. "Why?" was all he asked.

"Read it for yourself," said T. L., handing Williams the addenda to tomorrow's fax.

Williams read it impassively. Finishing, he said, "I see."

"What will we do?" T. L. asked.

"Do?" responded Williams. "That's just it. We *do* everything Mrs. Safar has asked." With that he began a systematic schemata, detailing everything the team would require in order to accomplish Deborah's order.

First they needed a plan of Senator Young's home. Simple. T. L. hacked into the central headquarters of the D. C. fire department, and filched the plans within five minutes. The homes of all the Legislators were on file there, in case of any emergency. Next, they needed to know how the Senator traveled from his home to the Senate Office Building each day. Did he drive himself? Unlikely. Did he even own his own car? His wife owned a Lexus, and she was away visiting her sister in New Orleans. That left livery services. There were 13 in the phone book. While T. L. hacked into each one, looking at client lists and schedules, Williams contacted Rusty McCaffry, Melvin Hogan, Mitsi Shigata, and Jan Christianson, other members of the assassination teams.

They all came directly to the Center. Williams told them about the change of plans. He assured them things would work perfectly, and they spent the next two hours rehearsing everything for the changed assignment.

By this time T. L. had found the livery Senator Young used. Records indicated the Senator was picked up at his home regularly at 6:30 a.m. sharp. His usual driver was a man named Hudson. Hudson's picture and home address was also in the file, and T. L. downloaded it for make-up and mask-making purposes.

Chapter 7

The Center. Eighth Street NW at College Street NW, one block from Howard University and Howard University Hospital.

In the early 1920s, the Presbyterians built a large stone church at the corner of Eighth Street NW and College Street NW. The sanctuary, with its long center isle, seated 650 comfortably. Office and educational space added another 4,000 square feet. From 1920 until 1960 that church served God and man. But by 1960, most or all of its founding members had either died, (and certainly gone to heaven), or moved away from the neighborhood. The few remainders who felt a certain loyalty to the old church attended sporadically. Finances fell away alarmingly, while utilities and maintenance costs soared, making a full-time minister impossible to fund. The steady supply of "guest" ministers did not generate any appreciable increases, and soon the church began to deteriorate. An all too familiar scenario, experienced by many major denominations. The congregation eventually dissolved, and the building became the property of the Presbytery of Washington D.C.

Finally, in 1967, an independent Baptist church offered to buy the building for the princely sum of one dollar. Presbytery gladly sold them everything, including the large adjoining gravel-covered parking lot. The congregation took the name 'Ebenezer Baptist Church' because that was the name of Dr. King's Church.

The all-black congregation renovated the building out of current funds, augmented by a considerable loan from the Federal Home Savings and Loan Association. Having done that, the Board of Deacons applied for and received a government grant to build an above ground, five-story parking garage on its half-acre adjoining lot. Congregational members parked there at no cost. The real purpose of the garage, however, was to help the congregation pay down its debt to Federal Home Savings and Loan, from the income generated by other users. Logical customers were people visiting patients at Howard University Hospital, located one block away.

The supporting pilings for the five-story above ground structure went five stories down into the ground. Plans called for the builders to create an enormous two-story underground warehouse facility, directly below street level. The congregation thought it could rent this warehouse space to furniture or appliance companies. The warehouse had its own loading dock and freight-size elevator shaft, which were never completed, off College Street.

The church renovations were completed in 1968 and the parking lot construction was completed in 1969. Projected income from the parking garage never materialized; in fact just the opposite happened. Garage usage dropped dramatically within months of its opening, as security was unable or unwilling to prevent thefts, break-ins, strippings, muggings, and lootings. Routine garage maintenance alone exceeded income. Salaries, insurance, and workers compensation soon put the church further into debt. Nobody ever rented the warehouse space, and so the elevators were never finished.

Unable to continue using the garage because of the negative cash flow problem, the Board of Deacons, in 1971, voted to close the facility altogether. Without the projected income from the parking garage, the congregation was unable to repay its debt out of current contributions, and defaulted on its loan agreement. The S & L ate the debt. What else could it do? In those days, even a nicely renovated old church with an unusable five-story parking garage had no resale value. Soon vandals and drug addicts were seen using the garage as a place to deal and to do drugs. Street people began to sleep in it. At night, small fires in old steel drums were common.

The Board of Deacons pondered what to do with the facility, and finally went to the Federal Government for another grant. This second grant would be used to demolish the garage built by the first grant. The garage had become a health and safety hazard. Result? Request denied. For the next 12 years the same grant application was submitted, and the same results came back. Denied.

Finally, in 1983, a grant was approved for $450,000 to demolish the garage and to haul away the debris. The demolition contract was awarded to General Contractor Harvey Hyde, chairman of the Ebenezer Baptist Church Board of Deacons.

Mr. Hyde hired the Chalmers Demolition Company to implode the structure. Sheldon Chalmers was Harvey's brother-in-law, and together they were going to make a small fortune. All the steel girders, railings and staircases, copper plumbing, wiring, and metal window casings in the office were going for scrap. Messrs. Hyde and Chalmers agreed to split that tidy sum down the middle. Rubble disposal cost only $8 a load at the landfill in nearby Cambria County.

Demolition day arrived. Mr. Chalmers pushed the plunger into the detonation box. A mighty roar sounded, followed by the usual billowing cloud of smoke. When the dust settled, the entire building had collapsed in upon itself.

The ground floor, and the below ground supporting girders, held all five floors worth of rubble above it. Sheldon and Harvey quickly covered the entire project with three inches of asphalt. Also buried, and quickly forgotten, were the two never-used, completely intact floors of underground warehouse space.

Three years later the Ebenezer Baptist Church folded. The city cemented and bricked all the windows and doors before the junkies and the homeless could move in. It was cheaper than demolition. The City did install two basketball hoops for the neighborhood kids. Nobody seemed to care that the building was a community eyesore.

Chapter 8

For quite some time, as her health continued to deteriorate and her incurable cancer worsened, Deborah realized that her remaining time was terribly short. She began to be plagued with a horrible, monstrous thought. She could not bid it away. It would wake her. Perhaps it was the medicine, or perhaps she was losing her mind. How could she have such a thought, when her whole life had been devoted to doing the right thing, and to preserving life?

When her mother-to-be was liberated from Treblinka, and her father-to-be was liberated from Buchenwald, each found a way into the land of Palestine. Hayim Mirsky and Judith Weiss met at kibbutz *Yahad*. *Yahad* meant "community, all together," among other things. Within weeks they married. Deborah Weiss Mirsky was born nine months later.

Judith Weiss died giving her daughter birth, and Hayim was crushed by Judith's death. Had he not seen enough death? Had he not lost everyone in his immediate family? Why his Judith?

At her funeral, Rabbi David Ravnitsky held the newly born Deborah throughout the entire ritual. Highly unusual! As he read or spoke lines from the Bible, he would then whisper something into Deborah's tiny ear. Each time that he whispered something to her, tears streamed down his cheeks and disappeared into his considerable beard.

When the service was over, Hayim Mirsky asked R. Ravnitsky what he said to his infant daughter. "Secrets," was his only reply. Then he pulled Hayim aside and spoke in a whisper that only Hayim could hear.

"Hayim Mirsky, this little baby needs your reserves' reserves. From so far within you that you dare not go there alone, you must pull out more strength than you ever possessed or used in Buchenwald." Such language! Buchenwald was not a word to be spoken, ever again. Hayim was furious. He took day-old Deborah and left the cemetery as quickly as possible.

That night, Judith appeared to him in a dream. She was so beautiful. "Hayim. Hayim. I'll tell you what Rabbi Ravnitsky whispered to Deborah. He said, 'Child, beautiful child, out of suffering you were born and into suffering you will go. One day, with much wealth, you will be responsible...'" Hayim woke before Judith could finish her sentence.

Not long after Judith's death, Hayim learned he had a distant cousin, on his mother's side, who had survived the concentration camps and made it to New York. He made contact and arranged to go to America. The cousin was Isadore Safar, Sr.

With a little luck, and more medical breakthroughs, Deborah's remaining time might be extended for another year or two. And when one's remaining time is known, it has a way of focusing one's attention on what really matters.

Deborah wanted to do something that would affect a significant mind change in the nation. She wanted to help people accept responsibility for their own thoughts and actions.

She had become extremely tired of all the excuses coming from every level of society. It seemed to her that an unwritten contract to fight existed in every segment of the country. It didn't matter anymore who threw the first stone. And the subject didn't matter. Pick one. Any one would do. Abortion? Instant fight. Gun control? Instant fight.

The results were everywhere. Name calling, hate crimes, and the inability to see beyond the end of one's nose, all eventually burned a horrible realization into Deborah's brain. How many times had she listened as criminals claimed that the reason they did their terrible deeds was because as children they were subjected to this and that? Never mind the reality of the video camera taping their crimes. These people accepted no responsibility for their actions. Everything was always someone else's fault!

It was the same in politics. Years earlier, a president had claimed that abuse in his childhood had caused his adult sexual addictions. And though he was found guilty of misconduct and lying, he was not removed from his high office.

Congress was just as bad.

Deborah was profoundly discouraged that there was not a system of strict accountability in place in any segment of society. She remembered what it was like to be the child of Hayim Mirsky. To him she would complain, "But so and so's father lets her..." only to be brusquely cut off by, "But you are not so and so's daughter. You are mine. *And my daughter will not....*" He had instilled in her a sense of responsibility, which she had come to treasure immensely.

She knew society was gravely ill, perhaps as fatally stricken as she was. She felt deep anger and frustration about this, and as she considered the short time remaining to her, unbidden thoughts began to arise in her mind. Serious illness requires serious measures, she thought. Appalling images came uninvited to her nightly. At first she pushed them away. But after a while, they made horrible sense, and she began to entertain them.

One day she received a letter from an old friend, Mitsuo Shigato, saying that her elderly mother had finally died. Mitzi had been born in 1942, somewhere in the middle of Idaho, in one of the detainment camps created for Japanese/Americans during the Second World War. Deborah and Mitzi had met at Princeton University, when Deborah was just a freshman. It was Mitzi's first appointment as an instructor in American History. She was four years older than Deborah. The women recognized that something existed between them before any words were exchanged, and they have been close ever since.

Mitzi had written to tell Deborah the horrible details of her mother's death. The letter broke Deborah's heart. Mitzi's father, Tanaka, had died many years ago, but her mother, Yoshuki, had lived into her tall nineties. Although Mitzi had cared for her at home for as long as she could, the time had finally come when she was forced to put her mother into a nursing home. With old age and memory loss, Yoshuki spoke less and less English and only a few words of Japanese.

The nursing home was owned by Health America, one of the largest managed care companies in the country. On one of her many visits, Mitzi discovered that her mother needed diapering, as she had lost all bowel and bladder control.

Budget guidelines at the home provided only two diaper changes per day per patient. No disinfectants safe for human skin were used to cleanse her or any of the other incontinent patients. Mitzi's offer to buy extra adult diapers for her mother was firmly rejected. Staffing limitations and time constraints were proffered as the reason.

As a direct result of the neglect, sores were common among the patients. The odor alone inside the home was enough to warrant arrests, but it was her mother's skin sores that made Mitzi cry. Eventually, they became so severely infected that they caused organ shutdown from the overload, and Yoshuki finally died in filth and in pain. None of that, of course, was on the death certificate. Heart failure and advanced age were the only reasons stated.

The last lines of Mitzi's letter crystallized every uninvited and horrible thought ever to enter Deborah's mind. Mitzi wrote, "Who's responsible, Deborah? Clearly the nurses did what they were told to do. I don't blame them. Some brought Phisohex from home and used it to clean mother. I blame the owners of Health America, but I blame Congress the most for letting Health America get away with making such large profits at the expense of people like my mother. You and I are not far behind her. Unless we find some way to do something about this, we could be next."

How prophetic, thought Deborah. *Little does Mitzi know.*

Chapter 9

Williams had been Deborah's confidant for many years, and she did not hesitate to talk to him. At first her ideas came out in large, vague blocks. The always imperturbable Williams listened silently, without visible emotion. Then Deborah told him the story of Mitzi's mother.

It affected the normally unflappable man like nothing Deborah had ever seen. He became visibly agitated, and when she finished he spoke.

His dear widowed mother, he told Deborah, had died while he was in Vietnam with the British Special Forces. His sister was there, too, nursing wounded soldiers. He had been horrified to learn that Mother Williams, still living in the mining town in Wales where he grew up, died alone because nobody ever checked to see if she needed or wanted anything. Poor circulation in her legs had caused them to swell, and gradually restricted her movements. He learned later that she had fallen in her small apartment, and she couldn't get up. Osteoporosis made her hip bone fracture causing her to fall. Her body was found nine days after she died because neighbors smelled something putrid coming from her apartment. For years Williams had had recurring nightmares about how long she had lain on the floor, and what she suffered, before dying, and he vowed then that given the chance, he would redress the social injustices that led to his mother's neglect and death. He and his sister were out of country, serving the country, and not one soul took the time to look in on his mother from time to time.

Deborah then spoke of an old legend about thieves and weasels. What's this all about? Williams wondered. Moses and plagues, and comparisons to the American Congress confused Williams even more.

But not for long.

Williams' finest feature was his organized mind. No matter what the problem, Deborah knew he would always recommend the best solution. But after several failed attempts to lead him to make a suggestion, Deborah gave up and spoke the unspeakable herself.

She told him she had concluded that the only way to right some of the wrongs in our country before she died, was to kill most members of the House of Representatives, high IRS officials, NRA officers, and some lobbyists for the NRA and the Managed Health Care companies. She was convinced that those particular groups were the most responsible for the nation's ills, and that they ought to be held accountable for their actions.

At first Williams was not sure he heard her correctly. He usually understood exactly what Mrs. Saraf was talking about, but never in his wildest imaginings would he have thought she could conceive an idea like this. This was not the Mrs. Saraf he knew and worked for. Perhaps it was the new medicine.

Deborah dropped the subject, and Williams left, his impervious calm deeply shaken. But as he pondered her words, his systematic thinking processes, and his own deep anger over his mother's terrible death led him to accept Deborah's idea. His intense loyalty to her sealed his final decision. A man of action by nature, he immediately began planning and exploring possibilities.

Days went by before Deborah broached the subject with him again. This time he was ready.

"There's a facility," he began, "at Eighth Street NW and College Street NW, one block from Howard University and the hospital. It's been vacant since 1986. It's a rather substantial building, with some very unique features."

Interrupting, Deborah said, "Williams, what does your rather substantial building have to do with my awful ideas?"

"Just give me a few moments, Mrs. Safar," he continued, "and if you say stop after that, I will."

He began with a history of the building and the parking lot. The church could be purchased from the city for little money. Substantial funds would be needed to renovate it, and to use it as a legitimate, privately funded social welfare agency. A non-profit corporation in a name of their choosing would serve as their front. The facility would need a director who had to be an integral part of the entire plan. Computer literacy classes would be offered there. Meals would be served, and after-school programs for latchkey kids and other at-risk children would cover things quite nicely. Tutors from nearby Howard University would be paid to teach children what they needed to know for their grade level. Clothing would be collected and dispensed there. A public bath would be installed in the basement. Counseling would be available. Battered women with their children could go there for shelter. All of the open space in the former sanctuary would have to be made useable for dormitory purposes. A paid security staff would see to it that order was maintained, and that nobody would get near a long forgotten, underground warehouse adjoining the old church.

Deborah was fascinated. Williams had not only grasped the enormity of the project, but he also had found the perfect headquarters whereby she could, and would, succeed.

The never before used two-story underground warehouse facility was the key to everything. It would serve as the Center of operations. Only a great deal of money and meticulous planning would turn it into a nerve center for the group of assassins Deborah and Williams needed. The warehouse had to be renovated at the same time the old church was being worked on, so as not to call attention to it.

With the help of Deborah's attorney, Williams purchased the old church from the city through a non-profit, social service agency they created, and which Deborah funded. The agency was to be known as *Been There, Done That.*

Construction workers came and went. Some worked on renovating the old church while others worked on the underground Center. All they knew was that they were finishing the old warehouse facility started long ago, so the social service agency could store donations. Air conditioning and electrical installations and plumbing were simply normal activities at such a job. Installing the freight elevator required no more explanation than anything else. It's true, all those construction permits looked legitimate, but the only real ones were for the old church. Everything else was bogus. Inspection approvals for all works were just for the old church. That the contractor accepted a very large extra cash payment not to document or report this underground construction activity, was just part of the cost of doing business. Williams paid $2.6 million extra to keep this construction out of sight and off the public record. When all was said and done, the Center didn't exist.

The two underground floors were 80-feet by 50-feet each—totaling nearly 8,000 useable square feet. Ceilings were 12-feet high. The first floor would be for all the computers, printers, and very sophisticated communications equipment needed. The photography lab, make up areas, and supplies were also there. T. L. Grimes, the old submariner, was in charge of all communications. Everything he needed was delivered at the same time the computers and other supplies were brought to the social service agency in the old church.

The lower floor was for training, and for all activities necessary to complete each assassination. It was there, too, that actual practice sessions for all the assassinations were conducted. Guns and ammunitions were stored there. Laboratories for making poison, bombs and bomb making equipment were also on this lower floor. So too was the paint and mechanical shop where the vehicles were maintained and repainted.

All supplies were delivered to the unloading docks in the rear. After unloading, the truckers pulled away just the same as they did from any job. Only then were the computers for the social services agency separated from the computers for the Center. So too were the guns, ammunition, and all other Center supplies separated from those needed to run the social service side.

When the oversized single freight elevator descended one floor, it opened to the left, into an open cavity under the church, which stored all donations and supplies for the social services agency. Shelving everywhere held foodstuffs. The great shower room was there. Used clothing was washed, ironed and distributed there. Paying jobs were had there. It was a city within a city. This space could be sealed off when necessary, by a padlocked, solid swinging gate.

To get into the Center from the same elevator, T. L. created a small transmitter that looked like a powerful light hanging from a key ring. All of the assassins had one. When the elevator door closed and the small light was pressed, the solid swinging door on the left side, leading into the social services storage area closed automatically. The entire right side of the elevator then swung open into a 12-foot long, 12-foot wide, 12-foot high corridor that led into the first floor of the Center. When larger items needed to be unloaded, the opening device was pressed twice, and the back of the elevator opened as well. Vans used in the shootings were brought in through this elevator, to be repainted and repainted.

Williams knew that money was not the problem. The real problem was recruitment. Who would join them? How could they all be trusted? Where was he to find the necessary number of people with the skills and knowledge and commitment to do this impossible job? For nearly six months daily discussions went back and forth between Williams and Deborah. How about this one? Why not that one? The two conspirators became one machine.

The first person hired was the *Been There, Done That* Director, Ms. Clarissa DeBeau. Ms. DeBeau was retiring after 30 years of service as a social worker. Nearly everyone in D.C. who had ever been in need, knew Ms. Clarissa.

Williams saw her on the 6 o'clock news: a pretty woman, smartly dressed, and very articulate. According to the news interview, Ms. Clarissa had worked her entire adult life for one social service agency or another. She'd seen and done it all. She called everybody "Shoog," short for sugar, but when she spoke Williams instantly picked up on her frustration, in the hidden irony of her politically correct statements. Yes, she seemed to say, I'm a doer of good. But I haven't really been able to accomplish much, because of the system.

Williams promptly contacted her via fax. If he could recruit her, her good name would give weight and credibility to the venture.

When she arrived at work on her last day before retiring, she found William's fax. It read, "Ms. DeBeau, please meet me at 3:30 tomorrow afternoon at the Mayflower Hotel. I wish to offer you a short-term job, for which you will be paid a handsome sum. Williams." Intrigued, she met Williams for tea the next day at the Mayflower Hotel.

Ms. Clarissa DeBeau was prompt. The maitre d' escorted her to the table Williams had selected. "How nice of you to come, Ms. DeBeau," he said. "I'm Williams. May I pour some tea for you?"

Clarissa smiled to herself. The fellow looked like that actor in the movie Who Killed Roger Rabbit.

Then he began to explain a plot to assassinate more than half of the members in the House of Representatives, as if he was discussing an innocuous business deal.

Clarissa had Cajun savvy, combined with very thorough D.C. smarts. After listening for only a moment, she realized she was in deep trouble. Perhaps she hadn't heard him correctly. But if she had, this funny looking little Welshman was asking her to become the first person in a group that planned to kill most of the members of Congress, high ranking official of the IRS, and the NRA, and many lobbyists for those groups. She herself would not have to kill anyone, of course. All she had to do was what she had done all her adult life - social work. She was to become the head of a legitimate social service agency that would be a front for the assassination scheme.

She was barely able to breathe as Williams explained the entire plan. It would not take more than three months to do the deed once the killing began, but it would take two years of planning, recruiting, and training before it was all over. She would be paid $5 million for her efforts. Ms. Clarissa, who had always enjoyed robust health, nearly had a heart attack when she heard the sum. The most she had ever made in any one year was $42,800. She reached for her tea but could not pick up the cup, her hands trembled so badly.

Williams continued, "In addition to the $5 million, you will receive a $7,000 monthly stipend. I'll need an answer before I leave, Ms. Clarissa. I would not want you to run to the authorities with my story."

Was that a threat, she wondered? This nice little man seemed harmless, but there it was. It went against every nerve and fiber in her body to think of participating in this evil scheme.

She could go to jail just talking about such a conspiracy. She wanted to bolt and run, but her feet seemed to be glued to the floor.

But she was so tired of getting nowhere with her work. The stream of needy people coming through her doors had grown larger each year, rather than decrease because of her efforts. She had testified numerous times before Congressional Committees who had oversight for this program or that. Not once had she left those sessions feeling as though she had accomplished anything. In reality, nothing ever changed. She had just been going through meaningless motions with her testimony.

"You did say $5 million? In American money?" she asked weakly.

"That's correct. Also," he continued, "a bottomless account for the *Been There, Done That* social service center has been opened at the Howard University Branch Bank of First City Federal. It simply needs your name on a signature card. You will be in charge of programming, hiring staff, buying supplies, and anything else you can think of. I'll hire contractors and the security people, and accountants will handle all paperwork, the payroll, et cetera. Your signature will be the only one that counts for everyday expenses. You'll never have to worry about subtracting anything in the checkbook. It doesn't matter what you spend. The checks will always be covered. You'll never have to submit an idea, or an item for purchase, to another committee or board for approval. We'd like you to start by going over to First City Federal and signing the signature card waiting for you. Then, go to work. We've bought the old Ebenezer Baptist Church at College and 8th NW. Just get the account opened, and we'll go from there."

Ms. Clarissa had been bombarded with too much information, but she finally asked, "We? You keep saying 'we,' but all I see is you. Who is the 'we' part of this? You aren't Mafia, are you?"

"Right," said Williams. "I mean, no. Does the name Deborah Saraf mean anything to you? No, I guess not. Well, Ms. Saraf is the prime mover, here. You'll meet her very soon. I've worked for her for a very long time. I'm sure you two will get along quite nicely. She is so tired of the excuses and lack of responsibility in this country that she sees this as the only way to change things before she dies. Is there anything else, now?"

"Why is she dying?" Ms. Clarissa almost whispered.

"Incurable cancer," was the also whispered answer. Then, "See you tomorrow at the old church. Ten a.m. sharp."

Ms. Clarissa sat for a few minutes after Williams left thinking of the thousands of souls she had watched suffer, and even die, because of a cold, uncaring, penny conscious government. She thought of her years of exhausting work to effect change, and her failure and frustration. Perhaps it was time for more drastic measures. And the *Been There, Done That* would be a legitimate, powerful agency where she might actually help people directly.

She knew how to make decisions under pressure. I'll be there, she said to herself.

Williams told Deborah that he needed a minimum of $600 million to complete the assassination tasks. The funds were to be withdrawn and re-deposited over a two-year period, in order to attract as little attention to the transactions as possible. Numerous new, numbered accounts, all offshore, would respond electronically, when needed, to each deposit or payment request. Monies would then appear in the vendor's account, and names would be completely eliminated. Each $5 million payment for project workers would be listed as a trust account for some individual, which the assassins and associates, like Ms. Clarissa, could access after all the deeds were done. Costs for the *Been There, Done That* and its needs were in addition to the $600 million. Its separate functioning would go on long after the project was completed. The endowment Deborah established would see to that.

The very first item needed on the long list Williams produced was a private and secure communications satellite, one that would not be susceptible to Echelon and its powerful, long range ability to listen to anything and everything that was transmitted and/or printed. Each year since Echelon had been launched and activated, it had received updates, making it nearly impossible for any form of communications to be safe from its ability to know everyone's business.

Williams had contacted a Japanese aerospace company, and informed them that an anonymous donor had made it possible to build and launch a small communications satellite that ostensibly would serve the Japanese embassies in the U.S.A., Canada, and Central and South America. Kishito Aerospace got the contract. The satellite's real purpose, however, would be to serve Williams and the Center. After the satellite was operational for about two months, the Center would destroy three-fourths of its capacities, the part that served all the Japanese embassies. The one-fourth of the satellite capacity that remained operational would respond only to the Center. On the satellite map, it would register as a non-functional failure, condemned to circle in its tiny orbit for many years into the future, emitting an aggravating white noise for anyone who cared to listen. In reality, it would be able to mask its messages in that white noise, and have them reassembled in the Center. This special satellite with its capacity to hide signals from Echelon cost nearly $40 million. The engineer who sabotaged the bird was Mitzi Shigato's younger brother, Nomo.

Chapter 10

Williams had served Ms. Safar for the last 18 years, and her husband Isadore until his untimely death five years ago. Isadore, a tall, slender, darkly handsome man with a scholarly demeanor that belied his acute business ability, had been surprised one morning when he entered his locked office and was greeted by a strange little man.

"Good morning, sir." Without the slightest hesitation in his speech, the man continued blandly, "I'm Williams, and I've taken liberty to serve tea and jellied muffins."

Isadore Safar, Jr. was not a man who liked surprises. He especially did not like to be caught off guard. This William character had managed to do both. And just how did he get past the security system and into his locked office? In spite of himself, Isadore responded, "Thank you, Williams. And in whose debt am I for this treat?"

The phone rang, as if on cue, and Williams said, "I believe there's your answer, sir."

It was Deborah. "Isadore, have you met Williams?" she asked.

"I have," he answered.

"Good," was all she replied, and hung up. It was settled.

"Will you be needing anything else, sir?"

"How about an answer, or a clue as to what's going on, here," he bristled.

"I'm Williams, sir, and I'm here to serve you and Mrs. Safar."

"Really? And just how did you get to do that?" Isadore asked.

"Let's just say, I came highly recommended," he answered. Without another word he was through the door and on to his next task. Isadore never again asked either Deborah or Williams about Williams' employment. Isadore trusted his wife's judgement completely, but in addition the little man's carriage and manner had impressed him. Isadore knew competence when he saw it, and in William, he really saw it.

Williams had contacted Deborah just the week before when Isadore was out of the country on business. He appeared at the mansion and asked to speak with her. She was disinclined to grant him the time, but his lovely accent and his audacious manner intrigued her. When he told her that her cousin Hannah Minsk had sent him, Deborah knew that she must at least see him. She would have hired him for his accent, alone, but there was something in the way he represented himself that made her listen to what he said.

"You and your husband need me, ma'am. I'll be your servant and protector like no other," he said.

"Protector?"

"Yes, ma'am, protector," he responded.

"You mean guns, and all that?"

"No ma'am, not unless that's necessary.".

"But you could and would use guns in our service if necessary?" she asked.

"In the blink of an eye," he replied.

"Why us, and why now?"

He replied, "All in good time, ma'am, all in good time. But I will tell you this much. You can count on me. Hannah knows that, first hand. She thinks I should now serve you and Mr. Safar. I think she's right."

The interview was over at the mention of Hannah. She was Deborah's only cousin, and the most interesting woman she had ever known. If Hannah thought she needed this fellow, that was good enough for her. She hired Williams immediately.

He told her he expected to be paid $9,000 per month, by electronic transfer to the National Bank of New Zealand in Auckland, and he detailed what additional expenses were to be covered. Deborah agreed. He would start at once by assembling his possessions and installing himself in the mansion, in rooms of his choosing. When Isadore returned from his trip, very late at night, Deborah and Williams had already planned their surprise introduction at his office the following morning.

He started by ordering a new security system and supervising its installation. He had existing fencing electrified, and made other hidden changes to create a strong defense against kidnapping and other crimes and indignities. He also served as chauffeur, butler, groomsman, groundskeeper, and Mr. Fixit.

Isadore was given a lesson in Williams' other assets only weeks after he was hired.

He and Deborah had to leave the symphony early because suddenly she felt ill. It was the first time Isadore could recall her ever feeling unwell in her entire adult life. She thought that perhaps something she had eaten for dinner wasn't agreeable. Little did she suspect it was the first sign of a fatal illness.

Isadore left Deborah in the lounge and walked toward the limousine parking area. He never saw either man. The large one grabbed Isadore from behind and held him motionless, while the other reached into Isodore's coat for his wallet. From nowhere Williams appeared, and in a blur of movement broke the thief's offending hand and arm. The second man dropped Isadore and started to run. Williams tripped him, causing him to hit his head on the curb and knock himself out.

"This way, sir," Williams said calmly as he led Isadore to the waiting limo. They drove to the front door and Williams waited while Isadore retrieved Deborah from the lounge. Neither man spoke a word to her about the incident.

Isadore Saraf was a tremendously successful aerospace engineer by training, temperament, and good management. He owned and ran 26 companies in 12 countries, and was looking to double his extensive holdings within the next two years. When he died in his sleep, Deborah was completely unprepared. After all, he wasn't the one who had health problems. Deborah suddenly found herself at the head of a global business entity, for which she had no training, and certainly no taste. It was Williams who suggested a management plan that would realize Isadore's dreams, and more than double Deborah's already considerable fortune.

The idea was to triple production everywhere. Williams' first action was to double the sales force. Third shifts were added to production lines. Large weekly bonuses were paid, based on production. Williams promoted, for example, the smartest tool and die makers to act as management intelligence. They stayed in production because they were excellent craftsmen, but management no longer said to them, "Do it this way, I don't care what *you* think." On-line production workers everywhere now had a large say in how the lines were run, and how people were treated. If production could be tripled using this new plan, then it was to be done. After all, bonuses were paid on production and sales.

At first, mutual respect was grudgingly established, but soon afterward they all wondered why they had not always worked this way. People actually looked forward to going to work.

With orders filled at their highest levels, and with new orders streaming in, Williams knew it was time to sell everything. Three logical buyers were approached. Each was willing to pay the asking price of $27 billion. However, none of the deals could be consummated when the word "anti-trust" began to appear in the media. Politicians were soon heard mouthing the same pejorative. All of the problems placed in the way of closing the deal emanated from Congress. Surprise! Congress said that if any one of the three buyers gained the entire Safar holdings, it would create an unfair trade advantage and hardship for the other two. In the end, the companies were broken up and sold piecemeal. When the sales were completed and the taxes paid, Deborah received only $9.5 billion. Had Congress not meddled in her affairs, she would have realized over $12 billion after taxes.

Chapter 11

The morning after Deborah's WSO fundraiser, she rose quite early and made some tea in her motel room. She also ate the bagel Ken Springfield brought to her from the deli across the street. At 7:30 she left the room. Ken made sure nothing was left behind that could possibly identify Deborah. He had been trained at the Center to use the powerful battery-operated tiny vacuum. No hairs could escape its suction. All dander from pillows was sucked into its bag. Crumbs met the same fate. Prints were wiped clean. Her cup was washed twice and dried with a towel Ken brought for that purpose. Drains were flushed twice with Drano.

It hadn't taken a lot to recruit Ken Springfield. A quiet man, deeply tanned from years in the sun, sinewy and powerful from constant physical work, he had been a farmer in Iowa, until he lost the farm three years ago. His great grandfather bought one square mile of land in 1886. His grandfather doubled the holdings in 1919, and his father, Kenneth Sr., doubled them again in 1941. Ken held onto his family's farm as best he could for as long as he could, but three consecutive years of drought dried up more than just his land. With no income, and no way to repay outstanding loans, Ken lost everything that had been in his family for 120 years. No amount of pleading with banks; no calls or letters to his congressman, had helped. He'd lived a righteous life and worked hard for the American Dream, but his dream became a nightmare when the bank foreclosed. Now new $230,000 homes littered his pastures and cornfields. It has become an all-too-familiar story.

Williams saw Ken on television, moving his family out of their spacious farmhouse and into public housing in a nearby town. He called information for Ken's new number, and contacted him immediately. Could Ken get away for two years for a job offer that sounded mysterious, if not downright shaky? Impossible. Why? Family and friends topped the list. Williams finally persuaded Ken to come to D.C. for less than 24 hours.

All he had to do was drive to the airport and pick up his prepaid ticket.

In the end, it was the chance to do something to right the terrible wrongs going on in the country that convinced Ken to join the team. The money was great, but it was the larger good he felt he could do that won him over. Of course, providing his family with a very healthy living wage while he was away didn't hurt. He was also able to negotiate college expenses for his children.

Deborah drove to the kill site in the rental Ken Springfield had driven to her motel. It was exactly 14 miles from the Quality Inn where she had stayed. Maxon Stroble, a second member of Deborah's team, had her firing cover and loaded rifle already in place. Max's only daughter, Betty, had been raped, shot, and stabbed to death in her college dorm several years earlier. Her murderer was not convicted because the police had failed to obtain a proper warrant before they broke down his door and arrested him. Max, a sensitive man, had withdrawn into himself to deal with his great loss and grief. The resultant strain caused his marriage to fail, and he was left adrift. His aloofness ultimately made him friendless. He had done odd jobs to survive, until this opportunity was offered.

Judy Morton, 46, an alert, short-haired brunette, the last member of today's St. Louis team, was the van driver. Her husband and three kids had all died in a drive-by shooting. It all happened so fast. She had run into the drug store to fill a prescription for her youngest daughter. When she returned to the car, she found them all dead. Gang bangers missed their target and hit her precious family instead.

Judy was tough as nails, and had faced her loss squarely. After finding her family dead, reality never again intimidated her. When Williams approached her she accepted immediately. An apt pupil, she excelled in the training. She liked what she had become part of.

Before first light, Max and Ken planted a tiny bomb where the rim touched the right front tire of Rudolf Mann's rental. Mann was the Executive Vice President of the National Rifle Association, and had come to St. Louis to address the Missouri

State Gun and Knife Show that morning at 9:30. A radio transmitter would explode the bomb and ruin Mann's tire. Max and Ken had practiced this operation at the Center for days. Each man knew exactly how to do everything.

Mann had elected to stay with childhood friends who lived in the suburbs, rather than in a downtown hotel near the convention center. That meant a longer, more secluded drive to the show. It was ideal for Deborah's purposes. The operatives knew the exact route he would take, and waited patiently in their positions.

From the van, Judy watched as Mann's car came into perfect position. She signaled Max, who pushed the transmitter's button that exploded Mann's tire. Mann's right front tire burst. He fought the beast for a few feet, and managed to pull the car off the road. Cursing, he walked to the rear of the car, opened the trunk, and took out the jack and donut-sized spare. When he knelt down to remove the hubcap with the end of the jack handle, Deborah fired, and Rudolf Mann was dead.

Deborah walked away from the scene and drove her rental to a downtown, metered parking space, where she left it and caught a cab to the airport. Judy, Max, and Ken would turn the rental in before they left the area. As before, the shooting scene was sanitized. Deborah's gun was in the van and the three were gone before the first motorist noticed anything wrong.

Senator Young's driver pulled into the Senator's driveway at precisely 6:30 a.m. Hudson had driven the Senator for the last nine years. A Hudson look-alike had been created back at the Center. The real Hudson had been induced to sleep late that day. With barely a nod to his driver, the Senator stepped into his car, busily reading the morning paper.

Suddenly Paul Young felt as though he was being crushed in a vice. Russell McCaffry, the youngest team member, a former Ranger who had been assigned to retrieve the mutilated bodies of his buddies while serving in Somalia, had removed the supporting material behind the Senator's seat. From his position in the trunk, Rusty thrust his powerful arms through holes in the seat he'd made earlier, and held Senator Young in a vice grip.

The older man, though very strong, was no match for the younger ex-Ranger.

Mitzi Shigato hopped over the front seat, where she had been crouching out of sight, and placed a net over the Senator. Rusty pulled the net's restraints through the armholes and tied them off inside the trunk. Paul Young wrestled and swore and tried to kick, but he only tangled himself more and more. Beaten, he lay still, awaiting his suspected fate. Perhaps he could reason with his captors.

He couldn't.

They drove the senator to a deserted soccer field parking lot not far from his home and held him upright, while the look-alike Hudson shot him once in the heart with his own gun. Rusty had entered the Senator's residence earlier that morning and removed the weapon from the gun case. Melvin Hogan, a Vietnam vet who lost most of his left leg to the VC's version of a Claymore mine, was the shooter as well as the driver. He turned the dead Senator's head and face so he could shoot the jaw off with a single bullet. Then all three got into the front seat and Melvin drove, as instructed, to the drop site three blocks away from the Washington CNN headquarters.

Jan Christianson, bent and round-shouldered, at 67 the oldest member of the team, was sitting in a car when he saw the Senator's vehicle approaching the drop spot. Jan's wife had died several years ago when her managed health care provider denied her treatment. They had classified the treatment "experimental," and anything experimental wasn't covered. Jan was very familiar with the health care system; his left knee had disintegrated to the point where it caused him to veer left when walking. He'd needed an operation for years. He was also an easy recruit.

Jan eased the boosted car he was driving in front of Senator Young's, and waited while Melvin, Mitzy, and Rusty finished their work. They left the Senator's .45 in the front seat, in plain view. When the team got into Jan's car he pulled away from the scene as though he and the others were tourists visiting the city for the first time. The Louisiana tag on Jan's "borrowed" car was a nice touch, they all agreed. Its real owners were still sleeping in their comfortable beds at the Twelfth Street Holiday Inn. Unless they were mileage-checking freaks, they'd never know the car had been moved from where they'd parked it the night before.

Chapter 12

Hermann Torrence, Deputy Director of the IRS, and four more members of Congress, all suffered the same fatal flat tire syndrome visited upon Rudolph Mann. The reports began to filter into the FBI, and by 10 o'clock it was very clear that seven more very public people had been assassinated.

President Huber called a Cabinet meeting. First to report was FBI Director Calvin Hunter. "So far, Mr. President," he said, "we have yet to turn up a shred of evidence that will help us identify the killers. They're real professionals, that's clear. We think we can identify some of the places where they hid, but there's not a twig or a hair or anything left that we can use. It appears as though sweepers came in behind the shooters, and sanitized the area."

An aide to President Huber entered the room and handed him a note. He cleared his throat. "Everyone, please. CNN is about to broadcast another message from the killers."

The four television sets in the room came to life. Johnny Marshall was in mid-sentence: "...this fax came in just moments ago from the St. Louis Convention Center, where the Missouri State Gun and Knife Show is under way. It reads:

Question: What do you call today's seven assassinations? Answer: Boring. Tomorrow's will be spectacular. We're sure we'll have your undivided attention, by then.

We're sorry it has come to this. But Congress will not change itself. The evidence is too great to the contrary. The NRA, for example, has lists of Congresspersons who are already willing to vote exactly as the NRA wants them to. The NRA also has lists of Congresspersons who require a little more "grease" before they get behind the NRA agenda. Grease. That was the actual word on Boyd Fuller's computer. The meaning is quite clear, wouldn't you agree? When the FBI removed his computer, that's the word they found. Ask them. We're sure they won't tell you, but we read that file before the FBI seized it.

Please listen to us very carefully. All of this killing could end immediately if Congress will go into session right now, and pass legislation prohibiting the sale of ammunition to anyone. The second requirement for us to stop is for Congress to pass legislation outlawing lobbyists. We want the penalty for selling ammunition, and for working as a lobbyist, to be death, but we'd settle for life in prison. However, we're sure that Congress, like Pharaoh of old, will only harden itself all the more. 'Nobody will intimidate me, huff and puff, and huff and puff some more.'

Either this Congress will pass such legislation, or by the time we are finished, those replacement Congressmen and women will. We are not sickos whose ideas are from Mars. Most of the American people agree that the Second Amendment gives law abiding citizens the inalienable right to own and to keep guns. Believe it or not, we support the Constitution. However, it says nothing about ammunition, and as we all know, it is really ammunition, not guns, not people, that does the real killing.

Most of the American people agree with us that lobbyists own and control Congress. I personally would love to run for congress on the 'Dishonest Ticket'. Elect me, not because I'm a public-spirited citizen committed to your good. Rather, elect me, and at the end of two years I'll tell you, to the penny, how much money lobbyists have left in my office to buy my vote. If those who carry money into congressional offices, where it is greedily awaited and eagerly received, are no longer welcome, think of the good that will be restored to the American people.

Now about Senator Young. Although we indicated in our first message that the United States Senate would receive a by, Senator Paul Young made a serious error. Should there be any others like him in the Senate, let his example speak to y'all. It upset us that Senator Young did not understand. All he really had to do was wait, watch and change. The death of Senator Young should tell everyone that we're capable of altering our schedule, should circumstances dictate just such a change. We're still of the same mind that the rest of the Senate is capable of fixing itself. More tomorrow.

"We're dealing with maniacs!" shouted Treasury Secretary Butterfield.

"Not so," answered Charles Newhouse, Head of Secret Service. Without asking presidential permission, Newhouse continued, "We are dealing with an extremely well organized, well financed, well trained group of seemingly ordinary people, who have proven their abilities to kill anyone they target. As evil as we know it to be, this group wants to get the attention of the United States Government. Believe me, it has mine."

Joe McNaughton, Chief of Staff lost it. "God damn it Charles, are you saying you agree with these monsters?"

Without rancor or malice in his voice, Newhouse looked at Joe McNaughton and said, "Yes."

The room exploded. "You're fired!" McNaughton shouted above the uproar.

President Huber sat like a stone. He was caught so off guard that National Security Advisor Gene Cummings filled the vacuum. "Joe, you don't have the authority to fire anyone, let alone Charles Newhouse," he said.

Newhouse rose from his chair and said, "That's all right Gene, I quit. Nobody listened to me yesterday when I begged almost everyone in this room to let me use the National Guard to protect members of Congress. Twenty-four hours, that's what I was told. Twenty-four hours and the killers would all be in custody. Calvin, your 24 hours have come and gone, and you've had another set of seven prominent people assassinated. Are you any closer to catching the killers today than you were yesterday? No? I thought not. I'll have no more blood on my head. But when every last member of Congress has been assassinated, perhaps then you'll wish you had listened to me."

As Newhouse turned to leave, President Huber found his voice. "Charles, I'm sorry that I didn't listen to you yesterday. You have my ear now. Please, tell us what you think."

Funeral arrangements were being made for the second set of seven victims. Two from the first group were to be buried the following day. It was well known that the funerals of Jennifer St. Claire and Karl Stilski would have large contingencies of congressional representatives in attendance. Stilski was from Chicago. He was a popular eight-term speaker who knew everyone, and who controlled power and authority to his advantage. More than half the Congress would fly into O'Hare for the few hours it took to bury him. St. Claire was from Miami. She wasn't well loved by her housemates, but they all agreed she did not deserve her violent death. Far fewer members of Congress were in Miami than were in Chicago.

As many as 75 members of the House stayed in D.C. Most were afraid to attend the services, and they excused themselves by playing the "pressing business" card.

Charles Newhouse was listened to. At all the funerals, on either side of each Congressperson, stood a National Guardsman. Few Congresspersons groused publicly. Most were grateful for the protection.

No legislation was passed that day, outlawing either ammunition sales or lobbyists. Nor would there ever be, by this Congress.

Chapter 13

That evening at the Center, Deborah met with everyone. As the group talked easily among themselves she regarded the efficient, dedicated crew she and Williams had assembled.

Floyd Briggs and Lawrence Craig, two of the shooters who killed some of the first 14 people, were ex-Navy Seals. Briggs, a black man, had been wounded in the right front shoulder in the Granada fiasco. Craig had been wounded in the abdomen in the Panama debacle. The two men were similar in other ways. Both were in excellent physical shape, and quick healers. Both were intelligent, and committed to what they were involved in. And both had left the service before retirement; angry at the Navy, and at the entire United States government, for its lack of simple intelligence, leadership, and courage. Neither man remembered who said it, but for them the expression was true: Courage makes all other virtues possible.

Williams sent these two men plane tickets for a job interview right after he interviewed Clarissa DeBeau. He had searched through VA medical files looking for people with their background, training, and temperament. Both men were unattached, and working in menial civilian jobs. When the one-way plane ticket to D.C. arrived in the mail, and the attached short note was read, each man was on his way.

Williams had felt Briggs and Craig would be the hardest to recruit. They were not. The $5 million paycheck was important, like it had been to Ken Springfield, but even more meaningful was the chance to make something right that was definitely wrong. Both men hated the idea of having to kill so many people, but it seemed to them the only option that would work. They, too, knew that nothing else would get Congress' attention. Nothing.

Wallace Kenan, tall and lean except for a slight potbelly, wore glasses and a distracted look. Physically not imposing, he was the apparent nerd of the group. But he was a nice guy to be around, and never showed off his considerable knowledge in his field. Kenan was a victim of company downsizing. He had been a respected chemist with the same chemical company for 27 years. At 52 he was too old to be employed elsewhere at his pay grade, and too young to retire. Deborah had found him via the internet resume search network. Inventive and practical, he used his expertise well when asked.

Floyd Briggs and Lawrence Craig had been pressed into the recruiting process. They were the ones who found Willie Batts, Cliff Craft, Rusty McCaffrey, and Jack Sparks.

Willie Batts, as physically powerful as Ken Springfield, had also been a farmer. And like Ken, when Willie lost his farm he too lost his identity. Farming was all he knew, and all he had ever wanted to do. How could he get only 11 cents for a gallon of milk when the stores got $2.68 for the same gallon? The injustice infuriated him. Willie was homely, with a disfiguring facial scar from a farm accident, but his appearance was deceptive. He was a complicated man, a serious, careful thinker, and a risk taker.

Cliff Craft was a pensioner whose company had been victimized by a hostile takeover. The new owners had raided the pension fund and left. It was all perfectly legal: Congress had seen to that. Cliff was left flat broke, with no recourse. Pudgy, scowling, often silent, Craft was morose and bitter. Revenge was his primary motive; he would do anything to get back at the bastards.

Lt. Col. (retired) Jack Sparks was from Special Forces. Sparks had been assigned to the CIA at times over his career, and he knew their tricks and crimes quite well. He'd been a part of them, off and on, for more than 29 years. The bean counters finally got him, something no armed enemy had ever been able to do. Sparks was not West Point, you see, so lieutenant colonel was top floor for him.

Nor was Terrence Laney Grimes, III, of the submarine service, a Naval Academy product. He had served, with distinction and had earned many commendations, as a communication specialist on every class of sub in the Navy's fleet. He knew all there was to know about satellite links and whatever gadgetry it took to run them. When he developed Meniere's disease, with its recurrent dizziness, deafness, and ringing in the ears, the Navy reassigned him to shore duty. After six months of that, T. L. Grimes, III, left the service with a medical disability pension. Williams told him to take 100 mg. of Dilanten three times a day and his Meniere's disease would be contained. He did, and it was. But his service career was over. T. L. readily joined the assassination team, and when asked to perform he shined. He was glad to be back where he belonged.

Hannah Minsk was Deborah's cousin, who enjoyed dual citizenship in America and in Israel. She was a true beauty, auburn-haired, lean and muscular, quite feminine when she wanted to be, quite masculine when she had to be. It was seemingly impossible to out-smart or out-think her; she was always miles ahead. Deborah admired her immensely.

Hannah's father, Mordachi Weiss, and Deborah's mother, Judith, were brother and sister. Mordachi had been moved from one concentration camp to another because his numerous skills were so useful to the Nazis. Like so many others at the war's end, he made it to Tel Aviv. By trade he was an exceptional jeweler/watchmaker/engraver. Hannah's mother, Harriet, a Brooklyn native, was visiting her maternal grandmother, Marion, in Tel Aviv, when she met Mordie.

Hannah was born in Israel in 1948. She split her school time in America with her summer vacation time in Israel. At 18 she joined the Israeli army, and promptly married her commanding officer, Benjamin Minsk. Major Minsk was killed in a terrorist bombing at the open market in Jerusalem, three weeks after he and Hannah were married.

She did not have to ride on her husband's coattails for the army to recognize her intelligence and physical abilities. Hannah Minsk was recruited by Mossad, Israel's CIA, where she served for the next six years. It was during this time that she met, and subsequently worked with, Williams who by then was a freelancer. When Deborah and Williams were recruiting their assassins, fortune smiled on them. Hannah was in D. C. with 25 graduate students from Tel Aviv University. For the next six months, she was available.

Wade Jackson, a lean, rangy, classic westerner with sideburns and mustache, had been a rancher outside of Butte,

Montana. He and his wife, Jennifer, had spent her inheritance and his life savings to buy 3,000 acres of prime prairie grassland where they planned to raise beefaloes, a mixed breed of beef cattle and buffalo. Wade lost all 3,000 acres, and every penny he and Jennifer had, to something called the Subsequent Purchaser Environmental Liability Law.

Over 300 acres of the Jackson's land had been a dumping site for the Butte Lead Company. The tailings and chemicals needed to extract the lead from the ore had all been dumped on what was now Jackson land. The good government of the U. S. of A. also added its treasures to the same 300 acres. The Defense Department stored benzene, styrene, and butadiene there, in rusted 55 gallon barrels left over from World War II days. Over many years, the toxic content of the old barrels had seeped and leeched into the soil on the Jackson ranch.

The government officials from the Environmental Protection Agency cared less that the realtor hadn't disclosed this information to Wade and Jennifer at the time of sale. Nor did they see anything wrong with tagging the Jacksons for costs to clean up the government's contribution to their land. Their Congresswoman, Sally Booker told them how very sorry she was for their loss, but her hands were tied. It was their land, now, and they had *inherited* the liabilities. Wade and Jennifer Jackson were responsible for a minimum of $45 million in cleanup costs. They lost everything, and Jennifer ended up in a mental institution.

Williams had been correct in thinking that Wade would be the easiest to recruit. An expert marksman all his life, he was only too glad to be the shooter of the Chairman of the Environment Committee, Representative Thornton Quigley.

Melvin Hogan was an under-the-bridge, down-and-out, homeless, alcoholic mess. Jack Sparks had been his commander in Vietnam, and Sparks knew that Melvin had intelligence and great personal courage. He asked leave to find Melvin, and to recruit him for this mission. In Nam, Melvin had pushed Sparks out of harm's way. The sniper's scope had given off the smallest glint, but it had been enough. Melvin's response had been instantaneous, and selfless. Sparks was on the ground before the bullet could tear his head off. In the process, Melvin stepped on a mine. Most of his right leg became instant hamburger. Sparks owed Melvin.

Williams and Deborah took convincing, but in the end Sparks prevailed. He found Melvin through his veteran's disability check mailing address. It was a post office box in Wallace, North Carolina. After Sparks found him, Melvin cried like a baby for two days. Sparks locked him down and dried him out. After three weeks of no booze, Melvin could finally hold down some eggs, toast, and tea. Only then did Melvin hear what Sparks had to say.

"Damn straight I want in, Colonel. Five million, and $7,000 a month from here until the job's done? Damn straight." From that moment on, he lost his taste for booze. He was a soldier again, and he had a mission.

Praise God.

The last two were very strange little men. Lloyd Evans was a Welshman from Williams' home village, and the only person who knew that Williams' first name was David. Evans and Williams had once served a hitch in Burma, where the two were trained by the Gherkas in the discipline called Bondo. He and Williams were swift, efficient, and quiet killing machines when necessary. Lloyd Evans' love for cars and trucks was exceeded only by his mechanical abilities and his artistic paint jobs.

Clarence Henry, slightly built but sinewy, was the angriest of them all. Long bitterness had made his features rigid and stern. For 18 years he fought the IRS over a tax bill he had paid in 1979. That year he had gone to work for an insurance company, as a salesman. After he sold policies to some of his family and a few of his friends, Clarence failed. He couldn't prospect worth a damn, and he was the worst closer the business had ever seen. He earned a measly $10,000 that year. And he paid his 1979 taxes on all $10,000, even though his W-2 Form said he only earned $5,000. Strange, he thought. Then, in 1980, Clarence received another W-2 from his former insurance employer, stating he had earned $3,000 that year. He threw it away. The following year he received another W-2 stating he had earned $2,000 in that year. Clarence threw that one away, also.

Then, in 1982, Clarence Henry received notice that he owed penalty and interest on his 1980 and 1981 taxes. He had failed to include those sums reported to the Federal government by his former employer when he filed his returns for those years.

For the next 18 years, Clarence tried to explain to a myriad of tax agents that he had fulfilled his obligation as a taxpayer by paying the tax on the entire amount he had earned in the year that he had earned it. What Clarence did not know, at first, was that his former employer was writing off his 1979 earnings over a three-year period, because they got a tax break by doing so. At one time, Clarence Henry owed the "Infernal Revenue Disservice," by their calculations, over $32,000 in penalty and interest on his $10,000 earnings from 1979. Once, an agent named Jesus Romeriz told Clarence he would destroy his family if he had to, but by God, Clarence Henry was going to pay. Another time he was told that Federal Marshals were about to seize his home, and it would then be sold at public auction to pay his past due tax bill.

Clarence was motivated. He also was the one who shot Ways and Means Chairman Martin Koyn.

One of the conditions for employment in Deborah's band was silence and anonymity. Names were changed; they knew each other only by their aliases. Only Williams and Deborah knew who was who. Nor did it further the project if people became friendly with one another. That's why teams changed on each assignment. Everyone had limitations. That was respected. No one was asked to do anything he or she did not want to do, or was not qualified to do. Chit-chat was minimal. Congratulations and high fives were unthinkable.

Deborah greeted everyone with a simple, "Good evening. As you know, a number of congresspersons have chosen not to attend the funerals, and have remained in D.C. Thanks to our resident chemist, 52 potassium cyanide hypodermic syringe units are ready to be fitted into the office chair seats of these people." She handed them a list with names, floor, and door numbers. "As we were all trained, we'll play our parts tonight. The razor-thin thumbprints in front of you are identical copies of the real ones belonging to the maids, janitors, and guards we are replacing tonight. So are picture badges and nametags. We'll install them just before we leave. It's very important that we do quality work on the seats. They must look as though nothing is out of place. When the congressman sits down, the weight of his body will drive the needle all the way into his fat you-know-what." Everyone chuckled because Deborah couldn't bear to say the word. "The plunger will compress, and the potassium cyanide will kill him within seconds."

Chapter 14

Wigs, make up, and facial masks had all been created for the night's work. The guards and cleaning people regularly scheduled to work that night were all called and told not to come to work. With so many congressmen and women away to attend the funerals, they simply were not needed. Nor would their pay be docked. Call it an unexpected bonus.

When the 11 o'clock cleaning crew and security people arrived, it looked like everyone was who he or she was supposed to be. All the thumbprints checked out when each person placed his or her right thumb on the scanner for identification verification. Not one of Deborah's assassins was challenged by the machine. Her guards stood post where the real ones were supposed to be. Her cleaners, including herself, worked quickly and quietly to accomplish their terrible goal. When 6 a.m. arrived, one full hour before quitting time and the shift change, all of Deborah's assassins found assigned exits and left the Capitol building.

Forty-six of the damned things worked. An alarm was sounded around 7:40 a.m., when enough dead congresspersons were discovered sitting in their office chairs. Security people ran through the halls shouting as loudly as they could, "Don't sit down in your office chair!" The FBI was called, as was D. C.'s finest. By that time, all the assassins were long gone. Each had faded into the woodwork. In two days they were to meet at the Center.

Calvin Hunter himself came to the Capitol building. Scores of crime scene experts from the FBI and the Washington D.C. police department fought for turf, and in the process contaminated at least a dozen offices. Fortunately for forensic purposes, there were so many other dead bodies that had not yet been compromised, and the FBI was soon able to eject the D.C. police with some measure of civility.

The press was the biggest problem. They were like male dogs that smelled a bitch in heat more than a mile away. And just like those male dogs, the press howled and growled for every whiff of good stuff they could get. Capitol Security, the real ones, who had reported for work at 7 a.m., finally ejected everyone who was not part of the official investigation team.

White House phones began to ring. The President's breakfast meeting with England's Prime Minister was interrupted with news of the 46 dead Congresspersons. Within minutes everyone was in the Oval Office.

"This has got to stop," President Huber began. "Perhaps we can appeal to some sense of decency in this group."

Joe McNaughton interrupted, "They have no decency. You'd be wasting your time. They're all hard-boiled killers who seem to enjoy what they're doing."

It was Charles Newhouse who again disagreed with the President's Chief of Staff. "Quite the contrary, Joe, I think it pains them to do what they're doing. Didn't you read and re-read their messages? We've shit on these folks for so long that we can't even remember what decency means anymore. We treat them as though they're dummies who couldn't possibly understand or appreciate what we do for them."

Gene Cummings, the NSA, picked up the clicker and CNN came on again. As before, news was quick to reach the network, and as before CNN's fax machine began to spit out the following, which was aired immediately.

Question: Are any of you familiar with the old truism, 'Anvils wear out hammers?' No? Well in this case, Congress is the anvil and we are the hammers. Were we to kill every member of this current House of Representatives, that once noble body would survive our hammering. We may dent its surface, but the great body of the anvil will survive. We undertake this terrible task knowing that the institution will outlive our puny efforts to change it. However, unless current members of Congress actually experience the very real danger of being shot and killed, the status quo will never change. The money from the NRA and other lobbyists will win the day each and every time. But when nearly 379 congressional representatives get shot or poisoned or killed some other horrible way, perhaps real sympathy and understanding for the common American, who has suffered from their outrageous failure to act on our behalf, will again surface. Congress must become responsible for bedding down with the NRA and other lobbyists, by coming face to face with what many of us have had to live through as a direct result of those unions. We intend to hold Congress strictly accountable for its choices. And we will not stop unless and until Congress divorces the lobbyists and re-marries the American people.

By now it should be clear to the government that it is not dealing with ordinary killers. The fact that you will not find any of us in a police arrest record book makes us extraordinary killers. Some of us have lost family to random gun violence. Some of us have lost property, the capacity to earn a living, and simple dignity. We are mothers and fathers, mostly, who simply must do this terrible deed because it is the only avenue left open to us. How was it stated by Mr. Jefferson? 'When in the course of human events it becomes necessary...' Well, for us it has become necessary, and we are now holding Congress responsible and accountable in a way we believe Congress has forced on us.

Until Congress becomes citizen-friendly rather than friendly to every lobbyist with money, we will not go away. Unless Congress acts, not from self-interest, but from the country's interest, we will continue our grim work. Statesmen and women need to rise up from the muck that has become associated with every facet of the political system. The greater good of the people must return.

When our work is finished, we will reveal all. Such knowledge will not bring the dead back to life, but we believe it will be instructive to Congress and to the American people. Individuals must co-operate with abuse in order for it to continue. Most of us citizens are so busy working to subsidize the government, we have no time to protest the abuses on a scale great enough to be taken seriously. However, when an abused citizenry no longer co-operates with their abusers, things do change. Never again will the IRS act as the rogue entity of government that it is. Never again will guns and ammunition be available to criminals; never again will innocent people be at the mercy of the EPA and a Congress that allows the innocent to pay for the dumping of the guilty. Never again will a farmer lose his land because Congress likes the continuous supply of money it gets from the banking lobby.

We've all seen how unity of cause has empowered the Civil Rights Movement, various handicapped groups, gays and lesbians, and others. When they formed a unified front they were empowered and caused meaningful changes in the way we are all governed. A number of years ago, a group of six or seven clergy met with Chicago's Mayor Richard Daly. In his office, they demanded better housing for the poor. They demanded jobs and educational changes. They demanded better police protection and garbage collection. Throughout the entire meeting, Mayor Daly took copious notes and nodded his head in agreement with each speaker. When the meeting ended, Mayor Daly shook hands with each clergy and assured him that he would address all of the grievances they voiced to him. Everyone left feeling good. NOTHING HAPPENED. NOTHING CHANGED. A year later the same six or seven clergy marched back into the mayor's office. But this time they did not come alone. Outside the mayor's office, over a million people appeared, demanding that the mayor listen to their leaders. Mayor Daly heard them this time, and Chicago began to change. Unity got results.

The only group in our country unable to come together in any appreciable way is the one which goes to work every day, raises families, pays taxes, gets old and dies. The saddest commentary is that every member of every other unified group just mentioned is also a part of this larger and unorganized body of taxpayers. The IRS and Congress know this very well. They count on it. We are all too busy earning a living to take years out of our lives to go to jail over taxes. But just think what would happen if 20 million Americans refused to file a tax return. There are not enough jails to hold them all. Think what would happen if another 20 million Americans refused to file a tax return the next year. The IRS and Congress count on that never happening. That's why we are shooting Congressmen and women and high officials of the IRS. We are the official protest group of ordinary American citizens whose voices have been drowned out by lobbyists, and who can't afford another day off to attend a useless protest rally against our present tax system.

Congress is the only body that can develop a fair system for taxation. We are not against paying taxes. We are just against those responsible for having developed and perpetuated this terribly unjust and unfair system under which we all suffer. Thomas Jefferson said that it was the **duty** of every citizen to pay as little tax as possible. Another colonialist, James Otis, was the one who phrased, "Taxation without representation is tyranny." If they were right, and we believe they were, then we'll posit a corollary. Every citizen has an equal and opposite duty to obliterate tyranny by getting our representatives to act for us, not in spite of us. If taxation without representation is tyranny, then tyranny with representation is taxing.

Unless meaningful changes take place in our national life, people making millions and billions will continue to pay little or no taxes, thanks to powerful lobbyists and tax loopholes. The national debt will continue to be borne by the majority of working people. This system has gone on too long. Proof of its over-long stay is the emergence of multi-talented assassins like us. In his 1787 letter to James Madison, Mr. Jefferson wrote; "A little rebellion now and then is a good thing." That's what we are doing. We are rebelling. Others may choose other ways, but this is the one we have chosen. Right or wrong, our course is set, and we will not waiver."

Chapter 15

White House Press Secretary Peter Hopkins stepped up to the microphone. "As you all know, 46 more members of Congress were murdered in their offices this morning when they sat on hypodermics filled with potassium cyanide. Fifty-two such devices were planted. Before I go any further, let me tell you that I will never again be interrupted or shouted at by you people. I will walk out of here like I did a few days ago. Whoever thinks he or she can break that rule just try me. At the end of my remarks, questions will be answered for 30 minutes. We'll do it in an orderly manner. First question will come from the first reporter seated to my left. Then the next reporter beside him will ask a question. Eventually you all can ask your questions, but I will not tolerate any more discourtesy.

"Now, the FBI has not harvested a single clue from any of the first 14 crime scenes. They were picked clean. Apparently, each shooter had sweepers who sanitized the kill site seconds after the bullets left the guns. How many sweepers? We don't know. What we do know about yesterday's killings is this. Small explosives were attached to the right front tires of each victim's car. They were radio activated, and at a spot preselected by the killers, the tires were blown. As each victim got out, either to change the tire or to look at it, he or she was shot in the head with another exploding bullet. Then the killers simply disappeared.

"As for today's killings, it appears that the regular cleaning staff and security people were replaced by identical lookalikes. From the security tapes at the entrances, everyone resembles exactly who they're supposed to be. We've learned that the real staff was called and told not to report for work last night. So many Congressmen and women were away for the funerals that the House was not dirty. Apparently, the caller had sufficient information on procedure that these loyal employees had no reason to question the caller's authority.

"The FBI has appointed Ellen Coast to be Special Agent In Charge of this manhunt. She will answer your questions, beginning with Myles Chastagne, on my far left."

"How did the killers get pictures and thumb prints of the cleaning and security staff?" Chastagne began.

Coast replied, "They probably downloaded them from the employment bureau's mainframe."

"But how did they get access? I thought this information was hacker-proof."

"Obviously, they are very good."

The next questioner asked, "Is the FBI hopeful of finding any clues in the Capitol building?"

"Yes, " Coast said, "but it will take weeks before family member prints and staff prints can be ruled out. Just maybe, one of the killers left a print. If it's there, we'll find it."

The questioning continued, each member of the media taking a turn.

"How would an odd fingerprint, not on file with the Bureau, be of help?"

"When we catch them, and we will catch them, it will place that person at the scene of the crime. In that regard, it will be of enormous help."

Next questioner; "What's being done to protect the remaining members of Congress from this group?"

"We think we've found something of a solution. We're sending 188 congresspersons on fact-finding missions. Forty-three from New York and 60 from California are traveling to France on a wine study. Twenty-two, most of whom are African/Americans, are going to Nigeria to establish better banking practices. Thirty-five Italian/American Congressional Representatives are going to Italy to try to mend fences for the cable car accident from 1998. And lastly, 28 will journey to Vietnam, to secure commerce orders, and to improve trade relations with that country."

The next reporter asked, "What about security for them while they're away?"

"The host countries have assured us that they will be safe in their hands. And frankly, we believe them. This group can't follow them around Africa, Europe and Asia, now, can it? We believe this will give us much needed time to work on catching the killers before the representatives return from overseas."

When the press conference concluded, Deborah called Williams on the house intercom. "Did you see the news conference?"

"Yes."

"I think we should travel abroad, don't you?"

"No," Williams answered. "We have acquaintances in Vietnam and in Italy who can supply us with everything needed, and they can do the job for us."

Deborah responded, "You never cease to amaze me, Williams."

Silence. Seconds later Williams said, "The cost will be significant, but the results will be worth it."

"Do it," she said, and disconnected.

Ellen Coast was at her desk going over skimpy preliminary field reports. Logical kill sites had been established for most of the hits, but nothing beyond the ambush places had been harvested. Her phone rang. "Yes? I'll be right over." She hung up and went to Calvin Hunter's office.

"Anything new?" he asked.

"Not really," she responded. "Preliminary reports are thin. As you well know, exploding bullets are everywhere on the black market. Anyone with a little cash and brains can get them. On the other hand, the information in the faxes is starting to give us something of a profile. We're probably looking for a mature male, 45 to 60, highly educated, and definitely not crazy."

Cal Hunter looked tired. Everyone had been screaming at him lately. Nobody was civil anymore. He could handle the President and Joe McNaughton, but it was the press that got to him. He was being vilified for not having produced the assassins by now. Vilified! And he was the good guy. Didn't they know that? Apparently, Cal Hunter had forgotten what it felt like to be the object of the press's sting. The media *loved* to spill other people's blood. They bathed in it. They luxuriated in it. They couldn't get enough of it. They didn't care if the killers were ever caught. All they wanted to do was to keep the blood flowing. Whose veins were let didn't matter. This was what sold. Big time.

Families of the dead Congressmen and women and their constituents grieved their losses. Many in this last batch of victims were not household names, so the news focused less on their records and more on their families. All decried the monsters that had murdered their loved ones in such cruel and unusual ways. Clergy had no problem eulogizing these good and, some said, great public servants.

Not surprisingly, however, the average-man-in-the-street interview produced many who agreed with the killers. The part in the fax about nothing getting through to Congress struck a familiar cord. Did the public approve of all the killings? Not really, but they sure could relate to the old Pharaoh and Moses story. They also thought the sale of ammunition was *the* answer needed for gun control. As Gabriella Fortunello from Queens said, "If those kids had been unable to get that ammunition, my son Vincent would still be alive." Several other parents who had lost children to guns expressed the same point of view.

Still more people had read the killers' messages and understood the wider point of view. They were the ones who expressed outrage and sympathy for citizens who had been gunned down without weapons, by the IRS, the EPA, and other functionaries of Federal government.

The results of the killings so far were quite measurable. Overwhelming public interest in democratic government was reborn. From everywhere, e-mail, faxes, phone calls, and old-fashioned letters began to pour into both houses of Congress. The Senate was stunned by the ground swell for the prohibition of the sale of ammunition. It was such a simple solution.

Simultaneously, another phenomenon arose. The ammunition lobby was reborn and empowered. Really obscene sums of money began to pour into the Capitol building. Meeting calendars were discarded, because the remaining House members and Senators could not get through the halls of Congress. They were crammed so full of gun and ammunition lobbyists that nobody could get from office to chambers. The two lobbies virtually shut down the House and Senate. A dozen senators finally called the FBI and the local D.C. police to have the lobbyists thrown out of the building.

The press loved it. Pictures did not have to wait till the 6 o'clock news. The media interrupted scheduled programs and went live with it. The fighting and name calling and ruffled outfits and torn uniforms confirmed every word Deborah had written.

When the American people saw the melee, their disgust with congress, the lobbyists and all they stood for became visceral. Rally after rally sprang up everywhere. Cries of "Kill them all!" were heard across America. "Go for 435," matched the other chants in intensity and number. Other than a few conservative clergy urging the killers to stop, most of the country's citizenry was firmly on the side of the unknown assassins.

President Huber knew he was facing an out of control crisis. Joe McNaughton suggested calling out the National Guard for a few days. The President vetoed that, saying he didn't think the Guard would respond to the order. How would it look for the Commander-in-Chief to be unable to order the National Guard into the streets, because they refused to stand against fellow citizens who were employing First Amendment rights? It wouldn't do. He had to go on national television, and he had to go on pronto.

All the networks agreed that the President could have half an hour, at 7 p.m., to make his case. His two favorite speechwriters were given the task of writing something that would appeal to the citizens' sense of decency and fair play.

For the first time, his speechwriters were at a loss for words. Leon Manchester thought the focus should be on pulling together in this time of crisis. Franklin James wanted to let it all hang out. He thought that the killers' messages needed to be taken seriously, and that perhaps the President should say he was sending legislation to the hill to outlaw the sale of ammunition, and the lobbyists, forever. At 6 o'clock not one word was on paper. Leon Manchester was the senior writer, and he finally said, "Just leave, Frank. I'll do this myself."

"It's your funeral," was all Franklin James said, and he left the room for home.

At 6:55, Leon handed President Huber his manuscript. The President had not read one word of it yet, but he had trusted Leon's judgment, and his excellent prose, for the last six years.

"Good evening," he began. "Our democracy has served us well for more than 240 years. We've survived through all kinds of wars and financial crises. I'm old enough to remember the massive, daily protests of the Vietnam War, which seemed to tear our great country apart. Students, mostly, were the sparks that ignited the debates that raged throughout the land.

"We've had three Presidents assassinated, and attempted assassinations on two and maybe three others. And yet none of that has had the effect on us as have the events of the last few days.

"Like you, I watched, earlier today, the ugly, disgusting scene unfolding as it happened at the Capitol building. Instead of pointing fingers at this group or that, let me assure you that such a scene will never happen in that hallowed hall ever again. I've issued an executive order, restricting entrance to the Capitol building to anyone who is not an elected member of that body or its staff. Now I know that some of you will be very upset with me for this order. But it is only temporary. Within the next 30 days, the Congress is to come up with its own rules regarding entry. I'm hoping each Congressperson and each Senator will have, say, 60 passes per day to issue to constituents. If lobbyists get 50 of them, then you'll know…"

President Huber stopped. He could not believe his eyes. The next few words of the speech were, "…that the killers are right, and that the lobbyists have more access than the citizenry."

He could not say the words. He coughed and reached for his water glass, trying desperately to think of a statement to substitute. "But of course," he finally bumbled, "that will never happen." From here on, he was on his own. Leon Manchester was history.

The damage was done. Everyone watching that speech could have finished the sentence for the President. Nothing of what he said from that point on was remembered. Leon Manchester became a hero, albeit an unemployed one. But he wasn't on the unemployment line for very long.

Chapter 16

It was Williams who addressed the group that evening. He and Sparky were leaving for parts unknown, to make arrangements to dispatch all 188 Congresspersons going on junkets. Everyone else was to remain at home, and concentrate on killing more IRS officials and lobbyists.

From a hacked-into fax machine in the Cathedral of St. Patrick, in New York City, Williams sent the following message: "Dear Fr. Pagano, the Holy Father has sent for me. Will arrive Vatican Square tomorrow at noon. Fr. White." He then left immediately for Italy in Deborah's private jet. When he reached Rome he went directly to Vatican Square. Wearing a priest's collar and black front shirt, he met another priest-like individual. They blended in so well that no one even saw them.

The man Williams met was Irish, not Italian. Italy just happened to be the best place for them to meet. Seamus Coglin was William's age and stature, although Seamus seemed much older. Williams was of an indeterminate age. The itemized list of deadly wares needed to kill 103 congresspersons in France was passed as though it were a common grocery list. The same was true for the 35 who were to die in Italy, and the 22 in Africa. Seamus could easily supply everything, including the manpower to do it. Monies would be transferred in the morning. Staging areas in the three countries, and escape routes for the assassins, had yet to be secured. Seamus assured Williams that by the time the monies cleared, he would have everything he needed. The two parted as they met. Casually.

With the help of T. L. Grimes, Jack Sparks gained access to another fax machine. This one was in the Federal Building in Austin, Texas. Texas held one of the larger Vietnamese populations, and communications between Texas and Vietnam were frequent. Because the fax was in Vietnamese, it passed as a typical message. Translated, it read, "Old friend, I'm dying, and would like to see you one last time. I plan to be in Ho Chi Minh City on Wednesday. I'll be at the Hilton. Ngu." Old friend was code for Huu. Huu had been one of Sparky's contacts years ago, when he was an operative in Vietnam.

Huu knew lots of money was soon to follow, and he was eager to get it. When Sparky arrived, Huu greeted his old friend warmly. But when he heard the proposal, he said no and stood up to leave. The whole scheme was too dangerous. It could not be done. Too many risks.

Of course, Sparky had expected this response. It was just negotiations, Vietnamese style. He told Huu that he was not doing this as part of the CIA. Officially, he was no longer working for them. This was private. No one would ever be able to connect him or Huu to the killings. And $50 million American was nothing to walk away from.

The number was even larger than Huu hoped to hear, which made him very suspicious. "Impossible," was all he said. But he sat down and thought quietly for several moments.

Sparky did not budge. Huu's lower lip quivered. The smile soon followed. They had a deal.

The first plane load of 103 congresspersons left Dulles International Airport for an all-night flight to Paris. As the plane cleared 10,000 feet, an audible sigh of relief could be heard throughout the craft. It had not been bombed (yet), and they felt safer. Conversations arose between old friends. Gossip and camaraderie gradually replaced abject fear. The passengers sat in small groups, talking and drinking wine.

But the banter for bragging rights, i.e., New York vs. California wine, was only half-hearted. The real topic finally surfaced. Would the FBI get the killers before the killers got them? Thank God they were getting out of harm's way, even if it was for just a few days. The longer the flight continued without incident, the more confident each person felt. Perhaps this trip was a damned good idea after all.

Similar scenarios were played out in three other aircraft. Most on board drank too much and laughed too loudly. The smell of fear reduced the possibility of meaningful conversation to small talk. The air filtration systems were swamped trying to get rid of the putrid body odor pouring out of everyone on board. Fear gripped and would not let go.

And yet, not one person on any of the planes suggested the obvious. Why didn't they at least consider outlawing ammunition and lobbyists? To broach such a subject would have branded the suggester a quitter or a coward, or worse yet, a turncoat. Although it was on everyone's mind, not one person had the courage to mention it.

Upon landing in Paris at 4 p.m., the New York and California delegation boarded two shuttle busses bound for a hotel near the airport. The luxury busses stood out because they were sandwiched between ugly personnel carriers full of armed soldiers. Shooters were stationed along the route to the Hotel Framoid, where the delegation to France would be staying that night. Everyone needed a shower and a bed for the next eight hours. Guarding this group was going to be easy.

The next day, everyone was loaded into the same luxury busses for the first tour of the first winery. At day's end, the delegation was to stay in several different hostels in the surrounding countryside. The small town of Chellonese had not seen so many armed soldiers since the end of the Second World War. For a change, the French were showing real concern for their American guests. The two senior members of the delegations were Gordon Nelson, of New York, and Wentworth Arndt, of California. Major wineries were located in their respective districts. Both men preferred beer, but neither would admit it. Over the years they had learned a great deal about wine, its history, and its value to an economy.

After three days out, the French delegation was getting somewhat ragged. The forced jolly good spirits on the plane trip over had dissipated into sniping that was funny at first, but now had a bite to it. Tempers were short, and the gentlewoman from so and so became the bitch from such and such. This was such a horse shit assignment, anyway. Voters would just see them as chicken. They all wanted to go home, even if it meant facing some kind of unknown firing squad. The further away from Paris the group traveled, the fewer armed soldiers accompanied them. On their return trip, they would pick up their escorts in the order they had dropped off.

The same dynamic was afoot in Italy, Nigeria, and Vietnam. Day four saw tempers unleashed, with a vehemence never seen in the hallowed halls of Congress. A few punches were even exchanged in the Italian delegation.

Day five was turn around day for all of the delegations.

Meetings with the Italians had gone nowhere. It was painfully clear that after all these years, nothing would ever satisfy them for the cable car incident, except blood. The delegates just wanted to go home.

The delegation to Africa had suffered great hardships. No one was prepared for the heat, or the culture. Energy seemed to be gone by 10 a.m. A general malaise fell over everyone. Bouts of dysentery humbled the strongest and nearly killed the weakest. All this group wanted to do was to go home.

Seamus Coglin, on William's orders, had contacted Maguboo Congeme, the most feared rebel leader in neighboring Chad. In actuality, Congeme was criminally insane. Nothing pleased him more than killing. He liked it better than sex. For whatever reason, Maguboo liked Seamus Coglin. Always had. Seamus made him laugh. Standing beside Maguboo, who was an enormous man, Seamus' head topped off half an inch higher than Congeme's belly button.

The Nigerian assassination plan was simple. On the appointed night, as close to 3 a.m. as possible, Congeme and his men were to go into the compound where 22 American Congressmen and women were sleeping, and butcher them with machetes and knives. No guns. Maguboo roared with laughter. He loved it. He would have done it for free, just for the fun of it, but he was a businessman. Besides, he had never been paid so much money to kill just 22 people.

Maguboo Congeme's eyes never left the clock. The time could not pass swiftly enough for him. But pass it did, and with 40 men, he entered the compound at Angalla and hand-slaughtered every man and woman there. Twenty-two, just as agreed upon. For free, he also killed every guard within two miles of the place. No one was left who could identify him or his men. They slipped over the boarder into Chad, where no one with any sense would ever have suggested Maguboo Congeme had been absent for as much as 30 minutes, let alone all night.

Vietnam was a different story. The Congressional Representatives succeeded with their given tasks. Promises of new business from both sides were signed. Computers headed the list of goods to be purchased from the Americans by the Vietnamese. But pharmaceutical research agreements far exceeded computers in value, by millions of dollars. Vietnam had rare jungle vegetation, full of medical cures just waiting to be discovered. Joint ventures, funded by the United States and private Vietnamese companies, were also inked.

In order for Huu to fulfill his end of the contract, he needed to get the Americans into the jungle that bordered Cambodia. But getting them there was not just difficult; it was almost impossible. Some were unwilling to travel because of snakes. Others didn't want to be exposed to water shortages, or unexploded mines. They all preferred to stay in the hotel, and meet business people during regular hours. Huu now realized why his payoff was so great. It took nearly half of his $50 million to get handlers to persuade the Americans that a trip to the border of Vietnam and Cambodia was a must.

There they were to see a pharmaceutical site, close to a Vietnam War monument that still needed to be dedicated. An undedicated war monument got everyone's attention. It was good press. The delegates dressed in jungle fatigues. The folks back home would love those photos. Besides, they were all going home in the morning, and the trip in and out would only take four hours.

To reach this remote site, Huu had to fly them in with helicopters. Six new helicopters were rented to carry the delegation. Forty-eight Vietnamese soldiers were to provide security for the group. They, however, flew in four Vietnam War-era choppers, whose replacement parts were fashioned from the equivalent of Coca-Cola cans, rubber bands, and chewing gum. Everyone felt queasy, except the soldiers.

At the last minute, three congressmen claimed diarrhea and stayed in the hotel. When Huu heard of this he reconfigured his resources and had his best assassin enter the hotel, to dispatch each victim with a silenced gunshot to the head.

When everyone had assembled at the handsome granite-like monument, a distinct pall descended on the delegates. The figure wasn't that of an American soldier. It was a Mung warrior, who, with hundreds of his tribesmen, had fought valiantly on the American side. As the delegates gathered nearer and nearer to the monument, one whispered to another, "That's it? All this way, for Mungs? Who were they, anyway?"

No answer was ever heard. The artificial monument exploded, killing almost everyone around it. Next, the ground under them exploded killing anyone who was not massacred in the first explosion. One of the explosives contained napalm, and it incinerated every single body. The four choppers carrying Vietnam soldiers lifted off as fast as they could. No soldiers were wounded. Staying around to see what had happened, or how they could help, was not in their definition of courage. The bomber walked over the boarder into Cambodia and vanished. No one sifted the area for clues.

Italy required more planning than all the other maneuvers together. Seamus directed this operation himself. Security was sophisticated. To kill everyone in this delegation at the same time was impossible. Meetings were being held all over Rome. Seamus needed to separate the delegates, and isolate them from hotel security if he was going to succeed.

On day two, Seamus learned that 32 of the 35 delegates had relatives throughout Italy. He contacted all of the relatives and persuaded them to invite their cousins, uncles, nephews, and nieces, to their homes for an overnight visit just before the delegates were to fly back to America. Arrangements were made, and 32 Italian-Americans set off to visit on the night before they were to return home. Cars were provided, and real guards traveled in each one. The drivers were also part of the legitimate security. The 32 members of Congress left feeling relatively protected, and all arrived safe and sound. The evening was spent in jovial story telling from both sides of the Atlantic.

When the delegates left in the morning to return to Rome, everything was as it had been. All the drivers and guards were in place. The cars were checked for bombs. Nothing was amiss. But it was the road at the end of the driveways that had not been checked. As the cars passed over certain spots, they were blown into the air by powerful dynamite bundles planted under new patches of asphalt. The stone roads were easier. Dynamite bundles fit anywhere. Within the space of an hour all 32 representatives, along with their drivers and guards, were dead.

Before news of their deaths could reach the three Congressmen who remained at the hotel, everything on their breakfast tray had been poisoned. Whatever they ate or drank would kill them, and it did. Seamus himself made up the breakfast trays. He had paid the regular assistant chef $5,000 American to stay at home that morning.

The two busses carrying the 103 United States Congresspersons to the Paris airport met a more horrible fate. Before the American delegation had arrived in Paris, Seamus had paid the head of transportation security, Monsieur Pierre Rousseau, $750,000 American to give his regular safety inspectors an unexpected holiday. That sum also purchased the right to re-staff the furloughed inspectors with Seamus's own people, who then certified that the busses were bomb-free and safe. These phony inspectors were the ones who planted the nail and shrapnel bombs in the ceilings, and the gasoline bombs in the floors of the busses. When it came time for everyone to board, the busses were still being checked for explosives by the very ones who had planted them. Of course they found nothing, and signed certification papers indicating their search had been thorough. Everyone boarding the bus that morning was relaxed and sure they were safe.

The trip was going nicely when suddenly the two busses exploded from within. The downward blast of the shrapnel through the ceiling of the bus shredded the clothing and flesh of all below. The upward blast from the floor ignited everything and everyone on the busses. The ceiling detonations were so powerful that some of the skull bones were missing on many of the dead. Those not killed instantly by the first explosions died from shock, smoke, flame, and an unstoppable flow of blood.

News of the deaths slowly reached a stunned world. It was generally felt that any assassin who could time all the killings to happen at the same time was more than a genius. He was undoubtedly the most organized killer the world had ever seen. Host governments began to apologize to the American embassies, and the embassies began calling Washington. Then CNN went on the air, to read yet another fax from the killers.

Our arms are long and strong. We would rather they all died on American soil, but we'll take whatever opportunity you give us to finish our work. By our calculations we only have 112 left. We are nearly two-thirds of the way to our goal. Again, it can all stop if the remainder of the Congress will simply pass laws outlawing ammunition and lobbyists. Should they come to their senses, we'll stop now. If not...

That same day, five lobbyists and two IRS officials were also killed. Five were shot. Two were bombed. President Huber was beside himself. This group was making him and everyone in the government look like the eunuchs they were. It would take months, no, years, to reconstruct the killings in France, Italy, Nigeria, and Vietnam. There simply wasn't enough manpower in the FBI to investigate this last group of killings.

Chapter 17

Ellen Coaster reasoned that finding the killers depended more on locating their funding source than in discovering a smoking gun. The FBI began to look for large sums of money transferred from accounts that matched what it thought these killings cost.

Deborah Saraf's name surfaced immediately. For the last three years she had been moving millions of dollars out of United States banks, into foreign banks known for their silence. Along with three others who had moved large sums of money, she was paid a visit by the FBI. Dr. Thompson was attending her when agents Hooks and Herford arrived. Deborah's cancer had gone out of remission, and new medicines were being dripped into her arm.

The large sums they were asking about, she told the agents, went to medical researchers around the world. She supported organizations or individuals who worked on finding a cure for her cancer. Without that elusive cure, she had one, but no more than two months left to live. The trust funds referred to were for individuals whom she knew and loved. Besides, what good would her money do if it were found in her accounts after she died? The United States Government would confiscate 67.5 cents out of every dollar!

The agents asked if they could look around. Of course they could. What they expected to see was unclear, but they walked through the mansion, poking here and there. An hour later they returned, as Dr. Thompson was adding a second bottle of medicine to Deborah's line. She was retching so severely into an emesis basin that the agents thought the bed would shake apart.

When she recovered enough to speak, she asked the agents if they had visited the *Been There, Done That* charitable institution she had established. She told them it had taken untold millions to renovate the building, hire the staff, and endow it in the name of her late husband, Isadore Saraf, Jr. No they had not, they said, but they would shortly.

They left knowing this woman was no killer. Nevertheless, they drove to the center and met Ms. DeBeau, who called them "Shoog."

Clarissa had not been warned of the visit. However, she had been told to expect one sometime, and to make sure that whoever showed up was given the complete tour, in particular the showers in the basement, the clothing center, and the freight elevator that took everything down for sorting and storage.

As usual, the *Been There, Done That* was crowded. The agents arrived just as meals were being served to homeless mothers and their children, and to the true dregs of society. Truckloads of good clean clothing were being unloaded at the docks as the agents pulled up, and computers were clicking and clacking all over the place once they stepped inside. The security staff was uniformed, but carried no weapons. They were big and burly and clean-shaven. Man Mountain Dean would have had a hard time with this bunch.

After the tour, agents Hooks and Herford asked the security guards numerous questions. Who came in on their shifts? Did anything suspicious go on, drugs, guns, that type of thing? The guards assured the agents that everything was above board, taking obvious pride in the part they played to guarantee everyone's safety and security.

Ms. DeBeau could not have been nicer if President Huber himself was visiting. She gave each agent a slice of home made peach pie with some vanilla ice cream on the side. They were umming and ahhing with every bite. If two agents had ever been hosed, Herford and Hooks were at the top of the list.

How much did all of this agency stuff cost, they asked? So many millions that Ms. DeBeau didn't begin to know. But this she did know, Ms. Safar was a saint. With just a few months remaining on her ticket, and so little strength left, she still never missed her turn at the serving counter on Wednesdays. In fact, Ms. DeBeau told the agents, she was thinking about changing the name of the place, after Ms. Safar passed, to the Isadore and Deborah Safar House. But don't let that out. Wouldn't want Ms. Safar to hear about it. She'd be real upset.

It was Ms. DeBeau's best performance.

When Hooks and Herford returned to their offices, Ellen Coast wanted to hear everything they had discovered before they wrote it up. While H&H had been out, she ran a check on Deborah Safar. Mother and father were holocaust survivors. Mother died in childbirth. Father emigrated to New York in 1947, and started to work for his second cousin twice removed on his mother's side, Isadore Safar, Sr. Deborah educated in private schools, graduated from Princeton University in 1968. Married Isadore Safar, Jr. same year. No children. Developed cancer four years ago. Given millions of dollars since to find a cure. Terminally ill. Gives liberally to WSO, and hundreds of other charities. Appears to be giving away her entire fortune, conservatively estimated at $12 to $16 billion. Still, she should be watched. But move on. This one seems, no pun intended, like a dead end. Cal Hunter thought so too.

President Huber was angry that Deborah's name had even come up. She and Isadore had enriched his coffers by countless sums over the years. The woman was a saint. If she weren't Jewish, he would start the movement to canonize her himself. Move on, Cal. Dead end, there.

Having received a clean bill of health, so to speak, from the FBI, Deborah was well aware that her time would most likely be at an end before she finished the project. As she lay in bed, exhausted, she told Williams that she certainly would be unable to go on any more assignments.

He assured her that he would see it through, no matter what. In thanks, she reached up from her bed and kissed him lightly on the cheek. It was the first and only physical contact she ever had with him. He was so moved it froze him like a statue. Later, in his room, he cried gut-wrenching sobs. Although he could easily complete the task without her, it would not be the same.

This would be his last assignment. When it was all over he was going to the North Island of New Zealand. Years ago he purchased a small but lovely home there, overlooking Waitemata Harbor. His older sister Mary lived in the house since the death of their mother. Mary wrote to him every month, and sent him pictures of the gardens. Perhaps there he could finally rest.

Ellen Coast was removed from leadership of the special investigators. She screamed loudly, but to no avail. Results were called for faster than she seemed able to produce them. But her replacement would fare no better, even though Rohan Holiday was all steak and no sizzle. Just what was needed, supposedly. He had been on medical leave for prostate surgery when the first shootings occurred. It was still too soon for him to return to work, but Cal Hunter could be insistent at times, and this was one of those times.

Holiday read and reread everything compiled to date. He started to ask questions of himself. Where would they find such a group? They must have a headquarters. Was it in D.C.? Was that possible? If so, where would it be? How many assassins were there? Were they military or CIA trained? Were any of the hits similar to anything known to the CIA? He called CIA Director Robert Benton and asked him these questions. Benton said he'd meet with Holiday the next morning, at CIA Headquarters in Langley.

Holiday was not surprised to learn that the CIA suspected several of its former operatives. The potassium cyanide made Director Benton name three men capable of creating and delivering such a system. Lt. Col. Jack "Sparky" Sparks, retired, headed the list. Director Benton and Sparks went back a long way. They had served together in Vietnam. Sparks was also fluent in Vietnamese, as well as Arabic and half a dozen other languages. But did Director Benton believe Sparks was part of this group? Definitely not. Jack was too patriotic. He could never do such a deed. Finding him, Holiday was told, would be the biggest problem the FBI would face. Unless and until Sparks wanted to be found, he would remain invisible. He was a ghost who materialized only when it suited him.

When Rohan Holiday got back to his office he summoned Wes Joshua, known as the mole. Joshua was in charge of the task force assigned to finding the group's headquarters.

"What have you found so far?" Holiday began.

"Nothing yet, Rohan, but we're looking for recent purchases of public buildings large enough to house such a group. So far, we've come up with nothing. The few suspects have all checked out as legitimate. Mostly foreign-born Asians, and some recent Russian immigrants, have profited by the downfall of properties in our fair city. For example, two Koreans named Kim and Han got a government grant to buy the old school at 54th Street. Damned if they haven't turned it into a first-class apartment building. It's fully rented and making them money hand over fist. I'm going back to re-visit an old church turned into a social service agency called *'Been There, Done That.'* Herford and Hooks visited the place last week, and they said it was a beehive of activity. It's run by Ms. Clarissa DeBeau."

Holiday interrupted the mole and told him he was wasting his time there. He knew Ms. DeBeau. She was a fine woman who could not possibly be mixed up with these killings. Besides, the President had told Cal Hunter to move on. According to the report, Ms. Saraf, the agency's benefactor, had only a few months to live.

Joshua acknowledged all this, but his instincts told him it was too pat. He reminded Holiday that the Safar woman's name had surfaced twice now. Once in the financial category, and now in the public building purchase.

"Then go for it," was all Holiday could say.

Joshua asked Cal Hunter to get a search warrant for the *Been There, Done That*. Hunter went ballistic. Joshua had expected that, and waited for the tirade to subside. Then he simply said that he wouldn't feel right if he didn't at least rule the place out once and for all. Cal Hunter reluctantly agreed, and told him to bring the results back to him immediately. He also told the mole that if he found nothing, it would be his ass.

When Wes Joshua arrived at the old church, warrant in hand and three agents with him, he was greeted warmly by Ms. DeBeau herself. She asked if there was anything she could do to assist them. This caught them completely flatfooted. She asked if they wanted her and everyone else in the building to leave while the agents searched. In return, all she wanted was for them to put anything they examined back in its place when they were done. She did not want to have to spend two weeks putting everything back together after they left. And could she get them a coffee?

Wes Joshua was charmed. "Just walk me through the place, Ms. DeBeau. If I need to examine anything, I'll do it gently, okay?"

"Ok, Shoog," was her reply.

They went everywhere. She opened doors and files and closets. She asked students to let these fine gentlemen look at their computers. When they got to the public showers in the basement, she told agent Joshua that she could not go in there from 11 a.m. till noon, because it was for the exclusive use of men, but he certainly could go in by himself. He did just that. Sixteen men of different sizes, ages, and races were enjoying this treat. Their clothes had been exchanged for clean ones. After they cut each other's hair and shaved, they'd get lunch and be on their way.

An hour and forty-five minutes later Wes Joshua called his agents together, and they left the building. If this structure housed the killers, then his name was President Huber. Wherever the assassins were housed, it wasn't in the *Been There, Done That*.

So close.

Chapter 18

That night, Williams told everyone that Ms. Saraf would not be able to go on any more missions. Her cancer had gone active, and had taken its expected toll. He only hoped that they would finish their tasks before she died. He was about to brief the group on the next assignment when T. L. interrupted to say he wanted them to look at a news tape he had made just moments before they all arrived.

Four congressmen had been shot and killed by unknowns, while the politicians were visiting their home districts. A fifth was only wounded, and the shooter was captured. He was a used car salesman from Indianapolis, Indiana. "I just wanted to let the world know I think the killers are right, and I only wanted to help them!" he screamed at the camera as he was arrested.

"Are you one of them?" a reporter yelled back.

"Hell no, I sell cars here! Everybody knows me."

It was to be expected, but it was not what Williams or any of them wanted. The news would just sadden Deborah. She especially did not want to be the cause of any citizens suffering because of her choices. But there it was. She would have to make a plea to the American people to stay out of this dirty business.

Nevertheless, they had their own work to do. Williams called them back to the task at hand. "It's time," he began, "to strike several more lobbyists. Five of the really big names are from law firms here in D. C. All are to be shot. They should be easy targets. They all live in the suburbs, and they commute daily. We can hit them in two days. Judith Proctor, of Flanagan, Lister, Adams, and Proctor fame, is first. Of all the lobbyists, she carries the most money for the NRA. Those who work for her and at her direction should look for other employment after she is dispatched."

When he completed the list and gave out the team assignments, he excused himself and returned to Deborah to tell her of the copycat killers. As expected, the news devastated her.

Jack Sparks drew the Proctor assignment. The plan called for him to be the shooter. With his team, he was to disarm Proctor's simple alarm system, and to kill her in her own bed. He'd done this deed several times before in his career, and it gave him no pleasure to do it again. The danger was not from the victim. She would be easy. The real danger came from neighbors. Someone was always walking a dog, or stargazing, or getting home from a party.

His only team member would be Hannah Minsk. She would take care of the alarm system while he took care of Ms. Proctor. They'd park the car in the driveway, in plain view. They'd also leave together, as if they had been invited guests. Ms. Proctor was known for her small gatherings. It happened often. Nothing unusual.

As expected, the plan worked. The other four teams also succeeded without incident.

CNN was waiting at the fax machine for its expected letter. But wait was all they did. This time, the fax was sent to the *Indianapolis Star News*, from a computer on that paper's publisher's desk. Deborah had reasoned that something printed had to go out. People needed to hold this, and to read it over several times. As always, she chose a simple declarative style to carry her message.

It saddened us to see decent Americans become caught up in our dirty work. Please, let no others get involved in something we've planned out, and are capable of finishing. We do not need, nor do we desire, your help. The four members of Congress killed were not assassinated by anyone in our group. The wounded one should let you all know that amateurs are a nuisance. They only slow us down. Should any others feel the need to kill congresspersons, please don't do it. You'll get caught, and we do not want you to suffer. Please, let us do our work. We haven't missed yet, have we?

Today we parted from our usual fare. We want the weasels to feel the sting of our work. Because of their influence on Congress, thousands of innocent Americans have died as a direct result of guns. Unless the remainder of lobbyists don't get the picture, let them ask themselves the question, 'Could I be next?'

Unless you get out of the lobbyist business, the answer is an unequivocal 'Yes.' Clearly, we can defeat any alarm system and get into any home we select. We are serious about killing lobbyists. It seems Congress will not get rid of you, so they've left that task to us.

If another group somehow got it into its head to kill drug dealers the same way we are killing congresspersons and lobbyists, then I'm sure they could rid us of drugs and their scourge as well. If I were to head such a group, here's what I'd do. First, I'd get a class action lawsuit against all drug dealers. Then I'd go to a grand jury and bring back an indictment for first-degree murder. Drug dealers are murderers, plain and simple. I'd then hold a nationally televised trial with a jury of 12 good men and women. They would find the dealers guilty of murder, and the judge would sentence them all to death. Then I'd go to the armed forces, and have all of their expert marksmen and snipers set themselves up where drug dealers work. When a drug deal goes down, a picture would be snapped and a bullet would go into the drug dealer's head. He would be placed in a Seal-A-Meal clear plastic bag and left on the spot. Same fate for all drug dealers. At the end of a week, the dead dealers would be piled up, doused with gasoline, and burned. All, that is, except the last one. He'd be left like the proverbial nest egg. After several months of this serious activity, drugs would be piling up all over America because no one would want to end up in a Seal-A-Meal bag. No dealers. No addicts. Simple. But that's for another group. I cannot lose sight of our agenda and targets. Back to Congress, tomorrow, and tomorrow, and tomorrow.

The remaining members of the House of Representatives were hiring armed guards to protect them day and night. Members of the National Guard were relieved of their duties, as it was clearly evident that they served no protective purpose whatsoever. Many remaining members of the House went back to their home districts, and hid someplace they considered safe. The pressure on Cal Hunter to find the killers was enough to explode Mt. St. Helen all over again. But day after day, no evidence was found.

And day after day, Deborah worsened. Agents Herford and Hooks returned to her home for one more interview. It was obvious to them that the woman had deteriorated quickly since they saw her last. Her color was ashen, and her voice was weak. H&H left without a word, and closed the book on her.

She rang for Williams. "Perhaps we should stop now. We've made our point, don't you think? So many congressmen and women have left town, and we don't know where to find them."

"That's true, we don't, but they can't stay hidden forever," responded Williams.

"Still," she added, "I'd like to be finished with this whole business, and make sure all our people escape."

"Whatever you say, Mrs. Saraf, you know I'll do. But I think a good beginning is far from a successful end. Wouldn't you agree?"

"We've made more than a good beginning, and you know it," she smiled. "The authorities will search and search and never find anything. They've been here and they've been to the agency, and they found nothing but a dying woman and a well-run, successful social service." Williams had to agree.

"Then call everyone to the Center," she said. "I want to tell them myself that we are finished, and that their money is ready for them."

None of the assassins could believe their eyes when they saw Mrs. Saraf. She was a stick. A bone. Williams pushed her in a wheelchair, and it was from the chair that she addressed everyone.

"Thank you all for coming, tonight. I'm ending our project as of this moment."

Shocked denials were voiced, and it took Williams' strong presence to call them back to order. "We've dented the institution," Ms. Saraf continued, "and it will be much improved as a direct result of what we've done. I want you all to establish yourselves wherever you choose. Williams has your pay packets, and instructions on how and where to access your money. Just remember, $5 million doesn't go as far as it used to." At that they all laughed. Then she added, "That's why I've added another $5 million, as a bonus." Astonished gasps of disbelief filled the room.

"Try not to call attention to yourselves," Ms. Saraf went on. "If you need to move, do so, but do it quietly. Those of you with families need to get reacquainted. Large cash supplies will cause you and them problems. Under no circumstances let anyone in your extended family know about your wealth. Cousins will emerge from everywhere asking you for money. Do things slowly, and in character with who you were at one time, before you knew me. Good luck to you all, and thank you for your help."

Jack Sparks could not believe his ears. He was stunned, as everyone was. He began to protest, but Williams stopped him to say he'd be back in two hours. First he had to take Mrs. Saraf home.

Those two hours seemed like an eternity. The group talked animatedly among themselves, everyone feeling as if the rug had just been yanked out from under them. Several suggested that they continue on their own, as though Mrs. Saraf had never existed. Collectively they had enough money to do it, didn't they? Others were glad to be done with it, and just hoped they could carry off the rest of their lives without getting caught.

When Williams returned, he told them all that Mrs. Saraf was sure to die within the next 72 to 96 hours. No one from the group was to acknowledge having known her in any way. The only exception to that rule would be her cousin, Hannah. They would have to mourn her passing some other way. Nor were they to make any memorials, or give any money to any charity in her name and honor. In no way were they to be associated with her. After all, in real life they would never have known her. Why, now, all of a sudden, would perfect strangers do something like that? The authorities would see such a gesture as a clue, and would be calling on them faster than the proverbial speeding bullet.

Bring no attention to yourselves, Williams continued. Don't pay cash for anything large. Use bank monies if you take out mortgages. Use credit cards sparingly, or not at all. Drive a good used car, but don't buy anything big or flashy for at least the next year and a half. Then a slight increase might be okay, but nothing that will call attention to you and your new wealth. The temptation to go large will be great, but restraint and discipline would better serve all.

He was, he told them, proud to have served with each and every one of them. They had reason to be proud, and even more reason to be careful. How much longer they could have carried on was anybody's guess. Even blind squirrels found a nut now and again, and the FBI had excellent eyes and ears everywhere. But he agreed with Mrs. Saraf that the game was over, and that it was time to go. He asked Jack Sparks, Melvin Hogan, Rusty McCaffry, Floyd Briggs, and Lawrence Craig to stay after everyone else left. They agreed.

Then goodbyes were said, and everyone left feeling whatever emotions came to them at the moment.

Chapter 19

"I need to destroy and then torch this place," Williams said to the men who had remained behind, "and I need your help. We can't do it all at once, and we can't do it in daylight. Small controlled explosions will ruin everything, first. Then, small fires will consume what we blow up. When that's done, I want this place flooded with cement. Any suggestions?"

"That's a lot of ceeee-ment," Melvin Hogan drawled.

"What else could we use," asked Williams, "that would seal this place forever and a day?"

"How about pig shit?" offered Melvin. The laughter was hearty. They needed a good laugh. But Melvin was serious. "Ever been to North Carolina, fellas? Nationally, North Carolina ranks No. 42 in teachers' pay, but it ranks No. 1 in pig shit. Pig shit is a big problem in that state. It's kept in holding compounds that are no more than earthen dams. When a hurricane or a bad storm hits, some of them dams break, and entire rivers are killed by the runoff. I know one farmer in Wallace who would pay us if we could take enough pig shit from him to fill these two rooms."

More uncontrolled laughter. But soon it ended, and the men began to think about pig shit in a new way. What about the smell? Surely someone in the neighborhood or in the *Been There, Done That* would get a whiff of the foul smelling stuff. Good question.

Melvin thought out loud, "If we can channel cement down the elevator shaft, and by-pass the car itself to pump in the ceeee-ment, then we can do the same thing for the pig stuff. But first we'll build plywood walls at the end of the corridor to seal off the smell while we fill the rooms. When the rooms are full, we'll pump cement behind the wooden retaining walls. Twelve feet of concrete that's 12 feet high and 12 feet wide will make it tighter than Tut's tomb when we're done." How many truckloads would it take, and how soon could Melvin get the stuff here? He didn't know the answers, but he was willing to find out.

While the others stayed behind to explode and burn, Melvin and Jack Sparks took one of the vans and drove to Wallace, North Carolina, that night. They got a few hours sleep before they went to the Bergemann Hog Farm, just outside of Wallace. The Bergemann farm was not part of a conglomerate, as so many of the hog farms were. Melvin had grown up with Bergie, and had worked on his farm before going to Vietnam. Over the years they had drifted apart. Bergie didn't recognize Melvin at first, but the two renewed whatever friendship they had very quickly.

Melvin introduced Jack as a business partner from D. C. He then told Bergie he was there because he wanted to buy a large quantity of pig shit, and have it delivered to D. C. as fast as humanly possible.

Bergemann was dumbfounded. He had enough product, that was for sure, but to get it to D. C. from North Carolina was another story. He liked the idea of swamping D.C. in genuine North Carolina pig shit, and the money was right. It alone would have made the effort worth while, but the opportunity to dump on D.C. was the real clincher.

Bergie needed tanker trucks. He called every trucker he knew within 200 miles of Wallace, and asked them to call every trucker they knew. In the end, Bergie contacted and hired 156 independent truckers who could keep their mouths shut when this thing was over. They were good old boys, every last one of them, and their large cash payments were none of the god damn government's business.

They made two runs. One hundred fifty-six tanker trucks carried enough liquefied pig shit to fill one floor of the Center. As each truck was loaded, it left for the Center. When it arrived, it pumped out its content and left for a second load. When the job was done, the trucks simply faded back into whatever town or farm or hamlet they had come from. Each trucker received $25,000 in cash, plus another $3,000 to flush the tanks. Bergie's take was $250,000. All cash.

After all 156 trucks had emptied their bellies of their foul-smelling contents, Williams had 12 cement trucks pour their entire loads behind the elevator shaft, just as Melvin had suggested, to seal in the manure. Williams had to pay the same

$25 thousand dollars per truck load of cement that he paid for the other trucks loaded with North Carolina's finest. Silence and forgetfulness had a price, and fortunately for everyone involved, Williams had the price. It took three nights to complete the project. Because the pumping system was sealed, and everything went into the rooms behind the newly constructed wooden wall, no odor was detected.

On the second night of filling, a D. C. police cruiser came by, and the officers asked what was going on. Williams knew that two innocents had to be sacrificed, and he and Lawrence Briggs did the job. The dead policemen and their car were taken down in the elevator, and a large opening was made in the plywood wall. The car was driven into the middle of the goo, to be sealed forever behind the cement wall. The plywood wall was hammered shut, and the pumping operation continued. The elevator car itself was left completely operable. It was still needed to carry goods into the *Been There, Done That*.

When they were through, Williams shook each man's hand, thanked him, and said he never wanted to see them again. And good luck. Lastly, he handed Jack Sparks a manila folder, and asked him to drive to New York City and post its content from a box of his choosing. Williams also told Sparks not to touch it bare-fingered.

When Williams went home that night he found that Deborah had died alone and in her sleep. He called Dr. Thompson, who came right over. The Puckett Mortuary picked up the body, and cremated it immediately. News of Deborah's death was given a small mention on the society page several days later. There was no service. Williams spread her ashes in the garden she had loved. He closed the house and left for the airport. His flight to New Zealand was both sad and happy for him. Deborah's attorney had instructions on how to dispose of everything left in her estate. Cousin Hannah was to inherit everything.

Always the good and obedient soldier, Jack Sparks carried out his final order as instructed. The letter was the last Deborah wrote. It read:

We've stopped for now. Everyone has gone aground, as have so many congressmen and women. However, do not think that we cannot reconstitute ourselves as an elite killing machine. I told you that once we were finished, I'd tell all. Well, I'll tell all that you really need to know. Revealing our names and numbers and place of operation would not be helpful to any of us. So that part will remain hidden for now. Maybe in some other time, one of us may tell all, but I doubt it.

Let me begin by saying that we had a lot of money to work with. For example, it took $50 million to kill the congressmen and women in Vietnam. The question is, did we get our money's worth? That all depends on what happens next. If we have not given the body politic enough pain to realize how typical Americans suffer because of the NRA and lobbyists, then we have failed miserably-- especially if no legislation is passed outlawing ammunition and lobbyists. If that proves to be the case, then we'll just have to pick up where we left off, after all the congresspersons come out of hiding. So to the survivors, and to those to be elected, we say do the right thing and put us out of business permanently. It was no fun doing what we did. Do we have any sadness for the families who suffered death at our hands? Absolutely. But our condolences are unwanted and unwelcome, I'm sure. I know that if I were ever to suffer anything like the survivors of these killings suffered, I would not want to hear anything from those who killed the members of my family. I'd only want them to hang, or become krispy critters in some god-awful electric chair.

We were headquartered in...oops, I can't tell you that. But if we are ever to get back together again and continue our work, we'll not return to Baltimore. That, of course, is yet to be determined by the next Congress. A lot of slots have been opened, that need to be filled with real statesmen and women. In filling these vacancies, please elect no politicians who say that all they want to do is listen to the people. She or he is not telling the truth. Past performances prove that politicians do not care about what we think or say. Question: How do you know when a politician is lying? Answer: When his lips are moving. No more politicians, please. The 13 colonies had a population close to one million. And yet statesmen like Thomas Jefferson, George Washington, John Adams, Benjamin Franklin, and many others, emerged out of that tiny number. With our hundreds of millions, surely others can emerge, through whose veins course the verve and intellect of our forebears. For example, elect a farmer from Iowa to Congress and let her or him sit on the committee that controls farming laws. That would be a good beginning. Every time you elect another lawyer to Congress, all you've done is elect someone who knows nothing about real life. Lawyers are trained to argue both sides of any issue. They are then susceptible to every lobbyist who carries the most money to argue his or her side more attractively than another, less endowed lobbyist.

Good luck. We'll be watching. And like the Terminator said, 'We'll be back,' if needed.

PART TWO

Chapter 20

New York Times editor Phillips Bell Ridley thought the two-page, double-spaced message was a joke. Which one of his staff was responsible? Negatives all around. It had been mailed from the post office at 12th and Broadway. Probably 20 people had handled the plain white, self-sealing envelope with its own printed stamp. What if it was real? Shouldn't they call the FBI?

In the end, like CNN had done, they rushed it to press, and it splashed page one. Nothing else appeared under the paper's identifying banner and date. No headline, nothing. And just like CNN, the *Times* was visited by another agent, who took the original document and its envelope to the lab. Again, nothing was detected that gave the Feds a clue. The paper was from Office Max stock. An inkjet laser printer had printed the letter. The envelope was standard issue, from any post office in the country. Prints belonged to postal employees and Times people.

Reactions to the *Times* splash were swift. The President called his cabinet together. Everyone was cautiously optimistic. "Baltimore!" was President Huber's first word. He repeated it with the same incredulous tone, "Baltimore! Who'd have thought Baltimore?"

Joe McNaughton interrupted the President of the United States, unbecoming behavior for him. With disgust in his voice he said, "For God's sake, Mr. President, you don't really believe they were headquartered in Baltimore, do you?"

President Huber looked wounded as he turned to his Chief of Staff, and sadly answered, "Yes, I do."

Joe McNaughton was the only person in the room who laughed uncontrollably at the response. He stopped quickly as he realized his mistake. "Sorry, sir. We've all been under a terrible strain," was his lame reply. But the damage was done. McNaughton knew, as did every other person in the room, that he would be replaced in the morning.

National Security Advisor Gene Cummings stepped in to fill the void by offering, "Perhaps Cal Hunter can give us an update!" President Huber agreed.

"Well, sir," Hunter said, "we've sent 50 agents to Baltimore to chase this thing down. If the killers really did work from there, we should be able to find their lair in days. But it's probably a dead end. I'm still convinced they are or were headquartered right here in D.C., and we've not given up looking here just yet. However, no real possibilities have surfaced. Personally, I think they worked out of several locations. Bombs and poisons and make-up and guns can't be assembled without someone somewhere noticing something. We're proceeding methodically, as always, and we will uncover their place or places of operations."

Chapter 21

Plans were made calling for elections to fill the unexpired terms of the assassinated congressmen and women. To no one's surprise, candidates began to emerge who had the backing of their respective parties. Campaign money for these select few also began to surface, from selective sources. Lobbyists. Ordinary citizens found it difficult to get into the game, and quickly went back to their televisions. One month for campaigning was called for, and every day was used to saturate the airwaves with this promise and that. All said they were for gun reform and ammunition control, but not one candidate even mentioned lobbyists. Several spouses ran to replace their dead husbands or wives. Few of them had any opposition. The public seemed to be fascinated with the political efforts dominating the news. And yet, no great candidates emerged to run hard against lobbyists and ammunition sales.

The FBI began to pull back its resources to find the assassins, because nobody seemed to care if they were ever caught or not. Particularly was this true in the Senate. They had been almost ignored by the assassins, except for the late Paul Young of Louisiana, and credited by them with having some common sense. Perhaps the FBI should move on, and back-burner this investigation. If something broke down the road, all well and good. If not, that was fine, too.

Rohan Holiday, Special Agent in Charge, was appalled. Wimps, all of them. No stomach for the long haul. And this was proving to be a very long haul. Baltimore was another dead end. If the killers were ever in that city, they had left it as clueless as the crime scenes they had created. Holiday told Cal Hunter to pull everyone out of Baltimore and bring them back to D.C., where they belonged. Hunter complied.

Cal Hunter called together all of the special task forces to report everything they had discovered to date. It wasn't much. And the only name that could now be firmly associated with three events was dead. First, Deborah Safar had moved a lot of money around in the last couple of years. Second, Deborah

Safar had bought a large public building. And third, perhaps the most interesting of all, the killings stopped when Deborah Safar died.

Even Cal Hunter couldn't ignore these facts. "Who inherited when Ms. Safar died?" he asked. It didn't take long to find out. Her cousin from Israel, Hannah Minsk, was to get everything that hadn't been earmarked for charity, research, or individual trust funds. By now Hannah Minsk had a large file, and the FBI was about to add volumes to it.

Hannah had made sure that her absence from Israel for the last six months was well documented. She had been on assignment from her university teaching position. She taught at Tel Aviv University in the diplomatic department, and had been in the United States with 25 graduate students, researching the history of American foreign policy as it applied to Israel. She and everyone in her group had been housed at George Washington University, and had made liberal use of the resources in the Department of State, and in the Library of Congress.

Rohan Holiday arranged to visit Hannah at her mansion, which she had inherited from her cousin, Deborah Safar. "I suppose," he asked her bluntly as soon as he arrived, "it's just coincidental that you returned to Israel shortly after your cousin's death?"

"The one had nothing to do with the other," she replied calmly. "My students' six-month visas had expired, and besides, our research was complete. I came back the other day for the reading of Deborah's will."

"Did you see or have contact with your cousin while you were in D.C.?"

"Of course. We had dinner several times, but she was so ill that it was impossible for her to get out. I didn't have much time to visit her at home, because of my own responsibilities."

"Did you know you were her sole heir?"

"No. I thought she was going to give everything to charities in the U.S. and Israel. I thought I would probably get a few dollars, but not the whole estate."

"Were you surprised?"

Hannah smiled. "Ever think you'd win the lottery? Surprise doesn't even come close. Astonished, yes. The lawyer in charge is still counting the money. I have no idea what the final sum will be, but I assure you, most of it will go to charities. I'll probably spend the rest of my life disposing of it."

Holiday took another tack. "Was your cousin political, to your knowledge?"

"No more than most, I guess. Of course she and Isadore donated money to major political candidates, but other than that, I never heard her say anything political, that I can recall. She gave most of her personal time to gardening, and to the WSO, until her long bout with cancer went into high gear four or five years ago. Then it seemed everything either slowed down or stopped. Isadore's death was a blow from which she never recovered. Deborah was a very private and withdrawn person. I wish I knew more that might be helpful, but I'm afraid I don't."

Holiday decided to catch her off guard. Watching her reaction closely, he asked, "Do you think it possible for her to have masterminded the assassinations of so many congressmen and women?"

Hannah was a consummate actress. With wide-eyed amazement she said, "What did you just ask me?"

"I asked you if you thought it possible for your cousin, Deborah Saraf, to have funded and masterminded the assassinations of so many congressmen and women?"

"Are you serious? Are you out of your mind? My cousin was a giver, not a taker. She couldn't hurt anyone, let alone kill anyone."

Interrupting, Holiday said, "Unlike yourself, Ms. Minsk! We know your military background, and your connection to Israeli Intelligence."

Not missing a beat, Hannah ignored Holiday's revelation and added, "Until she was confined to her wheelchair, she went on Wednesday afternoons to the *Been There, Done That* and served meals, for God's sake!"

"Yes, we know all that," Holiday said brusquely. "But did she have another side?"

"No. She was what she appeared to be. I can't believe that anyone would think her capable of such horrible deeds. What makes you ask such questions?"

"I'll ask the questions, Ms. Minsk. Now, tell me about any of her associates you may have known."

For the next two hours Hannah answered each and every question put to her by FBI agent Holiday. He failed to trip her up, along with everyone else who had ever tried. But when he finally left, he took with him the horrible feeling that Deborah Safar had been responsible, although he couldn't figure out how. He also had the strong gut feeling that Hannah Minsk wasn't telling him everything. Perhaps she was in on it.

When Rohan Holiday left, Hannah called El Al Airlines for the next flight to Tel Aviv. It left in five hours, and there were still two seats available in first class. She booked one and decided to leave for the airport as quickly as she could lock the doors. It would be a long time before she would return to this place. Her past training, and years of experience in the Mossad, had made her wary of agent Holiday. Hannah felt he might try to follow her, and if he discovered her destination was the airport, he might find some reason to detain her.

Her cab arrived 20 minutes after she called. The driver seemed too eager to ask her where she was going, and how long she would be gone. Hannah's suspicions were aroused. With nearly four hours remaining before her flight left, she decided to avoid the airport temporarily, and asked the cabby to take her to the Israeli Embassy. Once there, she deliberately tipped the driver inadequately, and he did not complain. Big mistake. The FBI was interested in her. And she knew why! She had to do something to refocus their search, and she thought she knew just what that was.

At the front desk she showed her Israeli passport and asked to see Ambassador Samuel Habel. Did she have an appointment? No. Could someone else help her? No, but she would talk to that someone else if they were available. The receptionist pusher her buzzer and asked, "Can you see a Ms. Minsk? You can? I'll send her up." The receptionist then told

Hannah to go up to the second floor and turn left. Zve Shimon, the ambassador's deputy, would see her immediately.

Hannah thanked her for her help, and walked up the elegant flight of stairs to the second floor. Zve Shimon received her himself. "How can I help you, Ms....?"

"Minsk," she answered. "You can get me in to see the ambassador, Mr. Shimon. My business is of a financial nature, and I must see him immediately. I'm talking about an obscene amount of money, and I haven't much time."

Somewhat flustered, deputy Shimon sputtered, "I'll see if he can see you."

Five minutes went by, and the ambassador himself arrived to escort Hannah to his spacious office. "What's this Zve was saying, about an obscene amount of money?" had to do for "hello."

"Thank you for seeing me, Mr. Ambassador. I'm Hannah Minsk, cousin of Deborah Safar, and sole inheritor of her entire fortune. To begin, I'd like to donate her mansion and surrounding gardens to the embassy. I'll see to it that at no time will the property require upkeep from Israel. Perhaps it could be used for cultural events. If you saw it as an asset, I'd like it to become a part of the Israeli Embassy complex."

Ambassador Habel was known for his smooth manner, but this offer from nowhere caught him without an answer. He babbled something about checking with his government, and if it were the right thing to do, certainly, he would receive the property. How could he get in touch with her?

Hannah extended her card, and the card of the attorney handling Deborah's estate. As the ambassador reached to take them, Hannah took his hand and arm, and gently but firmly guided him into the nearest chair. The ambassador was shocked at the ease and grace of her movement. He was too smooth to show fright, but she did have his undivided attention.

"Mr. Ambassador, " she said, "I need something from you, and I need it immediately. I'm being followed by someone who thinks I'm carrying valuables. Would you put me into a car and have me driven to the airport? It's not that I couldn't handle the person myself," she smiled, "but I don't want my private business to get public notice that could prove both inappropriate and dangerous. I mean, how would it look if I disabled some zealous American hanging around the Israeli Embassy?"

"I see your point, Ms. Minsk. Yes, we can assist you. I'll have two decoy cars leave by the front gate. I'll put our receptionist in the front seat. She's about your height and coloring. The second car will be my deputy's, and I'll send him shopping. You'll be in the third car, five minutes later. Your driver is specially trained in defensive driving. Actually, he's my driver and personal bodyguard."

Hannah thanked the ambassador, and asked if they could begin immediately. She had a plane to catch.

Chapter 22

As soon as Deborah's last communication left his hand and went into the mailbox, Jack Sparks knew he needed to vaporize. His instincts told him that his name had already surfaced, and a lot of people would be, or already were, looking for him. But first he had to set up his money.

He spent some of the day in the Chase Manhattan Bank, where he opened an electronic account. It would allow him to deposit funds from anywhere in the world. He then tied the account to a new Visa Card. The only really small problem, for him, had been a name and social security number. He had learned, over the years, to make any kind of phony identification papers he needed. The only one he had never tried was a passport. In his hotel room, before he went to the bank, Sparks cut and pasted and re-arranged his driver's license, and phony social security card, producing a new name and address. In less than three hours, Jack Sparks fell off the planet.

By the end of the day, Sparks began to think of the best way to get out of the city. He reasoned that the commuter train to New Haven, Connecticut, would be the perfect first step. Sparks had one of those bland faces that can only be described as ordinarily uninteresting. In his business that was a blessing. He seemed to be invisible. People would look directly at his unremarkable face and promptly forget him. At just under five feet nine inches and shrinking, Sparks looked the part of a commuter. His tie was unknotted after a hard day at the office. Reading a paperback like many other commuters, he did nothing to call attention to himself on the 45-minute ride. When the train doors opened, several hundred bone-tired executives and salesmen disgorged from one set of seats only to be reseated in waiting cars for the ride home.

Home.

For the first time in a long time, Jack Sparks realized that he didn't have one. His three ex-wives all had fine homes, thanks to his generous nature and his unwillingness to get into pissing contests with skunks. And although his equipment worked most of the time, he always fired blanks. He was sterile. There were no Jack Juniors anywhere, or any Jackies, either. He began to feel sorry for himself.

But then the thought of his money put a smile back on his face. The $10 million financial package from Williams had been deposited in the Banco Di Caribe N.V. on the island of Curacao. Sparks left $2 million there, and moved the rest, in $2 million increments, to four other banks, whose reputation for secrecy was legendary. They were the Bank of Estonia in Bermuda, the Finter Bank of Zurick in Monaco, the Caymanx Trust Company in the Cayman Islands, and the Maerki, Baumann & Co. AG, a very private bank in Zurich.

Using none of his former contacts because they would doubtlessly be watched, Sparks decided to travel and plan on his own. He needed no passport to go into Canada. Via Greyhound he left New Haven for Boston, where he caught another bus to Bar Harbor, Maine. He paid cash for each ticket. In Bar Harbor he caught the ferry to Yarmouth, Nova Scotia, a place he'd never been to in all his years. Sparks felt he could have a nice safe rest there, for at least a month. During that time, he could decide what he was going to do with the rest of his life.

His newly issued Visa Card identified him as Steven R. Purvis, and with it he could access $200 cash at a time, from any ATM anywhere in the world. The bills he created with his card would be paid automatically from the account he had set up in the Chase Manhattan Bank, at Broadway and 70th Street. Electronically he moved $8,000 into it from his account in Bermuda, and would add to it from time to time. Nothing big, Williams had said. Sparks knew that $10,000 was the cut-off figure that made bank officials take notice. But $8,000 was just right. He could let that run down to several hundred before he hit it again, with maybe $6,000 more from one of his other accounts.

His army retirement checks were automatically deposited each month, in another account in Rochester, New York, his hometown. That money would remain untouched. From now on, if he so much as looked at that account, someone would nail him.

But right now he was going on holiday. Not leave. Holiday. It was something he could not remember doing since he had been a kid, when his parents had taken him camping. He intended no such rough outdoor vacation this time. Hotels were the order of the day from here on in.

His two and a half-hour trip to Nova Scotia via the ferry named *The Cat* amazed and delighted Sparks. The big ship traveled at speeds of 55 miles an hour as it glided over the water on a cushion of air. Fellow passengers were all festive. The large bar, though crowded, had enough staff to serve all drinkers quickly. He drank two double Scotches in a booth as far away from the bar as was possible. Company of any kind was the last thing he wanted. But that was not to be. Too many people. Three sisters from Halifax were on their way home to attend their father's funeral, and they just plopped down into Jack's booth. Between drinks and stories and tears, they somehow sucked him into their misery, and he was forced to listen to daddy stories for the next hour. I've already disappeared, he thought wryly.

Chapter 23

Meanwhile, Hannah received a call from Deborah's estate attorney. He assured her that nothing was wrong, and that the accounting was moving forward at all possible speed. He thought he would have a final accounting for her within the next two months. The reason he had contacted her at this time was to let her know of a visitor to his office, a man by the name of Holiday, as in FBI Agent Rohan Holiday. The agent had wanted a copy of all financial dealings conducted by Deborah for the last five years. The attorney didn't know how he could possibly comply, and needed Hannah's advice. Could she please return to D.C. to see him?

Indeed, she could. She'd get the next flight.

It did not surprise her when Rohan Holiday met her at the gate. With an agent on either side of him, he asked Hannah if she would accompany them to the FBI building for a few questions. She assured Agent Holiday that she did mind, but she would gladly see him the next day. Her business prevented her from complying with his request just then.

Holiday was not a man to be put off once he felt an unacceptable stall was being played. "I'm afraid I have to insist, Ms. Minsk. You see, we think the money you've inherited is all kosher, if you know what I mean. It's just that the sums spent before you inherited it stink, and we need you to help us sort things out."

Sensing things were not what they appeared to be, Hannah asked as coolly as she could, "How could I possibly be of any help to you, Agent Holiday? I'm not an accountant. Talk to my lawyer. He'll help you, I'm sure." With that she began to stride away at a brisk pace.

It caught all three agents completely off guard, and they practically had to run to catch up with her. "Now just a minute, Missy," Holiday blustered, as he grabbed for Hannah's arm.

She spun around quickly, and with her extended right elbow caught Holiday squarely in the nose, breaking it. Blood spurted everywhere. The other two agents went for their guns, but too late. Hannah now traveled with two bodyguards, who were close behind Holiday and his two goons. They flattened the FBI agents with billy clubs before the men knew what hit them.

Hannah nodded thanks to her bodyguards as they stepped forward and waited for her to disappear into the crowd with them. But before she left, she pulled the wounded Holiday to the ground by his hair and whispered into his ear, "You smooth talker, you, Rohan. I'll see you tomorrow, as promised. Nine o'clock, Director Hunter's office. Don't be late." With that she walked away, bodyguards closely behind, leaving Holiday holding his bleeding and broken nose in one hand and trying to dial for help on his cell phone with the other. Not a pretty sight.

Cal Hunter was furious. Holiday had not only embarrassed himself, but the Bureau as well. "What were you thinking, Rohan? Those tactics went out when Mr. Hoover died. One more mistake like that, and you'll be removed from this case. Clear?" Holiday nodded meekly.

True to her word, Hannah Minsk appeared at the Hoover Building at 9 a. m. the following morning. But she was not alone. She had retained the services of internationally known and universally respected Attorney Martin Barringer. Her bodyguards were also with her. As instructed, Hannah was to say nothing. Mr. Barringer would do all the talking.

They were escorted into Cal Hunter's office, where Agent Holiday sat mute and sullen with an ugly bandage over his nose. Both eyes were swollen to little black and blue slits. He looked like he'd gone ten rounds with Mike Tyson. Hannah had to smile in spite of herself, and in spite of stricter warnings from Martin Barringer.

"The Bureau," Director Hunter began, "offers its apologies to you, Ms. Minsk, for any inconvenience caused you at the airport yesterday." She started to say something, but her attorney cut her off.

"Apology accepted, Mr. Hunter. I'm Martin Barringer, Ms. Minsk's attorney. I've been retained by Ms. Minsk to answer any questions the Bureau may have of her, which she is more than willing to do." Barringer then handed a business card to

Calvin Hunter and said, "Just submit them in writing, and mail them to this address. You'll get an answer promptly."

Having said that, both Hannah and Martin, who had not sat down, turned around and walked out of the door. The bodyguards followed, two steps behind. Cal Hunter realized he'd just had his nose broken and his eyes blackened, and there was nothing he could do about it. If he were a petty man, which he wasn't, he'd cause Martin Barringer serious anguish. But he knew that Barringer was not the problem. Solving this case was the problem, and he didn't have time to waste on Attorney Barringer. It was time to fish elsewhere.

Special Agent in Charge Rohan Holiday, however, was a cat of a different stripe. He decided he was going to bring Hannah down if it was the last thing he ever did.

"Do you think we'll hear any more from the FBI?" Hannah asked Barringer, when they were safely out of the building.

"Probably," was his one word answer. Then he asked her if there was anything he should know before the written questions arrived. Hannah recounted Agent Holiday's visit to her at the mansion, shortly after Deborah's will had been read. Martin Barringer was shocked that anyone could imagine Deborah Saraf capable of anything like the congressional killings. He'd represented her numerous times when anonymity was essential. Certain charities were never to know who their benefactor was. Once, Barringer recalled, Deborah had called him and asked him to represent a young mother who worked in one of their factories. She had killed her abusive husband one evening, in self-defense. Deborah never knew the poor woman, but could not in good conscience let her go unrepresented. And Agent Holiday thought Deborah was somehow involved with all those recent killings?

"That's the sum and substance of it," Hannah assured him.

"Rest easy," was Barringer's reply, as he nodded understandingly. "I'm here, and they'll have to go through me to get to you."

Before her flight back to Israel, Hannah visited the Israeli Embassy. This time she was expected. Ambassador Habel met her at the door. He had the warranty deed, transferring ownership of Deborah's mansion outside Old Alexandria, Virginia, to the Israeli government, prepared for her signature. One stroke of the pen and it was done. Naturally this transfer had to appear in the local paper, but who would ever notice?

Hannah directed her estate attorney set up a trust in the amount of $75 million, to care for the property and the grounds. The interest from that sum would care for everything for many years into the future. The ambassador assured Hannah that anytime she was in D.C. she need not stay at a hotel. The mansion would always be home to her at any time.

When the Israeli government took possession of the property, it was surprised by the quality of the mansion's security system. Whoever had installed it knew what he/she was doing. All it needed from them was a tweak here and a tweak there. Those tweaks only cost $3.5 million more. Hannah gladly paid the bill.

But the transfer was noticed. Deborah's former neighbors noticed, and they let it be known in the best circles that they were not happy about it. What if some Arab terrorists tried to bomb it? Maybe they'd get hurt in the process.

When news of the property transfer reached Cal Hunter's desk, he called together everyone who had ever worked the Congressional Killings case, as it had now been dubbed. What did this property transfer mean to their investigation? Were they unable to find the headquarters of the killers in D.C. or in Baltimore because it had always been in Old Alexandria? Was Deborah Saraf's mansion, now Israeli soil, headquarters for the killers? With that thought, everything got ratcheted up several notches. The 'What Ifs' fairly flew around the room. Something real, they thought, could finally be attached to the case. Their euphoria suddenly evaporated when the realities of off-limits began to settle in. Short of a declared war with Israel, nothing could open the mansion to their investigation. Not even the Supreme Court of the United States could, or would, ever issue a warrant to search that property. It was no longer American soil.

Cal Hunter thought it was time to call in the Department of State and the CIA. Perhaps they could help by gathering some new information inaccessible to the FBI. He'd call the Secretary of State and the director of the CIA to find out. He'd also send a new set of questions to Martin Barringer. Time to play hardball the only way he knew how.

Secretary of State Cooper "Red" Bryce returned Hunter's call the following morning. He'd been out of the country when Hunter called, and that was the reason for the delay. How could he help the FBI? The Director asked if he could come right over, because the urgent matter required a face to face, not a phone to phone. Certainly, was the answer.

Twenty minutes later the two gentlemen were seated in the Secretary's spacious and comfortable office. No one else was present. "Thank you, Mr. Secretary, for seeing me so quickly," Hunter began.

"Nonsense. Glad to do it. How can I help with whatever it is?"

Director Hunter began the long narrative of the Congressional Killings investigations. As Hunter warmed to his subject, the Secretary of State sat fascinated, until the name Deborah Saraf and the country Israel were mentioned in the same sentence, in a not-so-nice way. His nickname, "Red," didn't come just from his once abundant crop of red hair, now sparse and faded to gray. His temper was legendary. He nearly had a stroke when Cal Hunter asked if the State Department would run an investigation for the FBI.

"Are you out of your friggin' mind?" he bellowed. "We're still eating crow over the Jonathan Pollard fiasco, and you want us to dig a new grave for ourselves? First off, Deborah and Isadore Saraf were personal friends of mine. I knew them for many years. I've been to their home on numerous occasions. So has the president, I might add. Deborah died one of the most painful deaths imaginable. That she gave a lot of money to medical research in the last few years is not anything to get excited about. Hell, she gave a lot of money to a lot of people over the years. I'm shocked and angered that anyone in his right mind would ever put her name in the same sentence with the killers. If you weren't the Director of the FBI, I'd throw you out of here myself. Now as to any investigation State might run trying to connect the Israeli government to the killings because the Safar mansion has become Israeli territory, let me remind you that Deborah didn't donate the mansion. Her heir, Hannah Minsk, did. What's the problem? Am I missing something here, Director?"

Chapter 24

Cal Hunter left Red Bryce's office wondering why so many important doors had been slammed in his face every time he mentioned the name Deborah Saraf. Could she have fooled all of her defenders for so many years? Or was she, as President Huber suggested, a real saint? He didn't know. But one thing he did know was that he didn't like the treatment he was getting as a result of this gentle and good woman, whom everyone seemed to want to canonize. Perhaps his meeting with CIA Director Robert Benton would go better.

It didn't. Benton's answers and responses were nearly carbon copies of Secretary Bryce's. The only difference was that Benton promised that if he turned up something inadvertently, he'd get back to him.

When Hunter got back to his office he was fighting mad. He shut his door and called an old friend, his brother-in-law Phillips Bell Ridley, editor of the *New York Times*. He was put right through to Mr. Ridley's office.

"Phil, its Cal. How are you?"

"Is this just a friendly call, Cal, or am I to assume that you want something?"

"Well, that's a fine how do you do! Of course it's friendly, and yes, I want something. How's my sister?"

"Your sister is just fine. Now can we get to it? I have a luncheon in 20 minutes."

"You'll make it, I promise. I want you to assign your best investigative reporter to the Congressional Killings case. Believe me, our files and results will all be opened to him or her. We won't hold anything back because of National Security. I'm running into stone walls everywhere I go, every time I mention a prominent name that we think may have something to do with the case."

Ridley interrupted. "And might I ask who that is, Calvin?"

Out of habit, and without thinking first, Hunter said, "I can't tell you that."

Ridley interrupted again. "Open, huh? Call me sometime soon, Cal, when you don't talk out of both sides of your mouth. Right now, I have a luncheon to go to." And with that he hung up.

Hunter hit the redial button on his phone. His call was routed through to Ridley's desk, but Ridley had already left. It was one of the things Cal admired about his sister's husband. The man had an independent streak, and he couldn't be intimidated by anyone. Besides, he was smart and could smell a great story when it hit him in the face. Hunter knew Phil would call back after his luncheon.

And he did. "Sorry, Cal, that we got off on a bad note, but I was hungry, and you know how I get when I'm hungry."

"Only too well," Hunter said.

"You said something about my best investigative reporter. Hell, Cal, you're the FBI. I'm just the *New York Times*. You must have thousands of investigators. How can just one of my investigative reporters possibly help you? I'm confused."

Cal Hunter was momentarily stumped. Ridley hadn't risen to editor because he was either stupid or independently wealthy, or both. Looking at things from Ridley's perspective, just what did he expect? He decided to begin with *the* name. "Deborah Saraf."

Dead silence. Then, "No." More silence. "Impossible. I knew her and her late husband, Isadore. "

Before Ridley could begin the usual litany of Saraf virtues, it was Cal Hunter's turn to explode into the phone, "God damn it, Phil, you're doing the same thing to me that every other person from the President of the United States on down has done. Before I can say anything beyond her name, I'm hog-tied, gagged, and hung from the nearest yardarm. I think we have some real solid circumstantial evidence, but I can't get to first base with any of it. President Huber told me that if she hadn't been Jewish, he'd start the process to canonize her. Officially she's out of it, but somewhere inside of everyone's gut in the FBI, we know she was behind this whole damn shooting match!"

"Easy, Cal, easy. Fly me down to your office this afternoon. I can get away around 4:30. We'll talk. I'll bring someone with me, but no promises."

"I'll have a plane ready for you," Hunter replied gratefully. "And Phil, thanks. You're the only one who's been willing to consider our case."

Ridley punched another button on his phone and his secretary answered. "Yes, Mr. Ridley?"

"Helen, get Muriel Brett in here. If she isn't in the building, page her, but get her in here pronto. I need to talk to her. Thank you." Several minutes later Ridley's phone rang. It was Helen. Muriel was on line three.

Ridley pushed line three and said, "Muriel, can you drop whatever you're doing and come to my office? It's not really an option, today. More like a command performance."

"I'll be there in 20 minutes. New York traffic is what it is." Ridley knew it would be at least 45 minutes before she would arrive, so he used the time to call home and tell his wife where he was going, and that he probably would not be back that night. She asked if she could go with him, and he told her to pack her bag and meet him in his office by four.

Muriel Brett had never heard Phil Ridley phrase a request like that before. He was always solicitous of another's welfare, and he was courteous to the core. His toughness was mental. He could persuade most people of the virtue of his opinion long before ego or temper ever entered the picture. He was fond of saying, "It takes no talent to be nice, but you have to work too hard to be a shit." She knew that she was in no trouble, and did not, therefore, approach the coming meeting with any dread. However, the mystery in the request made her eager to know why the editor wanted to see her immediately, if not sooner.

"Ah, Muriel," he began. "Thanks for getting here so quickly. I hope I haven't inconvenienced you."

"Not at all," she began. "For you," and she paused, "anything." They both laughed, knowing that the amenities were now over and the real meeting could begin.

"Muriel," he began, "I've had a request from my brother-in-law, Calvin Hunter. You know he's the Director of the Federal

Bureau of Investigation, yes? Good, good. Well, Cal called me today and asked for my help. Can you imagine such a thing? He wants me to put my best investigative reporter at his disposal to solve the Congressional Killings case. For whatever reason, it seems the FBI is stumped and needs our help. I want you to fly with my wife and me to D.C. in about half an hour. Interested?"

Pulitzer Prize, was all Muriel could think. Interested? Is he crazy? Damn straight!

Chapter 25

Elections were just five days away, and voter turnout was expected to be heavy. Some precincts anticipated a 95% or higher count. None believed they would see less than 65% at their polling places.

Most of the candidates resembled rats, running aimlessly inside a maze. They all looked haggard. Their smiles were beginning to sag, and it seemed to pain them to show teeth one more time, but they were all troopers. Speeches began to sound canned. But there was an upside. There was less mud to sling in this election than in any other in memory. The short time available was one factor, but no public record to criticize was another, for many of the candidates. Several districts pitted two housewives against each other, women who had been friends since grade school. They wished each other the best, no matter what. Their friendship meant more to them than a congressional seat. The media, however, focused on those races where some dirt was being scratched up and tossed around.

Attention was also given to several races where the Christian Right showed great interest in the candidate. Christian fundamentalist candidates, and their supporters, especially, were gasping for their last breaths, trying to push their outdated agendas as hard as possible. But in the blinding light of reality, they were playing just to themselves. They merely didn't know it yet. To the majority of the populous, Christian fundamentalists were religious schizophrenics. Their beliefs came from an earlier century, when the existing technology was soft and easy to use. Horses were the fastest transportation available when their beliefs made any sense. Now it is hard for them to sustain a belief system from that earlier era, when today's technology makes it impossible to live in such a divided way. Fundamentalists use today's technological advances as though they were common, which they are. But somehow the fundamentalists cannot pull their 18th century theology into the 21st century with any ease. More and more of them realize on their own, that their theology and their lives barely intersected, if at all. The only good part about them is that they are truly benign. How did the old song go? "...more to be pitied than censured."

Half way around the world, Williams was resting and enjoying his sister Mary's company. She waited on him as though he was visiting royalty. "Stop, Mary, please," he found himself saying often. " I can't take all this fussing."

At first Williams slept long, undisturbed sleeps. He was more tired than he realized. But after several weeks of pampering and rest, he began to feel lazy. He followed the elections in America as best he could. The New Zealand press did a credible job covering its progress.

Before leaving America, Williams checked his own financial package. He knew Mrs. Saraf would be generous, but never in his dreams had he ever expected to have $110 million with his name on it. To his $10 million for the project, she added a bonus of $100 million. The handwritten personal note in his folder brought tears to his eyes, for a second time. It read, "Dear Williams, your selfless service to Isadore and to me can never be compensated properly. The enclosed is merely a reflection of our admiration, and appreciation for your time with us. I remember the day you told me that all you ever wanted out of life was 'a few kind words.' So characteristic of you. Here they are.

"You always made me feel safe. No matter what, I knew that somehow you would protect me at any cost. You were the big brother I never had. I loved you that way. Live well for both of us. Deborah."

Williams had moved the money several times, until he felt it was broken up sufficiently to call little or no attention to it. Deborah had deposited all of his money in the Bayshore Bank & Trust on the Island of Barbados. It is known as a bank for individuals who are loaded. He left $50 million in it, just because. The rest of it he moved in increments of $5 and $10 million. Should Mary outlive him, which seemed likely, he made provisions for her care. She had access to $2 million in her own trust account in the National Bank of New Zealand. At her death, anything left in that account was to go to the New Zealand

Conservancy, whose main purpose was to preserve as much of the wildness as was left on the two islands. Williams also set up numerous trust funds, to benefit charities and institutions. They were already beginning to receive benefits, and after he died those funds would be supplemented with the residue of his estate.

As for himself, Williams changed nothing. His lifestyle belied his true wealth. He lived simply and inexpensively, as he always had. He bought nothing for himself out of the money he received from Mrs. Safar. He guarded his anonymity with as much energy as he could.

One morning he and Mary were sitting on their open porch overlooking the harbor, when an Auckland police lieutenant walked up the path, and asked if he could speak to Williams for a moment. "Of course, officer," Williams answered calmly. "How may I help you?"

The lieutenant asked if they could go inside, where they might have some privacy. Mary excused herself and left the two men alone. "Mr. Williams," the officer began, "we've received an inquiry regarding you, from the Federal Bureau of Investigation in America."

"Really?" Williams' puzzled frown could not have been more genuine had it been real.

"Really. Were you in the employ of a Deborah Saraf for the last 18 years?"

"Yes, I served Mrs. Saraf and her late husband during that time. When she died several months ago, I officially retired, and came home, here, to live out my days with my only sister, Mary."

"Yes, I see. You bought this house many years ago, with this very purpose in mind, did you?"

Williams nodded assent.

" Well, the FBI asked us to call on you and ask you a few questions. Would that be alright with you?"

"Yes, of course."

"They want to know if you ever saw anything unusual going on in Mrs. Saraf's home during the past few years. Particularly, did a lot of strange people come and go in her home?"

Williams laughed out loud. "Absolutely not!"

Puzzled by William's response, the policeman asked, "Would you elaborate, please?"

"For the past few years," Williams said, becoming serious, "Mrs. Saraf was in the throes of dying. She was terribly weak from the cancer. Her energy was very limited. The only visitors she had were Dr. Thompson, nurses, and old friends on a very limited basis. The last few weeks of her life, Mrs. Saraf was nearly bedridden. Her cancer had reduced her to perhaps 80 pounds when she died. Her strength was minimal. The only people who came in then were nurses and Dr. Thompson. She had no visitors, not even old friends. Every effort was made to disturb her as little as possible. I maintained the residence, myself."

"I see. So you're saying that nothing strange went on in the residence at anytime you served her, and especially not during the past few years, just prior to her death?"

"That is correct." Williams knew full well where this was leading, and he had rehearsed the scene numerous times in his mind.

Sure enough, the lieutenant asked, "Mr. Williams, were you and/or Mrs. Saraf in any way connected to the Congressional Killings?"

Williams immediately changed his demeanor, becoming cold and firm. "No, sir, I was not, nor was Mrs. Saraf. I was her chauffeur, gardener, and housekeeper. Any time that she felt well enough to do anything, it was for one charity or another. She was a major contributor to the Washington Symphony Orchestra. Her last big party at the mansion was a major fundraiser, which she sponsored and hosted annually. I believe $1.6 million came in that day. But you'll have to call the WSO to confirm that amount."

The lieutenant was tiring of this seemingly useless exercise. Where did the FBI get the idea that an extremely wealthy, dying, and now dead, woman and her house servant masterminded the killing of hundreds of congressional representatives?

Williams instantly sensed the man's shift in attitude, and he broke the flow of questioning by offering him some tea. The lieutenant dropped his formal tone upon hearing the request. "Yes, thank you, I'd like that," he smiled. Williams instantly retreated into form, and demonstrated that he had always been, and still was, just a servant.

But the lieutenant wasn't quite done. "The FBI also wants to know about your finances. Did you inherit a lot of money from Mrs. Saraf?"

"Yes," Williams replied, coolly. In addition to his own $110 million, Williams was still the custodian of over $200 million left in the fund Deborah had created to kill the congressmen and women.

"Would you care to tell me how much?" the lieutenant pressed, obviously uncomfortable at being both inquisitor and guest.

"No, I wouldn't," Williams said firmly. "But I will tell you that nearly all of it has been set up in trust funds, for charities right here in New Zealand. One of the charities that has received $25 million American is the inadequately funded pension plan for police officers and their families."

"You don't say!"

"Oh, but I do say. The money is already drawing interest in the Central Bank of New Zealand. I've not made this public knowledge, and I ask that you say nothing anywhere. A path will be beaten to my door by people thinking I can fund everyone's favorite project. Your word, sir?"

"Yes, certainly, sir, my word. But you surely don't expect me to keep this under my hat at headquarters, now, do you?"

"I suggest you talk to your captain, lieutenant. He is the only other officer who knows about this. Also, in two months time, you and every other policeman on the islands will receive a significant raise in pay. I've created another trust fund that begins paying out immediately. If I were the killer the FBI seems to think I am, would I be creating beneficial programs all over New Zealand? The police are not the only underpaid public servants around here. Our hospitals will all be upgraded, and our own symphony orchestra will now have the means to rank with other world class ones. I tell you this just to give you some idea how my supposedly killer brain works. Our schools and universities will also benefit from the inheritance Mrs. Safar left to me. You see, I have no children, and my sister is my only living relative. Mrs. Safar would have approved, I'm sure."

The lieutenant was thunderstruck. "Mr. Williams, I'm truly astonished. I had no idea, of course, and I'm just doing my duty, here, today. I mean no disrespect."

"I do know that, lieutenant. What I don't know is your name," said Williams.

"Robert Charles, Mr. Williams. My name is Robert Charles, and I've been with the force for the last 12 years."

With that, Williams stood, extended his hand, said he hoped he had been helpful, and told the lieutenant he could come back for tea anytime.

After the officer left Mary joined her brother and asked, "What did the policeman want, David?"

Brushing her question aside as though it was nothing, Williams said, "Oh, not much. He needed to fill out some report about my employment in America before I retired here."

Calvin Hunter was not pleased or satisfied when he received the report from Lieutenant Robert Charles, of the Auckland police. According to the lieutenant, Mr. Williams was a simple servant type who had done his mistress' bidding. He appeared to be aging at a normal rate, and the only thing of merit the lieutenant could recommend to the Director was William's generosity. "If more citizens were like Mr. Williams, we'd all be better off," he wrote. Without realizing it, Hunter responded silently in his head with Pooh Bear's phrase, 'Oh bother.' Can't anyone see any criminality in any of these people? he wondered.

Chapter 26

The oldest member of the assassins was Jan Christianson, whose wife had died from lack of treatment while in the care of her HMO. His role in all of the killings had been to drive whatever vehicle was necessary, and to assist Lloyd Evans and Cliff Craft with painting and repainting them. When he received his financial package he went back to his apartment on K Street, where he sat staring at the papers as if they contained some kind of deadly disease. He was afraid to touch it for fear of contracting something horrible. He didn't know what to do with so much money. He almost wished he didn't have it. But unlike the others he didn't think he had a lot of time left, and if he was ever going to enjoy any of it, it had to be soon.

Mrs. Safar had warned everyone not to flash money around, or to call attention to themselves by buying expensive items. It took Jan two days to get the courage to access his account. The instructions were quite simple. His money had been deposited in the Banque de Gestion E. de Rothschild, 2, avenue de Monte-Carlo, in Monaco. It was in his AKA name of Noah Slutski. Noah Slutski, for God's sake. He had never liked the name, and wondered why Williams couldn't have come up with one more American-sounding. And then he laughed. Who cares? It had worked so far, hadn't it? His account number was 398-18503-j104-496, and all he needed to get his money was a fax machine.

Although he had enough money in his present account to see him through several months, Jan began to think of all the things he could do if he had more. He'd never been to Arizona, for example. And the more he thought about it, the better Arizona sounded. He'd go there, and just maybe he'd buy a house there. He called a travel agent and asked her to get him a first class ticket on the next available plane to Phoenix. Within minutes she found him a flight leaving Dulles for Atlanta, then on to Phoenix. His plane left the next morning. How was he going to pay for the ticket, the agent wanted to know. Was cash, okay, he asked? Cash would work. Drop it off this afternoon, please.

Jan went to the public fax at Kinko's, and instructed the Banque de Gestion E. de Rothschild, to wire $250,000 to his account in the Jefferson Bank on G Street, Washington, D.C. He did not ask for any confirmation that the transfer had actually gone through, he just walked over to his bank and asked for his current balance. To his delight, the money had already arrived, and was immediately available to him. He asked for $3,000, in $100 bills. The teller counted out the money and handed it through the glass.

Jan never looked at the money or the withdrawal slip. Without counting it he simply folded it and stuffed it into his right front pocket, where it bulged somewhat. To his delight there had been no hassle; no one seemed to pay the slightest mind. Maybe Mrs. Safar had been a little over-cautious in this catagory. He headed for the travel agency to pay for his ticket.

Perhaps his head was a little airy, his step a little bouncy. But neither he nor the businessman walking beside him saw the garbage truck whose brakes failed at the moment the men stepped foot into the crossing. The truck flattened both men, and killed them instantly. Police and paramedics were on the scene within minutes. Each man was loaded into an ambulance and taken to Howard University Hospital, where they were pronounced dead on arrival.

The Jefferson Bank informed the Departments of Treasury and Justice of the unusually large wire deposit that had come in from a Monaco bank. When the police arrived at the morgue to go through the victims' pockets for identification, they were surprised by the large amount of cash in Jan Christianson's pocket. His expired driver's license said he was from Hagerstown, Maryland. When they tried to contact anyone at the address on the license, they found out that he had moved from there several years ago, and nobody in that area knew where he was. Did he have any family? Not that anyone knew about. Someone remembered that his wife had died shortly before he left town. What about children? People just couldn't remember any.

FBI agents Herford and Hooks called at Mr. Jan Christianson's apartment the next day. No answer. A neighbor lady heard the knocking and informed the gentlemen that Mr. Christianson was one of the two men killed in that terrible accident yesterday. The agents left quickly and called the information in to their office, then headed for the Jefferson Bank.

There they were escorted into the manager's office. Sheila Cornwall had Mr. Christianson's account information on her desk, and handed it over to the agents when they arrived. They inspected it closely.

Mr. Christianson had opened the account two and a half years ago, with an initial deposit of $7,000. His rent started at $2,200 each month, and had gone to $2,600 three months ago. Weekly cash withdrawals totaled $200. Some weeks he took out $250. He sent $1,800 monthly to the County Home in Fredricksburg, Maryland. A call there led the agents to Rosey Christianson, 92 years old and senile, and Jan Christianson's only living relative. Further investigation revealed he had no written will. No lawyer in Hagerstown had prepared one, and a quick check in Christianson's neighborhood found none had been prepared in D.C.

News of this unusual death was sniffed out by *Washington Post* cub reporter Lynn Smolen. Her beat was the city morgue, and anything that smelled like a talk show subject. It was a tough start for a beginner; for the last six months everything had been overshadowed by the Congressional Killings. The only exception had been the disappearance of two policemen and their patrol car. They had just disappeared from the face of the earth. Among Lynn's readership, speculation was high that aliens had swooped down and taken them to another galaxy. The policemen's last reported call-in was from Howard University, where they had stopped to check out an alleged bicycle snatching. They had not been heard from since.

Lynn's column, which usually ran near the back page of section D in the Sunday paper, got moved to the front page of that section. Her editor thought she might be on to something.

"An elderly gentleman named Jan Christianson," it read, "was killed two days ago by a garbage truck, whose brakes failed at the red light on G Gtreet at Wisconsin Avenue. What makes this story so interesting is cash. Lots and lots of cash. Mr.

Christianson had just withdrawn $3,000 from the Jefferson Bank on G Street, moments before he was killed. But even more interesting was the fact that he had had $250,000 wired into that account from a bank in Monaco, minutes before he withdrew the $3,000. Until two and a half years ago, Mr. Christianson lived in a rundown neighborhood in Hagarstown, Maryland. And until his death, he lived in a nice apartment here in D.C. Who was Jan Christianson, and where and how did he get all of this money?

"Mr. Christianson, a widower, had no family, other than an older sister who is in the County Home in Fredricksburg, Maryland. Each month he sent $1,800 there, to pay for her care. Neighbors indicated Mr. Christianson seemed to be retired. Where did this money come from? The Monaco Banque de Gestion E. de Rothschild will not comment on the wire transfer. Treasury officials are trying to find out more from the bank about Mr. Christianson's account. Besides 'No comment,' the only thing the bank will say is that they have no money in any account under the name of Jan Christianson. The obvious next question is, under what name did they transfer $250,000 on the day in question? Their response? 'No comment.' Was the account emptied? Again, 'No comment.' What will become of any funds left in that account, assuming there is still a balance? 'No comment.'"

Wire services picked up Lynn Smolen's story, and several days later it reached the New Zealand press, where Williams read it in horror. All the others in Deborah's group were equally upset when they heard of it. Williams had retained the account numbers and names of all of the original deposits, but if Jan Christianson had moved the money before he had accessed it, Williams would never find it. He used his battery-powered laptop and called Jan's name up on his screen. Mrs. Safar had deposited Jan's money in the Rothschild bank. Williams needed to know if Jan had moved the money.

He told Mary he had to go into Auckland for a while, and left immediately for the nearest public fax. He knew that the Monaco Bank would not give out any information whatsoever regarding any of their accounts. He punched in the Slutski account number, and asked that the balance of the money be wired to his numbered account in the Clariden Bank in Zurick. Confirmation of the transfer came back to him moments later.

But the game was far from over, and his retirement had just gone out the proverbial window. He wished he had T. L. Grimes by his side, but that was not to be. From his laptop, Williams called up the instructions Atlas had programmed for Williams to use in a pinch. This was definitely a pinch.

He went home and switched his computer from battery to regular current. Next he plugged it into his telephone line, and woke up a sleeping computer in the most elite antiterrorist unit of the Pentagon. This unit, known only as Delta Force, is a phantom, because to the world it doesn't exist.

Williams and T. L. Grimes had gained access only once, through a wrong turn on Williams' computer. At the Center one evening, they had been hacking for travel and security status of the congressmen and women on junket. They figured the Pentagon was a good place to check. T. L's finger had hit two keys at the same time, instead of one. He reached for the "e" key and his fingernail snagged the "4" key simultaneously. All of a sudden his screen went crazy. After several seconds, T. L. realized what unit he'd contacted, and disconnected instantly. But he never forgot who he'd contacted, and how to do it. He and Williams decided that only in dire emergencies would they ever attempt to access that computer again.

From the Pentagon connection, Williams contacted the computer on Ambassador Habel's desk in the Israeli Embassy. The time difference between New Zealand and Washington D.C. is 12 hours. It was three o'clock in the morning in D. C., and Williams presumed the ambassador was asleep. The fax read: "Noah Slutski's contribution will arrive when needed. Regards, Weiner." Hannah Minsk would get the fax, and would know instantly what it was about. Weiner was William's identification name, which Hannah and he had used for many years. After Deborah's death, Williams had shared all of the operatives' names with Hannah, just in case. At the time he didn't have a specific reason for doing it, but he felt it was important. Little did he imagine he'd need to use them so soon.

Chapter 27

Williams would never put Hannah at any risk, but this situation called for some tiny exposure. Perhaps the communication would slide unnoticed by the Echelon satellites. One could hope. Unfortunately, Echelon had been told to monitor any and all communications that went to or came from Hannah Minsk. So significant was Williams' fax that CIA Director Robert Benton asked President Huber for an early morning meeting at the White House. He also asked that Cal Hunter attend.

FBI Director Cal Hunter met his brother-in-law Ridley at Dulles at 6 p.m. Hunter was delighted to see his sister Margaret. He'd never met Muriel Brett before, but he had admired her work for many years. A good choice, he thought. Cal Hunter was always the gracious host, and he took everyone to the Café La Tort in Georgetown. His wife, Marsha, was already at the table when they all arrived. The menu was extensive and suited most palates. Amenities over and orders placed, Cal plunged right in, with a synopsis of the case to date. With Hunter's permission Muriel ran a small tape. She did not want to miss anything he said, and later she wanted to be able to take notes and to reflect on the tape's content. The food came. Everyone, especially Phillips Bell Ridley, dove into it, and silence was observed for the next 10 minutes. Everyone was famished. Coffee and desert, and the two wives left for the Hunter home while Cal, Phillips, and Muriel headed for Hunter's office.

"The killers have stymied us at every juncture," he began. "They knew how to clean a kill site better than anyone I've ever encountered. Their timing has been perfect. And their faxes are so damn reasonable." Hunter went on to tell them about his meeting with the Secretary of State and the CIA Director.

"They were right, you know," said Ridley. "State can't do anything. Israel would bloody our nose over this kind of investigation. And we don't have anyone, anymore, who has the courage to take the blow and to hit back. Why the hell is that, Calvin? I remember a time when our country had some backbone. Now our so-called leaders seem to be a bunch of pansies." Hunter agreed with Ridley, but felt obliged to make a lame excuse on behalf of the administration he served.

It was Muriel Brett's turn. "I'm intrigued by the Israeli government getting the Safar mansion. Tell me more about Hannah Minsk. What's her background? Where was she when the killings went down? Things like that, Cal." Again, Hunter detailed what he knew. Just then the red button on his phone lit up, the one that was the direct line to the president.

After listening silently for what seemed like a full minute, Hunter said, "Yes sir. I'll be there." Turning back to his guests, he said, "Well, it seems Ms. Minsk has received an unusual fax from the Israeli embassy. I'm meeting with the president and CIA director Benton first thing in the morning. I'll be back here shortly after 8:30. Be here. I'll let you know what it's all about."

President Huber and CIA Director Benton were sipping coffee when Cal Hunter arrived in the Oval Office. "Good morning, Cal," said the president. Benton had a mischievous smile on his face as he asked Hunter if he had enjoyed his dinner last night.

"Yes, thank you," Cal answered. "Are you monitoring my movements, these days, Robert? I didn't kill all those congressmen and lobbyists. I don't care what the press says."

"Yes, I've heard that before." Both men laughed. President Huber was in the dark regarding this banter, so the two men let him in on the information. "Cal had dinner last evening with his brother-in-law, none other than Phillips Bell Ridley, the editor of the *New York Times*," Benton said. "What's the matter, Cal, can't solve the case with your own staff?"

There was general laughter. "Something like that," Hunter smiled.

All business again, Benton began, "As you know, we've been interested in Hannah Minsk for reasons other than the Congressional Killings. She was, and probably still is, a good intelligence agent for the Israeli government. Her donation of the Saraf mansion to Israel waved all kinds of red flags for us. We've tracked her movements and her communications ever since. Everything was normal until last night. About 3 a.m., a fax left the Israeli Embassy and went directly to Hannah Minsk's office at Tel Aviv University. It read, 'Noah Slutski's contribution will arrive when needed. Regards. Weiner.' We haven't been able to translate the coded message yet, but we're working on it.

"But the interesting part of the communication is in the prompt. This message originated from inside the Pentagon. Our elite antiterrorist group, commonly known as Delta Force, sent it. We know they really didn't send it, but we're at a dead end to know who prompted them. It's virtually impossible to get inside of Delta Force's computers, because on paper the group doesn't exist. Our watchfulness didn't include Delta Force because they're impregnable. Until last night. These folks are good. Real good. Why would anyone go to such lengths to contact Hannah Minsk, unless it was to warn her, or to advise her? About what?"

The president sat listening uneasily throughout the entire recitation. He knew who Hannah Minsk was. He also knew how many times he had told Cal Hunter to back off Deborah Safar. Finally he spoke. "Robert, I'm wondering if you will give Cal, here, your complete files on Hannah Minsk. We all know she's Mossad. But let's do this as quietly and as carefully as we can. I don't want to tip our hand to the Israelis, or to Ms. Minsk. Agreed?"

"Of course, Mr. President, I can do that. I'll put everything I have on her in a file and send it over to you this morning. Okay, Cal?"

"That will be fine, and thanks, Robert," Hunter replied. He couldn't help adding wryly, "It isn't everyday we get such cooperation from you folks."

But the meeting didn't end on that nicety. Director Benton had more. "We've been watching a lot of money fly around the world in the last few weeks. For example that old man, Jan Christianson, who was killed a few days ago by a garbage truck, moved $250,000 from a bank in Monaco, for God's sake. Where and how did he ever accumulate that much money? We've just recently developed a technology that lets us get, ever so slightly, inside the world of electronic banking, and it seems that Deborah Safar set up an open account worth $5 million, two years ago, for a man named Noah Slutski. Just before she died, she moved another $5 million into that account. That account was never accessed until recently. And do I have to tell you the amount that was withdrawn? Right. $250,000, and it was wired from the Slutski account to the Christianson account, right here in D.C."

He had the full attention of both listeners now. "Yes, and it gets juicier! A week after the first transfer, the balance in the Slutski account got moved. Where, and by whom, our technological wizard hasn't figured out yet, and he may never uncover it, because we haven't been able to get behind the Delta prompt. But now, the soup gets real thin. It's a stretch, but I'm of the opinion that the fax sent to Hannah Minsk was to let her know that Jan Christianson's, or Noah Slutski's, account had been erased, and that nothing could tie her to the money."

"Holy Toledo!" exclaimed the President.

Chapter 28

Wade Jackson could hardly wait to get out of Dodge. The morning after the assassins had been disbanded and given their financial packages, Jackson had moved $1 million from his account in the Caribbean Bank of Commerce Ltd., on St John's Island, to the Bank of Antigua, also on St. John's. He wanted to see if he could do it, and if in fact the money was really there. It was.

Then he flew to Montana to see his wife. She looked so old, and so pitiful. There was not a single sign that she recognized him. In addition to her deep depression, Alzheimer's had set in, and Jennifer Jackson simply vegetated all day every day. Wade left the sanitarium feeling yet another great loss. His once beautiful wife didn't even know who he was.

He drove his rental car out the institution's front gate as fast as safety allowed, and headed straight for Las Vegas. All his life Wade Jackson had wanted to play in a high stakes poker game. But something had always prevented it. No more. Nothing was going to stand between him and that card table. Nothing. By the time he reached Nevada he'd cried his last tear. They were replaced during the last 10 miles before Vegas, by an itch that was barely recognizable at first, which his mind told him he'd ignored for too long.

So much glitter confused Wade's senses. All the casinos looked alike after a while. He got tired of looking for any one in particular, and decided to pull into the next one on his right. It was an enormous enterprise. It looked like the pictures he remembered of the Taj Mahal. In fact, it was actually called the Taj Mahal II. The parking valet grabbed the $50 and handed Wade his retrieval ticket. Not one word was exchanged between them. Not even a fake "Hello."

Wade had been driving for several hours without a break, and he felt a little dizzy when he took his first step. One of the bellhops thought Wade may have had a few too many, and went to his assistance. Wade waved him off with a tip to his hat. When he walked through the big doors of the casino, a rush of excitement washed over the big man. It took him several seconds to get his bearings, but he managed to see the gaming rooms opening to his right, and the crowded reservation desk getting more crowded by the minute on his left. Not wanting to wait his turn, and fearing that he might not get a room, he walked back outside and found his would-be helper. This time the young man came all the way over and asked if he could be of any assistance. Jackson handed him a $100 bill and asked him if he could get him into the manager's office. For a hundred bucks the young guy would have whistled *I'm a Yankee Doodle Dandy*. "Follow me, sir," he said.

The manager of the Taj was two inches taller than Wade Jackson. He looked like he'd just stepped out of G Q magazine. The only blemish Wade could see was a three-inch scar above the left eyebrow. It was a knife-fight scar if Wade had ever seen one. This dude was not just pretty.

"Mr...?" the manager began.

"Jackson, Wade Jackson."

"Yes, Mr. Jackson, I'm Billy Jelks. I run this place. How can I help you?"

"Well, you can call me Wade, to start with. Then you can tell me if I can put $1 million in your house bank."

Jelks did this every day, and replied, "Of course. We can take a cashier's check if you have it, or we can arrange for a wire transfer if you prefer." Wade was a bit disappointed at the blasé reply. He thought his $1 million opener would get a more enthusiastic response, but evidently it was just a run-of-the-mill item for this big guy.

"You can use the fax in my office if you like," Jelks continued, "or you can go to any bank, or Kinko's, and use theirs. It's entirely up to you. When you're finished let me know, and we'll take you to your suite. Do you have luggage?"

Jackson shook his head negatively, and said, "I assume you'll have everything I need in house, and that I can charge it against my account."

"Correct."

"Where's your fax?" Wade asked. " I'll just use yours if you don't mind."

Jelks led Wade into a small alcove inside his elegant office, where a single fax machine sat at the ready. "You privacy is important to us, Wade. We keep this machine away from everything else in the casino. The next account number printed on that first sheet of paper will be yours. Just hand-print your name, account number, and the amount you want to withdraw. Dial your bank's number and press 'send.' The money will appear in your Taj Mahal account within the next few minutes." Then Jelks left the alcove.

It took only a few minutes for Wade to complete the paperwork. It had been a long time since he'd had $1 million at his disposal. It felt good. His itch began to assert itself again, ever so slightly. The fax machine jumped to life as he inserted the page. From memory, Wade punched in the numbers connecting him to his account in the Caribbean Bank of Commerce Ltd., on St John's Island, requesting the transfer of funds. The account was under the name of Edmund Sergeant Reynolds.

Although it took only a few minutes for the money to fly around the electronic banking routes, it seemed like forever to Wade. When the fax spit out his confirmation sheet, he picked it up and exited the little 'private' room. Billy Jelks was seated behind his desk waiting for him. "Everything okay, Wade?" he asked.

"Perfect. Appreciate your courtesy." He hesitated. Jelks, sensing there was more, pushed his throne-like chair back and motioned for Wade to sit down, which he did. Then Jelks simply waited.

"I'm wondering if we might have a chat?" Wade began. Jelks nodded. "It's like this, Billy. I've been away for some time, now. I'm sort of rusty, if you know what I mean."

In truth, Jelks wasn't sure what he meant. The 'rust' could have come from several sources: prison; not having had an opportunity to gamble for some time, or just isolation in a rural setting. When Wade realized he'd have to spell it out, his face turned a deep red. Jelks knew, then, and saved Wade any further embarrassment. "I see," he began. "Are you in a big hurry to get to the tables, or are you in a big hurry to get to your room?"

"Neither," said Wade.

That did catch Jelks off guard. Usually, his clients were in a hurry to satisfy their needs. "How can I help, Wade?" he began in earnest.

For the next 15 minutes, Wade Jackson gave Billy Jelks a veritable shopping list of wants. He needed proper clothing, both informal and something appropriate for the high stakes poker games he wanted to enter. All he had were the clothes he wore. He needed a haircut and a proper shave, by a good old fashioned barber. His teeth needed to be cleaned, too. But could it all wait until tomorrow? Right now he was so very tired. All he wanted to do now was sleep. Was that okay? As he reached the door of Jelks' office, he turned and thanked Billy for all his help. "Just one more thing," he said, with some confidence. "I'd like a lady tomorrow evening, who'll stay with me for as long as I'm here. I want her to be around my age, too. Someone nice. Someone who ain't in a hurry."

"Gotcha," was all Jelks said. He hit the buzzer on his phone, and another young bellhop appeared at the door, with the key to Mr. Jackson's suite.

Elegance was the only word that could come close in describing the Taj Mahal II. The view from Wade's suite on the 41st floor was breathtaking. Every exterior wall was glass, from floor to ceiling. Grotesquely large baskets of fresh fruit and flowers were everywhere. Godiva chocolates overflowed candy dishes. The bar in his suite was larger than most neighborhood bars. And it was better stocked, too. Clickers were everywhere. This one made the drapes open and close. That one opened the home-theatre sized television and entertainment center. In all his born days, Wade Jackson had never been in such opulance. It took him 15 minutes to walk through all eight rooms and four full baths. Gold faucets glittered. Waterford figurines sparkled. The place was so clean a surgeon could have done surgery on every bathroom floor. It was too much.

But he was so very tired. He went into the bathroom, stripped, and showered for a long time. He felt so dirty. All the mirrors in his bathroom were steamed when he got out to dry himself. Naturally the towels had never been used before, and they were plush plus. So was the bathrobe hanging on the door. Wade wrapped himself up in it and walked to the bar, where he filled a big glass with ice. The Glenlivit appealed, and he poured a big one. Life was good.

Before he was half finished with his drink, his eyes got very heavy. Within moments he was sound asleep in the big chair beside the oversized bed. He never moved until 4:44 a.m. the next morning. The need to urinate woke him. At first he was disoriented, but it took just a second for him to recover. When he finished in the bathroom, he came back and got into the gigantic bed. He slept another five hours.

What woke him this time was the sound of people in his room. It seemed like an entire army had arrived. First, though, his breakfast was served at the lovely all-glass table beside the bar. How'd they know he liked his eggs over lightly? The Canadian bacon was perfect. And the coffee! Hell, everything about this place was perfect. But who were all these people?

The old black man introduced himself as Clarence, and he was there to cut Mr. Jackson's hair, trim his mustache, and give him a proper shave. While that was being accomplished, a tiny oriental woman, very young, began carving on Wade's fingernails, and damn, when she was done there, began fixing his toenails, too. Several men brought in pants and shirts and shoes, of all styles. Underwear and socks were stacked in several piles, from which Wade was to choose. Others brought in formal wear, and suits with matching shirts and ties. In the end, Wade asked each vendor to pick out for him the things they felt would make him look his best. And could he have some of them right away? He was anxious to get downstairs. "Yes, Mr. Jackson. Of course, Mr. Jackson," was the reply to everything.

The last person in the room was the dental hygienist Wade had requested. Jelks hadn't forgotten or missed anything. Ruthie Friedmeyer worked for a local dentist, but that day she came to the Taj Mahal II before she went to work. With only a few of her office tools at her disposal, she was at a distinct disadvantage, but she did her best to remove the plaque and tartar buildup on Wade's teeth. Mr. Jelks had said he'd make it worth her while. When she left the casino, he handed her three $100 bills.

When Wade Jackson descended in the all-glass elevator, he looked and felt like a new man. No more killings for him. Time to enjoy some of the money he had earned. When he walked out of the elevator, he asked the first bellboy where the high stakes poker game was played. The youngster led Jackson through the casino to the card rooms reserved for the really big moneyed players. The doorman told Wade that it cost $250,000 to buy into any game in the room, and could he get his chips for him? Wade told the doorman his name, and asked him to charge his house account for that sum.

Within seconds, Wade Jackson found himself seated at a high stakes poker table with five other men. There was a minimum of $1.5 million on that table. It took Wade three hours to lose his first $250,000, and three hours more to lose his second. He won several hands in a row, and was up almost $40 grand before his luck turned. But what the hell. It was only money, and he had lots more where that came from. Besides, it wasn't really real. It seemed more like Monopoly money to him. He excused himself and left to get something to eat.

Billy Jelks, dressed in another great suit, greeted him on the other side of the door and asked him how he did.

"Not so good, but I had a lot of fun."

"That's the spirit. Can we go to my office and talk?"

Once there, Jelks asked if Wade was hungry. Starved, was the reply. Was he up for a couple of great steaks, right in the office? Bring 'em on, Wade answered.

When the two men had finished their meal, Billy Jelks brought out two Cuban cigars. Wade was a non-smoker and declined the offer. Billy put both cigars back in the humidor. "Wade, I've been thinking about your last request for a woman your age. I have several in mind, but I'd like to hear what you want."

Wade didn't know what to say. He hadn't thought that far ahead. Just a nice lady was fine by him. Jelks continued. "You know what I mean, don't you? Blond, redhead, white, black, French, Oriental, tall, short, big tits, that type of thing."

Wade thought for several minutes before he answered. "I'd like a very pretty woman. I don't care about much else. I'd like her to be about a head shorter than me. Color of hair doesn't matter. I don't want anyone with silly-cone implants. Natural, you know? Size isn't what's important. Just not real big. I want someone who likes to talk and listen. I want her to make me scream with pleasure when we get there. Other than that…" he stopped short, and laughed heartily. Jelks joined him.

"I'll have someone to your liking within the hour," Jelks said. "If you're through gambling for now, I'll send her up to your room. If you want to try your luck again, I'll have her meet you in the casino. And remember, if you don't like her for any reason, just say so. No use spending your time and money on someone who doesn't suit. Agreed?"

Wade agreed.

He wasn't through gambling, but instead of poker he wanted to try his luck at blackjack. Maybe he'd do better there. By now everyone on the staff knew that Wade Jackson could have as many chips as he wanted, anywhere he wanted them. When he got to the blackjack tables, he was seated at the no-limit table. He asked for and received $50,000 in chips. It took him 20 minutes to lose it all. He asked for another $50,000.

After 50 more minutes went by, Wade had about $4,000 left in chips. He felt a hand rest on his shoulder, and he turned to look at its owner. Smiling back at Wade was, by far, the loveliest lady in the room. At first Wade thought this must be the one Billy Jelks had sent. She was nearly as tall as he, and her creamy chocolate skin made Wade stare in spite of himself. Was she the one? She wasn't. This beautiful person was one of the showgirls from another casino, and she was in the Taj to gamble, just like all the other suckers.

It was moments later that Wade realized he had a bulge in his pants that hadn't been there before Margo sat down. Perhaps he'd better finish out these next few hands and retire to his suite. He was definitely ready for some action of another kind. He looked around, but didn't see anyone in the room looking for him. He sent word for Billy Jelks.

In minutes Jelks met Wade at the door. He began, "Billy, I thought you were sending someone into the casino to meet me."

"Sorry, Wade, I got a phone call that I had to take. Shall I send someone up, now?"

"I'd like that."

His pulse picked up considerably as he rode the elevator. He practically ran to his suite. His hand began to shake as he tried his key in the door. Over the years he'd been with a few women other than his wife, and while he was in D.C. he'd been with several more. But none were going to be like this one. He was sure. He had to go to the bathroom again. When he stepped out, there was a knock at his door. An adrenaline shot hit him everywhere, but he slowed everything down. After all, he didn't want to appear too anxious.

When he opened the door, Wade was greeted by a woman who exceeded every fantasy he'd ever had. She was not just pretty. She was perfect. Her hair was red and tightly cropped. Her clothes were business-like. Not gaudy or suggestive. She extended her hand and said, "I'm Candy, Wade." Wade Jackson took her extended hand and told her how pleased he was to meet her. They stood staring at each other for a few awkward moments until Wade found his voice and said, "Come in, Candy, please, come in. Would you like a drink, or something to eat?"

"No thank you. But I would like a kiss." There it was. She folded into Wade's arms and held him firmly as he bent his head and lips to meet hers. Jackson thought he was in heaven.

Candy broke the kiss after 15 seconds, and turned her head to his shoulder. It was obvious to her that Wade Jackson was a good kisser. He was also easily excited. She turned back to him for another kiss. This time she slid her right hand down and felt his dick as it tried to stretch out in his pants. That would not do. She said, "Why don't we satisfy this right now, Wade?"

"Okay," was all he could get out. They were both out of their clothes as fast as fingers could move, and Wade Jackson knew his luck had turned for the better. Candy was a real beauty. She pulled him onto the bed and rolled him on his back, and began to suck his cock slowly, and then more vigorously. He could not remember when he had ever enjoyed himself more.

When she mounted him Wade didn't try to control anything. He simply let nature take its course.

For the next five or six minutes Candy rode Wade, and enjoyed every animalistic growl and sound of pleasure she could get out of him. When he finally came, Candy kissed him throughout his entire orgasm, then lay quietly on top of him as his entire load ran back out of her and down his cock and balls, to puddle right there in the bed. Neither one moved for a long time.

Wade didn't stay hard for long. Candy suggested that they get into the tub and clean up. He could stay there while she drew the bath. That sounded good to Wade. Within seconds, he was asleep. Candy knew he would do that, so she wrapped herself in one of the great robes already in the room, drew the bath, and waited several minutes before she woke Wade. But she didn't just let him walk to the tub. Taking his dick in her hand, she walked in front of him and led him to the tub. All the time, she had him hold her breasts, and kiss the top of her head. This, indeed, was a passionate woman.

The bath crystals and soaps were scented with fragrances unfamiliar to Wade's nose. But he liked them. Candy liked the water very hot, and she told Wade to expect it. Both descended slowly into the huge tub. It took several minutes for them to get used to the water's temperature, but finally they were comfortable.

"Thanks," he said.

"My pleasure," she responded, with a big smile. "We're going to have so much fun together. I promise. Let me wash you, and then you do the same thing to me that I do to you, okay?"

Again, "Okay" was all Wade managed to get out. For the next half hour Candy and Wade played in the tub, gently touching and rubbing soaps and bath oils over every inch of each other's body. Then, "Stand up," she said, and Wade Jackson was immediately on his feet. Candy began to suck his cock again, and he began to feel weak from it all. She told him to sit on the pillow on the edge of the tub, and she would finish him there.

For the next 10 days, Wade and Candy were inseparable. Candy asked Wade for, and received, hundreds of thousands of dollars of her own chips. She gambled away only a few thousand of them, and quietly asked the croupier to cash in the remainder and bring her a check. Wade kept going to the little fax machine in Billy Jelks' office and wiring more and more money to the casino. He didn't care that he was $6 million down. He was in lust again, and he was having the time of his life.

When two treasury agents showed up in Billy Jelks' office, asking for one Edmund Sergeant Reynolds, Billy told them that he'd have to check, but he couldn't remember anyone by that name ever having been in the casino. The agents asked, did he know where Reynolds went? No. Did Reynolds win a lot of money? Can't say. Did he lose a lot of money? Don't know. The agents thanked him for his time.

Billy said, "That's okay, but why are you asking about a Mr. Reynolds? Is he in some kind of trouble?" They answered his question with another thank you, and left.

As soon as the agents were out the door, Jelks called head of security for the casino. Big Al was a formidably strong man whose best quality was his mind. No question, Big Al could beat you in the physical department, but he was always three or four steps ahead of you in the mental game.

"We've got a problem, Al," was the opener from Jelks. "Two treasury agents were here asking about Edmund Reynolds, known to us as one Mr. Wade Jackson. I told them no one here was registered by that name, but I'm sure they didn't believe me. Make the records reflect that Wade Jackson checked out two days ago. And then check him out--for good."

"You got it, Billy," was all the big man said.

Jelks was curious if Jackson, or Reynolds, or whoever the hell he was, had anything left in his offshore account, and he looked at the duplicate copies of all six transactions Jackson had executed from the fax machine in his office.

While Big Al was taking care of the Wade Jackson problem, Jelks told the front desk that he would be gone for a few hours, and asked them to inform assistant manager Tommy D'Agilio of his absence. Jelks had to think. If he moved money from Jackson's account to the casino, it would show, and he'd only get his cut from it. If he took all of it and didn't inform the owners of his intentions, he could get a visit from Big Al's counterpart. What to do?

Greed won out. Jelks went to the Kinko's office furthest from the Taj Mahal II, and sent the fax requesting the balance of account #LY932-841V-065 be sent to his personal account in the Mizrahi Bank on the Cayman Islands. Moments later, he got back the confirmation sheet that $3 million had been transferred to his account, and that the account in Caribbean Bank of Commerce Ltd., was now closed. He could not believe his good fortune.

When Jelks returned to the casino, Big Al was not yet back from his grim business. Al knew the biggest problem in getting rid of a body was that the damn thing didn't disappear all at once. If simply buried out in the dry desert, it would take a hundred years for it to decay beyond a forensic lab's ability to identify it. Besides, kids and prospectors were always finding them. Big Al's solution was grim, but very effective. He kept a truck, and the largest Davy tree-grinding machine manufactured, in a garage facility 45 miles out in the desert. Every body Al needed to get rid of got the exact same treatment.

Usually, he broke his victim's neck. Rarely did he ever shoot anyone. Cleaning up the blood was a problem. Then the body was ground up, feet first, into a firebox. The public would be amazed at the heat generated by sagebrush and gasoline in a steel box, vented at the top and bottom. After grinding the body, Big Al just kept grinding sagebrush, and all evidence of flesh and blood passing through the blades got scraped, then burned, away. When everything had been successfully incinerated, Big Al opened the two side panels of the firebox and let the wind do the rest.

Chapter 29

Cal Hunter returned to his office, where he met with his brother-in-law Ridley and investigative reporter Muriel Brett. He knew that no matter what he told them, or, conversely, did not tell them, he would forever be tagged as the leak in the FBI, so he decided what the hell. He told them everything he knew.

Just before they were ready to leave Cal's office, his secretary buzzed him and indicated a Ms. Lynn Smolen was waiting in his outside office to see him. She was with the *Washington Post*. Ridley asked if there was any way he could get out of the office without being seen by Ms. Smolen. Certainly. Cal buzzed his secretary and asked her to come in. Could she take Mr. Ridley out the back way, please. Muriel asked if she might stay, and pose as an agent or something, just to see if Ms. Smolen had anything of interest.

When Ridley was safely out of the building, Ms. Smolen was shown in to Cal Hunter's office. It was highly unusual, she knew; she was well aware that her chances of seeing "the man" didn't exist, but nevertheless here she was. The woman with Hunter looked familiar, but Lynn couldn't place her, and besides, she was an agent named Kohler.

"How may I help, you, Ms. Smolen?" Cal asked. She was so taken aback by everything in the office that it seemed as though she hadn't heard the question, or realized the time she was wasting. Her head snapped to and she nearly blurted out, "Huh!" but caught herself in the nick of time.

"Mr. Hunter," she said, "I'm a rookie with the *Post*. I cover the morgue and anything unusual. When those two D.C. policemen disappeared some time ago, my readers became convinced, and remain convinced, that they were simply abducted by aliens. What else could explain their complete disappearance, including the D.C. police cruiser they were driving that night?"

Cal's eyes began to cloud, but Muriel's widened. She ventured a question. "Ms. Smolen, is it?" Affirmative nod.

"Ms. Smolen, where did this abduction take place, and at what time?"

"That's the strange part, Agent Kohler. Police records show the cruiser had responded to a call about a stolen bicycle at the Howard University and Hospital area, somewhere around two in the morning. They called back about 2:10 and said it was a hoax. Then, nothing. They were never seen or heard from again."

Cal Hunter abruptly sat bolt upright in his chair. "Will you excuse us, Ms. Smolen, for just a moment? I need to get Agent Kohler going. It'll only take a moment, and then we'll finish the interview." Smolen didn't understand what was happening, but she knew full well that some nerve had just been struck, and that she was being given the fast shuffle.

As soon as Ms. Smolen was safely reinstalled in the outer waiting room, Hunter said, "Muriel, the *Been There, Done That* social agency, funded by Deborah Saraf, is only two blocks away from the Howard University Hospital. There's got to be some connection. I suggest you go undercover somehow, and find out what really goes on there. Call me anytime."

"Alright," was her shocked response.

"I'll have some of my people pose as street people, so you'll always have adequate protection," Hunter said. With that, he buzzed for his secretary to come in and show Muriel the same exit she had just shown his brother-in-law. Next he called Rohan Holiday and asked him to report to his office immediately. "Get some of your best undercover types to get inside the *Been There, Done That*. Have others linger around the building. At all times I want Muriel Brett protected, got that?"

"Yes sir, but who's Muriel Brett?" Damn, Hunter thought. Pictures on file. Get them.

Lynn Smolen was shown back into Director Hunter's office, and apologies were offered for the interruption. How could Mr. Hunter help Ms. Smolen?

"Mr. Hunter, what I really wanted to ask about was that old man, Jan Christianson. I just used that police story to let you know something about the people who read my column. Anyway, the old man ended up in city morgue with 30 crisp, new, $100 bills in his pocket. But you knew that. We've learned that he had just transferred $250,000 from a Monaco bank. Moments after the transfer and withdrawal, he and another fellow were killed by a garbage truck whose brakes failed in the very intersection both men were crossing. Was that just an accident, or do you and the Bureau think he was targeted to die?"

Before he could answer, Lynn Smolen asked another question of merit. "I've had some help chasing down the old gent's background, and there's no way he could have squirreled away that much money in his lifetime. Until his wife died, they lived in the same paid-for $28,000 home for nearly 40 years. No kids. He worked as a truck driver. I know this is a leap, but could he have been one of the Congressional Killers? I mean, his wife died because her HMO wouldn't pay for her treatment. And the messages from the killers said they were just ordinary people, remember? My readers want to know if the FBI killed the old guy, or was he killed by someone within the group of killers to make sure they were never found?"

Cal Hunter was fascinated. After another 10 minutes of Q & A with Lynn Smolen, he indicated his time was limited just then, but told her that in another week he'd be glad to see her again, if she'd call and make an appointment.

As soon as she was out the door, he buzzed for Rohan Holiday. Within minutes Holiday was seated across the desk from his boss. "Rohan, what do you have on Deborah Saraf's financial affairs so far? I'm not really concerned with the estate. But, what do we know about money that went into medical research or trust funds, and who the people are that benefited from her largess?"

Holiday began to carp and wine about Hannah Minsk, but Hunter cut him off. "Enough, Rohan. Just tell me about the money *before* Saraf died."

"Sorry, Cal. I just get so mad every time I think about Minsk. Anyway, over the last three years Deborah Saraf has moved slightly more than $1.5 billion offshore. We've been able to track it from here to several major banks, but from there it's been more than a struggle. By calling every cancer research facility here and abroad, we've learned that she gave more than

$300 million trying to find a cure for her cancer. But all of that money came from banks here in America. Not even one offshore bank received more than a $20 million deposit at any one time. But she sent enough of those $20 millions over the last two years to total a little more than $1.5 billion. We think most of it was moved several times, making it nearly impossible for us to follow to its final destination. Over the last 10 days, however, we've watched an account in the Caribbean Bank of Commerce, Ltd, on St. John Island, wire nearly $6 million to the Taj Mahal II in Vegas. Treasury sent two agents there, but the manager never heard of any Edmund Sergeant Reynolds. The only thing the bank would confirm about the money was that it had been transferred as requested, and that the account had been closed hours after the agents visited the casino. And when we hacked into the casino's computer system, we found out that one Wade Jackson had been registered there, up to and including the day the agents visited the casino, and that Jackson had gone through $6 million in 10 day."

"Holy Toledo!" Cal Hunter was impressed.

"It gets better, Cal. Edmund Sergeant Reynolds has no social security number. But Wade Jackson does. It's 187-46-5071, issued June 9, 1959, in Cheyenne, Wyoming. Until several years ago, he and his wife tried to raise beefaloes in Butte, Montana. They lost everything because the EPA, on a tip, discovered that 300 acres of their land had really toxic pollutants, left there by mining companies and the U.S. of A. Federal government. And to add insult to injury, we made them clean it all up. They lost everything.

"His wife went crazy and ended up in a sanitarium, and Wade Jackson disappeared, until now. Jackson flew from Dulles just 15 days ago to Montana, where he visited his wife for the first time since he admitted her there two years ago. The woman had developed Alzheimer's during Wade's absence. She didn't know him. He left in tears. His rental car ended up in the Taj Mahal II parking garage. That's an oversight on someone's part, and we'll find out whose, to be sure. We've checked around, here in the Capitol, and one Edmund Sergeant Reynolds had an apartment on L Street, one block north of Jan Christianson's, whose address was on K Street. What we now know about Christianson is that he had his apartment in the name of Noah Slutski--the same name on the account in the Monaco Bank that wired $250,000 to Christianson's Jefferson Bank account, just moments before he was struck down by a garbage truck and killed."

Cal Hunter smiled. Perhaps, he reflected, the worm had turned.

Election Day promised more than it delivered. Surprise, surprise. Voter numbers were up slightly when compared to previous elections, but not as dramatically as had been predicted. People tend to be quick forgetters. Bad weather kept many of the faithful away in most of the Northeast, while a power grid failure shut down large segments of the Southwest. Middle America was more interested in the newest Country and Western phenomenon's pay-per-view, day-long charity concert held in Nashville. The Deep South elected many NRA supporters, who quietly gave a wink and a nod, as only they can do. Only two of the spouses of dead congresspersons were defeated at the polls. More men were elected than women, and the majority of them had law degrees.

Williams watched the news with a heavy heart. So did Hannah Minsk and Jack Sparks. When those 248 newly elected replacements arrived, Washington D.C. was in for more chaos than even it could handle. Bud Abbot and Lou Costello's 'Who's On First' routine was about to play nicely once again. Congressional leadership was going to look more like the old football game children played when they didn't have enough players for two teams. It was called 'Throw up and kill.' One kid would throw the ball up in the air, and all the others would try to tackle, or 'kill,' whoever caught it.

If Deborah Saraf's assassins had done nothing else, they had caused Congress to recreate itself. Past seniority systems and horse-trading loyalty bonds no longer existed. Old ropes were gone. It would take many months, perhaps years, to replace the broken congressional "Good Old Boy" system that had been destroyed. Just maybe some of those newly elected would have bright ideas about governing. One could hope.

Chapter 30

Muriel Brett spent two unsuccessful days trying to find a room near the *Been There, Done That*. She wondered if Jan Christianson's apartment had been rented yet. It had. Muriel ended up in the Kalafut Family Motel on N Street. It was only one room and a bath, but she could walk to the agency from there. It took another week to assemble her clothing from Goodwill and Salvation Army secondhand stores. Everything she bought was at least two sizes too big, including underwear. She skipped meals and baths. She dragged her new wardrobe through mud puddles and made rips and tears in several places, including seams. Her hair matted and her teeth scummed up. Her hands browned and her nails broke. By the time she made her entrance at the agency, Muriel looked and smelled like the street urchin she had become.

It was the silly straw hat, however, that completed her image. Broken on one side, with an old pigeon tail feather sticking out of its dirty pink band, and pulled down tightly to her eyebrows, the hat made Muriel Brett evaporate. What emerged was a goofy character who looked lopsided and off kilter. The broken glasses gave her that certain wacky, scatterbrained, unable-to-focus-on-any-one-thing-for-very-long look. Pictures of her transformation were taken by a *New York Times* photographer assigned to capture her story on film. Could a Pulitzer be far behind?

Rohan Holiday's team of protectors were more than impressed by her efforts and commitment. Muriel didn't know any of them, and on purpose had not been introduced. All she knew was that Special Agent Holiday's people were in place, and it was safe for her to do whatever it was that she was going to do at the agency.

Muriel reasoned that her only truth was hunger and filth. The agency didn't care about identity as much as it cared about real need, and after nearly 10 days of deprivations, Muriel was truly hungry. It would play. She did not have to act that part.

Her name? Let's see, how about Muriel? The *Been There, Done That* knew that most of its people had several names. For fun Muriel thought the last name Ringer sounded perfect. She was now Muriel Ringer, from Union, West By God Virginia, if necessary.

To her surprise, that first day she didn't even need just plain Muriel. Lunch had already been served when she arrived, and only a few stragglers were left in the dinning hall, but she was admitted and fed nevertheless. Not one soul or worker wanted to know anything about her. After all, they'd been there and done that. Maybe in time, if she stayed around, someone might ask for her name. Right now, she was hungry. Very. How about some homemade ham bone, bean, and potato soup, hard bread, and coffee? Perfect. Bring it on.

To her surprise, the soup was delicious. The bread crusts were yesterday's unsold loaves, donated from a local bakery. The coffee was excellent. A girl could get to like this place, she thought. She ate hungrily and sloppily, spilling broth on her open sweater and dress front. The butcher-paper tablecloth under her bowl began to wet and stain from her efforts to eat. When she finished she asked for more, like Oliver Twist had, but unlike Oliver she got it. Everyone in the room recognized her for what she was at that moment: a hungry, slightly off, funny looking, dirty woman. Without realizing it, Muriel stuffed a bread crust into one of her grimy pockets. It did not go unnoticed, but nobody cared. They'd all done just that at one time or another.

The new director of the agency came over and sat down beside Muriel while she noisily slurped her coffee. She introduced herself as Laura Isaacson. Muriel got a wild-eyed look on her face and attempted to move away from Ms. Isaacson.

"It's okay," Laura said. "I'm not going to hurt you. All I want to know is, would you like a big slice of peach pie?"

"With some ice cream?" asked Muriel.

"Sure," was the quick reply. Laura stood up and walked back to the kitchen, where she scooped a big dollop of vanilla ice cream and put it beside the pie. This time, after setting the pie and ice cream in front of Muriel, Laura sat across the table from her. Muriel's tiny smile was thanks enough for the other woman. To Muriel's surprise, Laura left without another word.

It took no real effort to finish the pie and ice cream. Muriel was truly hungry. Her eyes darted around the room now, and she could see several other women and men in her condition. All hungry, all dirty, all untrusting of everyone, even those who had served them food and coffee. One of the women stood up and bolted for the door. No one tried to stop her. Not wanting to overstay her first visit, Muriel decided that she would just walk out naturally. However, the room began to spin as she stood up to leave. So much food in her stomach after a 10-day fast was more than she could handle.

Muriel fell backwards onto the bench behind her at the next table, and then forward onto the floor, breaking a tooth when her head hit the floor. The pain was immediate, and she reacted like a cornered animal, flailing her arms and legs in all directions. Blood spattered from her lip and face, where two small cuts bled freely. One of the burly guards was at her side immediately. Where did he come from? she thought. Was he one of her protectors? "Let me help you, miss," was all he said.

"No, no!" Muriel screamed. "I can do it myself. Get away! You'll be hearing from my lawyer, so you will. Damn slippery floor!" Everyone backed away from her, giving her as wide a berth as possible as she staggered to her feet and left.

What was she going to do now? She needed medical and dental attention, for sure, but if she got it, her efforts would all be lost. It took all of her will power to walk back to her room.

Someone had contacted Rohan Holiday, because he was sitting in the only chair in her tiny room when she opened the door. "My God, Muriel," he said, shocked. "You look and smell like hell."

"Thanks, Rohan, you sure do know how to sweet talk a girl," she replied.

"I'll get you to a dentist," he countered, but Muriel cut him off.

"No, I don't work for you, and you can't order me around. I'm in charge here, remember?" Rohan began to protest, but Muriel would not listen. She asked only that he go to a dentist and get a small rubber cap, that she could slip over her broken tooth. It would have to do for now. Within the hour, Agent Holiday was back with the prophylactic she had requested. It fit perfectly. The tooth would have to be capped later. Holiday left without a single question. He had already been briefed by his own people regarding the accident.

The next day Muriel again appeared at the agency. It was very crowded. The menu on Friday was fish sticks, pizza, and Coca Cola, everyone's favorites. Muriel stood in line with the rest of the clients this time. No one talked. An exception was an old, insane, nameless woman who babbled to herself in a language nobody recognized. When Muriel's turn came, the server asked how her lip was. Instinctively, Muriel hid her mouth with her hand and mumbled something that sounded like, "It'll be okay."

An empty table near the kitchen door caught her eye. Trying not to trip or spill anything on her tray, Muriel negotiated the distance from the serving line to the table without mishap. After she swallowed several bites, she noticed that three other people had selected her table to eat at. No one spoke. The silence was unlike anything Muriel had ever experienced. She did not want to do or say anything that might give her away, so she said nothing.

Laura Isaacson appeared and sat down at the head of the table. She had a cup of coffee with her that she sipped now and then. Wild eyed, goofy looking Muriel glanced at Laura quickly, and then looked away so as not to get caught spying. Too late. Laura had been expecting the look, and smiled slightly to indicate it was okay.

"Nice to see all of you today," she began. "I hope you like the food. If you need anything more before you leave today just let me know. For anyone new, showers are in the basement, as well as new and clean clothes. Your privacy will be respected, and you need not rush anything. Men have the showers from 11 a.m. until noon daily, and women have them from 2 p.m. till four. If you need help finding anything, just ask any one of the security officers, and he will take you wherever you need to go.

Bye for now." Speech over, Ms. Isaacson rose and went to another table, where she delivered the same message.

Chapter 31

As soon as Clarissa DeBeau received her financial package, she made one phone call. It was to her former deputy director, Laura Isaacson. She asked Laura to come by the agency after work that day. When Laura arrived, Clarissa told her that she had become too old and too tired to run this enormous project. Did Laura want the job? It was that simple. Clarissa had the new bank card ready for Laura's signature, gave her the keys to the building, and left.

For as long as she could remember, Clarissa DeBeau had wanted to watercolor. As a child she loved art classes in her school, but as she grew up her interest went no further. A hole was left in her soul, over which she grew a patch called reality. But the patch was beginning to fray. She needed to paint. Not knowing how long she might be needed at the *Been There, Done That*, but wanting to be prepared in case anything went wrong, she had applied for and received a passport just several months into the project. Now, with Laura Isaacson at the helm, the world lay before Clarissa. She needed only to decide.

The town of Arles, France, suddenly popped into her head. She remembered that van Gogh had spent time in Arles. And though he painted in oils, nevertheless she loved his colors. Always had. She'd try a visit, and if she liked it, perhaps she'd stay a spell. Enough money was in her personal checking account for a ticket to the south of France. Additionally, from the same account, she signed out another $10,000 and converted it into traveler's checks. She did not need to access her $10 million just yet. Never married, the only daughter of Maurice and Bridgett DeBeau had no ties or family to answer to.

Air France carried her first class to Paris the following day. After she breezed through customs, she asked her taxi driver to take her to a lovely hotel near the Louvre and Notre-Dame Cathedral. Using his best English, the driver said there was only one place for mademoiselle to stay, the Hotel le Ambassador on rue Dauphine. And he was right. It was perfect. Her large room afforded Clarissa the comfort and grace she had earned, and deserved, at this time and stage in her life.

It took her 12 days to visit all the sights within easy walking distance of her hotel. Her favorite activity was meals at the nearby world famous café, les Deux Magots. But after 12 days, it was time to go.

She rented a car and drove south to Grasse, where she booked a room at the Hotel des Parfums. Clarissa's $10,000 worth of traveler's checks had dwindled down to a mere $700 by now, and she realized that she'd need more cash if she were to continue on her quest to reach Arles. But that journey was not to be. Clarissa DeBeau fell in love with the small hotel, its charm and grace. Totally smitten by the place, on impulse she wondered how much money it would take to buy the 71-room facility. Surely it wasn't for sale, but could it be purchased? Who owned it? How could she find out? It would come to her tomorrow. Right now she needed a long hot bath, a great meal, and some sleep.

At breakfast the next morning, Clarissa asked the consergier if he would turn in her rental car. Of course, madam. Next, would he help her find a major bank? Of course, madam. The Banque de France, he said, was only two blocks south of the hotel, and she was well able to walk there. And walk she did, directly. At the information center Clarissa asked to see the bank manager. She wished to open an account. Of course, madam. Right this way, madam. To her great surprise, Clarissa was actually ushered into the bank manager's office, rather than into the cubicle of an account executive whose job it was to open daily accounts.

Jacque Gruier rose quickly and extended his hand to Clarissa. In perfect English he introduced himself and asked for Clarissa's name. Would Ms. DeBeau please be seated? Would Ms. DeBeau care for some tea? No? How can we help?

Clarissa began with a series of questions. "Can I transfer money into your bank electronically?"

"Yes."

"How much money can I transferred without causing authorities in France to ask questions?" $50 million was the answer.

"So, $5 million would not pose any problems?"

"None, madam," he replied.

"Then I'd like to open an account with you by depositing $5 million American, which I'll wire here later today. I'll need an account number, yes?"

"Certainly, madam, and is there anything else?"

"Yes. Do you know who owns the Hotel des Parfums on Boulvard Eugene Charabot?"

"No, madam, but I will inquire for you."

"Discreetly?" she asked.

"But of course, madam."

"Good. See you at three this afternoon."

She started to leave, but M. Gruier reminded her that she needed an account number. Right. He buzzed an account executive and asked him to come back to his office. Moments later a young man appeared. In French, he was ordered to open an electronic account for Ms. Clarissa DeBeau, and to bring the account number to the manager immediately. Address and identity confirmation matters could wait.

That was certainly painless, thought Clarissa as she left the bank. A nice walk around the town would give her plenty of time to think about her rash decision to buy a small hotel in the south of France.

Each step she took made Clarissa realize that this was one less-than-well-thought-out decision she was not going to ignore. If the joint was available, and if she had enough money, she was going to buy it. Although she knew nothing about Grasse, the town itself was enchanting. The air was scented from millions of flowers growing everywhere. The buildings were old. Narrow streets, lovely shops, and no apparent rush to get anywhere or to do anything, began to sink deeply into her consciousness. Thank you, Deborah Saraf, wherever you are, she thought.

By noon, Clarissa had walked far enough. She was hungry. She hailed the first cab that came along, and asked the driver to take her back to the hotel. From her room she ordered lunch. The waiter could not have been any more courteous.

When she finished eating, Clarissa knew it was past time for her to look at her financial package, and how to access it. All she needed, Williams had said, was a fax machine. The hotel had one, she presumed. Yes, it did. Deborah and Williams had not needed to change her name into anything. She was the only legitimate part of the dreadful business that she was so glad to be rid of. She was in France; Ms. Saraf was dead, and Williams was who knows where.

Life was good.

It only took two minutes for $5 million dollars to fly from the European Federal Credit Bank Limited on St. John's Island to the Banque of France, Grasse, branch. True to her word, Clarissa arrived at the bank at three o'clock sharp. M. Gruier was pleased to greet her at the door, and to usher her into his office. Yes, the money had arrived. Thank you for your business. You've made a very wise choice in banks, Ms. DeBeau. We need you to fill out a few forms, all right? Not even $5 million could make those forms disappear. It only insured that they would be there.

The worst of it all was citizenship. The United States of America required large sums of transferred monies by American citizens to be reported to the Treasury Department.

"Any way around that?" she asked.

"Yes, become a French citizen," he answered.

"Can I do that quickly?" she wanted to know.

M. Gruier indicated that it had happened before, with the right amount of cash changing hands in the right places.

"Could M. Gruier make that happen?"

"Certainly, madam. Come back tomorrow morning at 9:30, and we will have all the necessary papers for you to sign, and viola, you will be a citizen of the great Republic of France."

"Now, she said, about the hotel. Who owns it, and can it be purchased?"

"Too soon to say. Tomorrow, perhaps," he indicated.

Clarissa did not sleep well that night. Several bad dreams of dead congresspersons haunted her. She had participated in an evil happening, and she was just as guilty of killing as were the shooters. For her, the end still did not justify the means, $10 million or not.

But at 3:54 a.m. she bolted upright in her bed, awakened by a good dream. She had always believed that dreams were more than psychological road maps into the psyche. Her Southern Baptist faith had informed her that dreams were also pathways that the Divine still used to speak to humans. But just what was it that God wanted her to know?

In her dream, Clarissa had watched masked and richly bejeweled party revelers bobbing for apples with tiny skewers. The enormous tub of floating apples had become *the* attraction at the party. But in her dream, tiny people (all similar in appearance to the 'Who' population in Dr. Seuss's *Horton Hears a Who)* were afloat on the apples, trying to hold on to stems, if any, or flattening themselves out for more traction on top of their rounded red rafts.

The object for the party revelers, it seemed, was to skewer the little people on the apple, and not the apple itself. The little ones, an eighth the size of an M & M, were the real delicacies to be had in this exercise. Partygoers could not get enough of them. They were better than alcohol or cocaine, of which both were there in abundance. Hours of poking and chewing, and laughing at the helplessness of the tiny ones, were needed to finish them off. Clearly, a good time was had by all.

At daybreak, however, when the party ran out of energy, and all the goodies had been eaten, a new sensation began to inflict itself upon the laughers, the skewers, and the chewers. One by one they began to fall down dead, in bathrooms, in cars, on sidewalks, wherever they happened to be at the time. The little ones had realized that if their families and way of life were to survive this taxing humiliation of constant roundup, death, and destruction, all of them would have to do more than just complain to their own authorities. They would have to, as Billy S. had said, "…take arms against a sea of troubles." So they all carried around with them the largest vial of poison they could, in case it ever became their turn in the barrel.

But what did any of it mean, Clarissa wondered? She was famished after all this dreaming and philosophizing, so she called the front desk and asked if it were possible for her to come down to the dining room, or to have something brought to her room. She didn't care which. She just wanted some eggs, toast, coffee, and orange juice. She could come down? Great. The chef was not due in for several hours, but the hotel had a policy that guests, for a price, of course, could visit the kitchen at any hour, if they were willing to prepare the food themselves. She was willing.

It wasn't until her tummy was full and she was enjoying the last sips of orange juice that it struck her. At that precise moment she realized that all was well with her soul. Her redemptive dream epiphany made her laugh out loud at its simplicity. The party going revelers was the American Congress. The tiny persons being skewered and chewed up with impunity and disdain were the American people. All of a sudden, Clarissa felt more proud of herself than at any other time she could remember. She and her tiny band of assassins had done good. Of that she was sure. She also felt the Divine *absolvo te.* And, like Moses of old, she felt the Divine had led her to a different land of milk and honey. This place had to be for sale. It just had to.

M. Gruier had good news for her. Papers were prepared for her signature, and a local judge would administer her oath of citizenship at 10 a.m. The cost for all of this was steep. The sums had already been subtracted from her account. The naturalization officer in Paris required $25,000 American. The couriers needed $10,000, the local judge required $15,000, and M. Gruier asked only $5,000 for brokering the deal.

In less than 24 hours, $55,000 flew out of Clarissa's account. That was more than she used to make in a year, before she went to work at the *Been There, Done That*. But, hey, it was only money, right? Clarissa thanked M. Gruier for his efforts, and indicated the sums were fine. She signed the papers as quickly as she could, never reading anything because they were all in French. At 10 a.m. sharp she renounced her American citizenship and swore allegiance to her new country and home.

Vive la France!

About the hotel, she asked. Currently, it was owned by the proverbial nere-do-well nephew who just last year, had inherited it from his great uncle. The skinny was, between the ponies and the tables in Monaco the young gentleman was strapped for cash, and would be willing to part with the hotel for the mere sum of $7,250,000.

Clarissa could not believe her ears. That was more than three-quarters of her fortune! Impossible. Her shock registered with M. Gruier immediately, and he sat mute for several moments, while Clarissa had a private moment to herself. When she looked at him almost teary eyed, he said, "In reality, Ms. DeBeau, it is worth almost every penny of the asking price. With proper management, it could once again make money for a *resident* owner."

What did that mean, she wondered? "Ms. DeBeau," he continued, "for a small broker's fee, I'll be glad to negotiate a more favorable price for you, but I need your permission to do so."

"By all means," she brightened. "What kind of a fee are we talking about?"

It was all M. Gruier needed. He said, "For every $100,000 I'm able to reduce the asking price, you'll pay me $5,000 American. It will give me motivation to bring that price down considerably, wouldn't you agree?"

Of course it made sense, but internally she resented the cost of doing business with this man. She thought, all the banditos don't work the streets with pistolas. Some of them wore three-piece suits, ties, and shiny shoes, and don't carry guns of any kind. Reluctantly, she replied, "Agreed. Just let me know how much and when. I'd really like to settle in, here, if possible."

"I understand," was the reply.

Three days went by before Clarissa received the call she was waiting for. M. Gruier had reduced the purchase price down to $5,250,000. Clarissa felt she had a good deal. She told Jacque Gruier to draw up the papers, and she would arrange to have more money transferred into her account to cover costs and transfer taxes. That same morning, Clarissa removed another $3 million from St. John's Island and transferred it to her bank in Grasse, France. That covered her costs of ownership. Her initial deposit of $5 million, less $55,000 for the citizenship papers, had left her $4,945,000. Add in the $3 million, and she had $7,945,000. Subtract the $5,250,000 for the hotel, plus M. Gruier's fee of $115,000, and the transfer tax of $52,000, and Clarissa still had $2,280,000 on hand in Grasse, France. She'd leave the remaining $2 million in her account in St. John's, in case she ever needed it.

That settled, where could she buy watercolor supplies?

Chapter 32

Weeks went by for Muriel. She went daily to the *Been There, Done That* hoping to find some clues that she could use to expose the Congressional Killers' base of operations. She finally took a shower in the basement facilities. Better fitting, clean clothes were also had there. She asked for and got a job in the laundry, where she worked for minimum wage, eight hours a day. With her first paycheck, she went to see a dentist who capped her broken tooth and gave her an antibiotic to handle any infection she might have contracted from it. She also moved into one of the vacant dorm rooms for battered women and their children. Laura Isaacson saw great potential in Muriel, and made her a pet project for rehabilitation. Slowly, Muriel allowed the tutorial to evolve. All the while, Muriel kept an eye open for anything that might let her know something was not right at the *Been There, Done That*. She saw nothing.

After nearly a month and a half of daily contact with the social service agency, Muriel Brett returned to New York City without having mined a single clue that might help solve the Congressional Killings. But was she disappointed? Not in the least. Her Pulitzer would come for a different story. It detailed the possibility of metamorphosis for almost anyone who arrived at that particular agency hungry, broke, and dirty, if they simply kept going back for more. The selfless contributions of staff and founders could not have been more prominently featured. Grudgingly and finally, Cal Hunter had to accept the fact that the *Been There, Done That* agency, founded by Deborah Saraf, was just what it appeared to be, and what all empirical evidence confirmed. Cal was not a happy camper.

The case, however, seemed to get a break. Ms. Clarissa DeBeau had recently moved $8 million to the Banque de France, in two installments, all within several days. By reconstructing nearly 20 of the $10 million so-called 'trust funds' for persons Deborah Saraf had never known before the Congressional Killings had started, the Department of Treasury, working in close conjunction with the FBI and the CIA, had long since realized the importance of watching each account's activity closely. They could not believe their good fortune when Clarissa DeBeau tapped into her account big time.

It was agreed that the FBI would pay a visit to Ms. DeBeau in Grasse, France. Arrangements were made, and Herford and Hooks once again came calling, this time at Hotel des Parfums.

Their unannounced arrival caught her flat-footed. They were sitting in the lounge, waiting for her to return from a morning of painting, when she saw them first. It gave her enough time to catch her breath before they could see her surprise. She walked past them as though they didn't exist. It was Hooks who watched her open a door and disappear.

Within seconds, she heard the inevitable knock. She'd make them wait for a few moments. A second knock. When she went to the door, she greeted the two agents with her usual smile and best "Shoog" routine. "To what do I owe this pleasure?" she gushed. "Can I offer you some refreshments?"

"No thank you, Ms. DeBeau," Hooks answered. "We've come to ask you some questions regarding the trust fund Deborah Saraf set up for you."

"Really," she began. "And just why do you want to know anything about that?"

It was the opening they had hoped for. "Well, Ms. DeBeau, we think Deborah Saraf masterminded the Congressional Killings. We think she ran the operation out of the *Been There, Done That*, and we think she paid everyone involved $10 million."

"What have you boys been smokin', Mr. Hooks,?" Clarissa asked, in her finest southern accent. "You've both been through that agency, and so has Mr. Wes Jordan, plus three other agents. As for Ms. Saraf, she was the kindest, saintliest woman I ever knew. That she was generous with me isn't any of your business," Clarissa responded, pouting. "Besides, you have no authority here."

"Well, Ms. DeBeau, on that count you're wrong," countered Herford. "We have every right to question American citizens on foreign soil when we get that foreign government's written permission, and we have that document right here." With the same satisfaction bridge players feel when they trump their opponents for a deciding win, the smiles on H & H outdid the Cheshire cat's.

"I see," was all Clarissa could manage. "Would you gentlemen hold that document for just a moment while I get two of my own?"

"Sure," was the quick, enthusiastic chorus. They had her this time. Revenge was sweet.

Clarissa left the drawing room. When she returned she handed her newly executed French citizenship papers, drawn up several weeks ago, to H & H.

"This can't be," offered Hooks. "You can't be a citizen of France."

"Oh, but I am, Mr. Hooks. Check with French Immigration in Paris. See that seal, right there? It's from Immigration Headquarters in Paris. All perfectly legal, and all final."

But it was the second document that really sank all hopes for Agents Herford and Hooks. She handed them the deed of title to the Hotel des Parfums, made out to Ms. Clarissa Debeau. That sealed the end of the interview. Not only was she a French citizen, she was also the owner of a substantial piece of real estate, which the French government was not about to have badgered, on some suspicion from the American FBI.

"Now," she said, "if you gentlemen will excuse me, I have a real life to live." The astonished agents knew they had been bested again, and were not about to stick around for another kick in the teeth. Cal Hunter was going to lose it over this one.

He did. "Bribes!" he shouted. "The lousy frogs are notorious the world over for giving them and for taking them! I wonder how much it cost her to become a French citizen so quickly?" No one answered. It really didn't matter. But for H & H there was a bright side. Clarissa DeBeau would never have to be consulted in this matter, ever again.

Chapter 33

In order for her to participate in the killings, Deborah's friend Mitzi Shigato had taken a year's sabbatical from Princeton University, where she was a tenured Professor. When Williams first fetched her from Princeton, New Jersey, to Deborah's mansion in Old Arlington, Virginia, Mitzi thought it might be the last time she would ever have any private time with her dying friend. She was wrong, of course.

Williams had prepared a simple meal of flounder, asparagus tips, and potato chips. The two women ate sparingly. Over coffee and apple cobbler, Deborah asked Williams to join them. She produced Mitzi's letter, which proposed an unknown action they should take to avoid being the next ones to suffer the fate of her dearly departed mother. Mitzi remembered writing the letter, and was pleased that Deborah had saved it.

For more than an hour Williams revealed the plan Deborah and he had developed, to prevent a repeat of Mitzi's mother's painful and degrading death. At first Mitzi thought she was missing something. This was not the Deborah whom she knew and loved. Rather, this was a monster sitting quietly across from her, urging her megalomaniac servant on.

Fear soon followed disbelief. Mitzi felt trapped. She asked if Williams would please stop and just take her home. There was no way that she could possibly participate in Deborah's scheme. What if they were caught? She didn't want to spend the rest of her life in jail. That would be a worse fate, she thought, than an evil nursing home.

But Deborah would not take no for an answer. She asked Williams to get Mitzi's first book, titled *America's Greatest Strength: A History of Political Opposition from 1914 to 1976.* When Williams read aloud pre-selected passages from Mitzi's book, she sat transfixed by her own words. Her heroes all went to prison, or were ruined financially, or both. Some of them, like Ghandi and King, had died for what they believed. At the end of the reading, it was not shame that Mitzi felt, but pride. It was not Deborah's prodding that convinced her to join, but it was her own powerful prose. The $5 million package at the end was refused. Blood money she didn't want. Williams convinced her to stay the night. He would drive her home in the morning.

As soon as the killings stopped, Mitzi tucked her refused blood money package into her suitcase and headed for Montreal. For several days she stayed in her hotel room and debated with herself regarding the money. At night, she walked. Passing an open computer store, an idea popped into her head. She asked if she could buy internet time.

Yes, for $12 per half hour. Done. Mitzi asked her search engine for a list of women's colleges in the northeast region of the United States. Two in particular caught her eye. Chatham College and Carlow College were both in Pittsburgh, Pennsylvania. Next she asked for a list of major banks in Pittsburgh. The name Mellon Bank appealed. How could she find out if either or both colleges had accounts there? Tomorrow she would call the banks and ask. If Mellon Bank handled Chatham and/or Carlow money, she'd wire each school $5 million, and feel righteous.

Both schools had accounts in the Mellon Bank. From the pay phone six blocks away from her hotel, it took Mitzi five minutes more than she would have liked to convince Rudolf Byers, manager of electronic accounts, in One Mellon Square, that her intentions were honorable. Finally, she asked Mr. Byers if he did or did not want her to deposit a total of $10 million in his bank. Well, yes, but one cannot be too careful, these days.

Right.

Mitzi told Mr. Byers to expect her wire transfer within the next 15 minutes. He thanked her and hung up.

The nearest Kinko was another block away from the phone Mitzi had used to call Mellon Bank. All of her money had been deposited in the Bank of Butterfield, in Bermuda. She followed Williams' instructions to the letter. First, she identified her account by number. Next, she asked the bank to transfer $5 million American to account # 58-d222-0193 in Mellon Bank, in Pittsburgh, Pennsylvania, and the remaining $5 million American to the same bank, into account #58-d222-0161. Charges would be paid out of accrued interest, and if anything remained in the account, give it to the local Salvation Army. Within five minutes, Mitzi's fax machine received confirmation of the money transfers, and a note indicating enough money existed in the account after costs were deducted to make a $22,000 gift to the Army.

The last thing Mitzi did not want was to stay in Montreal another moment. She had already packed her bags that morning, paid her bill, and asked the concierge to have her bags loaded into her car, and the car ready to go by 11 a.m. It would not take the Treasury Department or the FBI very long to figure out that the fax transferring all that money had come from Montreal. Time was on her side for at least another two hours, she thought. Instead of heading south for the boarder and going home, Mitzi decided to head west. She'd cross back into the United States from Windsor, into Detroit, and from Detroit she would drive to Idaho to see if the detainment camp where she was born still existed.

It didn't.

How could Mitzi live out the rest of her life knowing what she had been a part of? It was a question she would wrestle with for many years to come--she hoped!

Bells rang and whistles blew in the Treasury Department as soon as $10 million moved in two installments from Bermuda to Pittsburgh. Agents in Pittsburgh were in Rudolph Byers' office in 43 minutes flat. "Who is Nyla Rae Pellett?" the agents wanted to know. He didn't know that name. "Really?"

"Really!"

"Well, Mr. B., she just wired $10 million into your bank not more than 60 minutes ago." Byers indicated he never asked the woman caller for her name. He did say that she had to keep adding money to the pay phone.

"May I?" Treasury Agent Blair Harris asked as he picked up Byer's phone, and dialed at least 16 numbers. "I need a phone identified. In Pittsburgh, Pennsylvania, phone 412-356-0922 received a seven or eight minute call from a pay phone in Montreal about an hour ago. I need to know the number and the location of that pay phone, and I need it yesterday."

No one spoke. Two minutes went by, and the phone rang. "Harris, go. Thanks." With that, Harris and his partner were out the door, leaving Rudolph Byers wondering what had happened.

Agents Harris and Speicer hurried back to the Federal Building on Grant Street. When they were safely back in their offices, Harris dialed D.C. and reported his findings. A hearty "Thank you!" was offered, and the line went dead. Cal Hunter's phone rang and he was told of the money transfer, the name in which the account was registered, and the phone number and city where the deed was done. He knew a guilty conscience when he saw one, and this one went off the charts. But what was the donor doing in Montreal, Canada? Avoiding immediate arrest, for one thing, he thought. By now, Nyla Rae Pellett, or whoever the hell she is could be anywhere, and probably was. He'd have to fish elsewhere.

Chapter 34

Willie Batts realized that he would be a caught man just as soon as he touched his money. Hadn't they figured out that old man Slutsky was one of the killers when he tapped into his offshore account? Willie needed to mosey back to rural Mississippi where he came from. He needed to unburden his soul with someone he could trust. Because he was such an uncomely man, he knew that if he flew, someone would look suspiciously at him. If he tried to rent a car, more suspicion. What to do? An older black man could travel unnoticed on the Greyhound Bus.

Willie left the next morning for the bus station, and boarded the first bus he could catch to Atlanta. In Atlanta he bought another ticket to Tupelo, Mississippi. From that bus station Willie called his brother Sunny; told him where he was, and asked him to pick him up. Questions flew, but none were really answered. Where were you? Why didn't you write? We thought you might be dead.

Willie had plenty of money in his pocket. He had spent little of his $7,000 monthly pay, and when he left D. C. He closed out his bank account and converted it all into traveler's checks, which he sewed carefully into the lining of his old coat. He felt no immediate need to do anything, and acted it.

Sunny gave Willie all the time he needed. After three days of just sitting around the house, Willie asked Sunny if they could walk from one end of the farm to the other. Sure. The first 300 steps were in total silence. And then Willie began, slowly at first, and then he gushed like a broken damn, pouring out impossible to hear and more impossible to believe information. Sunny became fearful for his life, and for the life of his entire family. Are you crazy, Willie? You'll bring us all to an early grave.

But Willie was prepared for this. Sunny was always the timid one in the family. That's why he took few risks, and why he was still living on the little farm he could call his own. It was safe. He had watched his older brother, Willie, try to expand,

and in trying, lose everything he had. But Sunny also admired Willie. He couldn't turn his back on his brother now, could he?

Sunny didn't say anything for hours after the two men returned home. Willie began to think Sunny might have ideas of turning him in just to save his own behind, and to collect any reward that might be out there for one of the Congressional Killers. But he was wrong on that score. Sunny was trying to process Willie's story.

Neither man slept well that night. Around 2:30 each went to the fridge for a snack, where they met unexpectedly. They looked awkwardly at each other. "That was some story, you told me," Sunny began.

"I know," was the answer. "Any ideas of what I should do?"

"One," replied Sunny.

"Shoot."

"Tomorrow," was all Sunny said, and he trudged off to bed not eating a bite of his ice cream.

In the morning, Sunny had breakfast all prepared and ready for his older brother when he came down the stairs. Willie loved good grits with heavy gravy and homemade biscuits. After his third cup of coffee, Sunny said, "Let's go." Willie followed without protest.

In Sunny's old Dodge pickup, Willie asked him where they were going. Sunny just said, "You'll see."

But Willie wasn't satisfied with that answer. What if Sunny had a bad plan? What if whomever they were going to see would turn him in? "Not good enough, Sunny. I need to know where we're going before I agree to go."

"Fair enough," replied Sunny. "We're going to old friend Nat Forbes' office. You do remember Nat? He's now the president of the Union of Black Farmers in America, and he's headquartered here in Tupelo. I figured if the $10 million came into one of our branch offices, say in South Carolina, or Georgia, it could eventually get here so you could buy your old farm back, if you wanted it."

Willie smiled immediately at the thought of getting his farm back, but that smile soon faded. It was too obvious. He'd get caught sure as shooting. Willie began to sweat profusely at the thought of jail, but Sunny exhibited a confidence Willie had never seen before. He'd have to trust someone, and if he couldn't trust his own brother and the president of his brother's union, well....

The brothers didn't have an appointment. Mr. Forbes secretary, Jameela, knew them both from grade school, and promised she'd do all she could to get them in to see Nat. In less than five minutes, Nat Forbes exploded through his office door and greeted the Batts brothers like long lost kin. He only had about 10 minutes, but he'd gladly give them that, and schedule more time later if they needed it.

Less than two minutes into the conversation, Nat paged Jameela and told her to cancel his entire day. He said he was leaving for the day. Something had just come up that called him away. No emergency, just something that required his personal attention. Jameela thought to herself, Yah, fishin, no doubt.

"Don't say another word," Nat told Willie, "until we're out of here and somewhere I think is safe."

The three men piled into Sunny's old truck and headed for Nat's smokehouse, located off the dirt road a quarter mile behind his farmhouse. Once there, Nat asked Willie to tell him the whole story, from start to finish. Willie did. It took him several hours. "That's why I came, home, Nat," he finished. "As soon as I touch that money, I know the FBI will be all over me like white on rice. Sunny's right. I've got to get it into the union. It's the only way any of us will ever benefit from it. I've already got enough in my pocket to make a serious down payment on my old place."

Interrupting, Nat scolded, "Your old place, my ass. That would be a dead giveaway. We'll figure out a way to get you a new place."

It was Willie's turn to interrupt. "Nat, I never wanted to end up with a lot of money, I think you know that. But I did want to be able to own my own farm and pay my bills. You know what happened before. All I really want out of this is a decent farm, with a chance to make a decent living. The rest of the money can go to help the membership with mortgage arrears, or equipment needs. Frankly, I'd like it if some of it could help get you elected to Congress, where I think we'd finally have a voice we can trust."

Willie extracted a promise from both men that they would not tell another living soul about the $10 million, or how Willie got it. They had no problem with that. They also agreed to go home and think up a plan whereby the money could get from the Nevis Trust Limited to the union's account in Greenville, South Carolina, without getting Willie arrested. Further, they all agreed that Nat should meet them at Sunny's home first thing in the morning.

Willie and his brother were truly out of their depths. But not Nat. Congress! He'd thought about it before this, and he realized he'd make a great representative, but he never believed he'd ever have the financial clout to run. God works in mysterious ways, he thought.

The three men sat at Sunny's kitchen table drinking coffee shortly after 7 a.m. The show was all Nat's. "Willie, I think I've figured out a way to move the money. I also think I've got a way for you to buy into an existing farm, and triple its size."

"How, and whose?" Willie asked.

"Your brother Sunny's, of course," replied Nat. "Sunny takes in failed older brother, who lost his farm. Sunny buys 400 acres from Nat Forbes, whose land runs side by side on his south pasture, and also buys the widow Sampson's adjoining 200 acres. She'd need a life estate in the place to make the deal work. You and Sunny would be partners. The cover story is seamless, and the deals would all be legitimate. Especially, if I'm going to run for Congress. I'll not be able to farm anymore, now, will I?"

The brothers just stared at each other. Partners. The sound of that word had never appealed before, but at this stage in their lives it had a ring to it. Partners. Sunny was afraid to speak, and he hoped Willie would say yes first. Willie did.

Nat continued, "Moving the money shouldn't be that hard. Any fax machine, you said, will do. But we can't do it from Tupelo. I think we should find a fax machine close by the Capitol building in Washington D.C., and access your account from there. I'm not willing to trust another human being to do that job for us, so I'm asking you, Willie, to go with me to D.C., fax the bank, transfer the money, and get the hell out of town. What do you think?"

What Willie thought, and what he said, were two different things. He liked the idea of rubbing the government's nose in it one more time, but he was afraid D.C. was too close for comfort. Agents would be at that fax machine within minutes of his accessing the money. "I like the idea, Nat, but I don't think we could escape if we went to D.C. I think we'd get caught. Paducha, Kentucky is a better idea. We can drive there tonight and return in the morning as soon as we finish. Tomorrow's Saturday, so you won't miss work."

As much as Nat wanted to see D.C., Willie's idea made more sense. Paducha it was. They'd leave that night at dark.

Nat drove. All night long the two men talked about farming. Willie had missed it so much while he was away. He wouldn't say a word about any of the others in the group, or who had funded the assassinations, but he did say that he learned a lot from all of them. Every now and again Nat brought up the idea of running for Congress, and Willie supported the idea enthusiastically. Playfully, Willie reminded Nat that if he didn't do his job, he knew a permanent way to remedy that failure. Both laughed. But Nat knew Willie was serious.

They rode into the outskirts of Paducha at first light. A big truck stop at I-24 and Rt. 60 acted like a magnet. It just pulled them into the parking lot before either man realized how hungry he was.

Plan was, Nat was going to find a Kinko's in the yellow pages once they reached Paducha. Willie chose Paducha because it was urban enough, close enough, and a place the Federal agents would never think of as a site where international banking crimes would ever take place. Willie and Nat would be in and out, and back in Tupelo, before anyone even realized they were gone.

But they didn't have to rely on the phone book. They passed a Kinko's at Fourth Avenue and Pine Street. It wouldn't be open for another hour, so Nat and Willie found a public parking lot two blocks away. It was a 24-hour metered lot that accepted quarters only, and a quarter in Paducha bought 30 minutes. Between them they had three quarters, and they jammed them all in just in case.

At 9:30 a.m., Willie left Nat's car and walked the two blocks back to the Kinko's. It had several customers already, and he did not need to get any cash to feed his fax. The machine was at the ready, and he simply fed the four $1 bills required for overseas communications into it. From memory, Willie dialed the bank's number. When it answered, he dialed in his account number and requested his entire balance, less charges, be wired to account #332-B773-82119 in Greenville, South Carolina. He pressed send. The machine came to life, and within two minutes, his confirmation sheet was printed out for him to grab and leave. He didn't speak to anyone, and not another person paid him any attention. He was in. He was out. It was as though he didn't exist. Sometimes not handsome and invisibility had its benefits.

Nat asked him if it went okay, and only then did Willie smile. He handed Nat the confirmation sheet and told him to read it out loud to him, as he was still too scared to believe he had just owned, and then given away, $10 million. Nat read it out to him and started the car.

The trip back to Tupelo was eventless. They stopped for lunch in Memphis, where they burned the confirmation sheet and trampled its ashes into the ground outside the restaurant. They were home for dinner that same night. As far as the world knew, these two old friends had been fishin' all day on Sunny Batts' pond, where it bends and meets the Tombigbee River.

Another $10 million withdrawal, moving from the Caribbean to the Greenville, South Carolina account of the Union of Black Farmers in America, drove Treasury agents in D.C. crazy. How could they ever catch anyone in the act? It had to be another of the killers giving away his or her spoils, and like the Montreal donor, this particular killer had just used Paducha to do his dirty work. The agents quickly found the fax machine used to do the deed, but no one could recall anyone using it. In truth, two others had used the fax since Willie Batts, but that didn't matter. There was so much black dirt on each key, from so many users, that it was impossible for anyone to leave a fingerprint anywhere on the keyboard. Agents were quickly on their way to Greenville, to talk to union representatives about their windfall. Was this donor like the one from Montreal, somehow connected to the recipients of their largess? Agents swarmed the Pittsburgh colleges and the Union of Black Farmers in America office, but came away empty. As far as anyone could tell, the anonymous donor had just dumped the blood money because it was blood money.

Maxon Stroble proved the blood money theory for them all.

Chapter 35

Maxon's daughter, Betty, had been brutally murdered several years before Max was recruited to join the merry band of Congressional Killers. Betty had been a lovely freshman co-ed, away from home for the first time in her life. At Arkansas State she roomed with two other girls, all three enrolled in elementary education. While she was alone in her room one Friday night, a convicted rapist named Jimmy Mathews, out on bond and awaiting trial for holding up a convenience store, raped Maxon's daughter, shot her and stabbed her to death. He got off on a technicality. He was convicted of the armed robbery of the convenience store and was currently behind bars. Max never recovered from Betty's death. He just drifted from place to place cutting grass or painting houses until Williams contacted him, and gave him an opportunity to do something about his grief.

When Max got his financial package, he felt that he and Lady Macbeth were kin. He simply could not stop washing his hands. His sense of guilt at wronging so many hundreds of families far outweighed anything he ever suffered losing his only daughter to a murderer. The surviving family members of so many other families had to hate him with as much hatred as he had ever mustered for Jimmy Mathews. In essence, he had done to them what Mathews had done to him. The simple math overwhelmed Max. He hated only one man. But the hate that he knew was directed toward him from so many began to crush him, and he found it difficult to breathe. He'd wake up at night gasping for air. Soon he slept in his recliner, finding it easier to stand from a sitting position than being startled awake in a prone one. Foods tasted like cardboard. Booze didn't help. The stuff tasted lousy and smelled worse.

One morning, after a particularly bad night, Maxon Stroble realized he could not torture himself any longer by simply staying alive. He had to end his life. But he needed to attempt some restitution for all of his terrible deeds. What to do? For days he wandered around his apartment trying to figure out his end.

One evening, out of sheer exhaustion, Max slept for a few hours, and in that sleep he had a dream. In it, he saw himself sailing out to sea on a handmade raft that he had tied together with thin, cotton clothesline. The shore was lined with hundreds of well-wishers. From the raft, Max was throwing handfuls of diamonds and pearls back to the people on shore. The folks there made sure everyone who picked them up had the exact same number of jewels as the next person. When his bag was empty, Max's raft came apart and he drowned.

When he woke up, he smiled for the first time in weeks.

Max cleaned up and walked to the local bookstore, where he picked up a do-it-yourself will, and promptly went back to his apartment. He read it, and it looked like it had all the whys and wherefores he thought all wills should have. Satisfied with the document, Max directed that all of the money in his bank account at the time of his death should go to the Treasury of the United States of America. Further, he stated that the Secretary of the Treasury should draft individual checks in the amount of $40,983.60 for survivors in the immediate families of the 244 victims he had helped kill. All monies left in his checking account should go to Arkansas State in memory of his daughter, Betty.

When he finished writing his bequests, he walked to his local bank, requested a notary republic to witness his signature, and asked if several tellers would also sign on the lines for witnesses. Next he left the signed, witnessed, and notarized will in his safety deposit box.

On the way home, Max stopped at a Radio Shack and bought a fax machine. He plugged it into his phone line, and fed in the following hand written message.

To CNN. My name is Maxon Stroble. I was one of the Congressional Killers. In a few moments, I intend to wire my $10 million financial package to my personal bank account here in D. C. When you open my safety deposit box, #5809, you'll find my bank account number there, plus my last will and testament. In it I direct that the total sum of my account be given to the Treasury of the United States. Further, I've directed the Treasurer of the United States to divide that sum by the 244 *victims I helped kill, and cut their surviving families a check for $40,983.60 each. The key to that box is beside my fax machine. When I have confirmation that the money has been successfully wired, I plan to sit down on one of the cyanide devices that we used in the Capitol building. I kept one, for reasons not clear to me then but crystal clear to me now. I'm unable to cope with what I've done. I used to be a good man. Now I'm a monster. Please have me cremated, and dump my ashes in a common grave somewhere, where the ghouls will never find what's left of me. The last thing I'd ever want is some kind of veneration from the sick set.*

True to his word, Max finished his financial affairs, sat down on the needle, and slumped over the desk. In less than 30 seconds he was dead.

All hell broke loose. At first the FBI could not believe its good fortune. A wire transfer had just been ordered from D. C., to arrive at a local D. C. bank. Within minutes, CNN called the FBI and told them of the fax they had just received, giving the D. C. phone number at the top of the page, imprinted by the fax machine. Within 15 minutes from the time Max Stroble contacted CNN, the FBI was at his front door, breaking it down. They found him dead at the desk. The fax machine was still plugged in, and the confirmation page sat in its cradle.

Lynn Smolen was all over the story. Every wire service in the world carried it. The consequent public awareness of the amount of, and reason for, the payoff sum, plus the number of donations identical to the Stroble figure, let the other assassins know how dangerous it was to have anything to do with the cash.

Chapter 36

After only three weeks of vacation in beautiful Nova Scotia, Jack Sparks was bored out of his mind. Doing nothing was mind erasing. He was beginning to feel dead, already. But what to do? No matter where he went, he realized the routine would not change. Nice hotel, sightseeing, move on to the next nice hotel, more sightseeing...but in truth, where could he go? What could he do?

Then it came to him. He needed to get to his bank in Zurich.

Jack erased as much of his stay in Nova Scotia as was possible before he boarded *The Cat* back to Bar Harbor. Everything he bought for himself in Nova Scotia, he either disposed of or donated to the Salvation Army bin, two blocks east of his last hotel. From Bar Harbor he bussed it back to Boston, and then to New York. Any agent with any brains would know that going to ground meant fleabag sleeping rooms and disguises, so Jack reasoned that Trump Towers would be perfect for a quick overnight. It was. He purchased new clothes and supplies to alter his identity once again. He taxied to JFK and used a public phone there to get the next available flight to Zurich. One way, please. He had to get to his account there. An in-house withdrawal would not be seen by those looking for him, if, that is, anyone was really looking for him. After a great supper, Jack went back to his room and to work. His plane left the next evening at 8 p.m.

In the morning Jack headed for Chinatown, in Manhattan. He needed a clean passport from someone who didn't know him. In less than 20 minutes Jack was seated in front of a very old man who called himself Wu. Just Wu. The old man spoke worse English than Jack did Chinese, so they conversed as best they could, given the circumstances. Seven thousand cash was clear in any language, but Jack quickly reduced it to half, with a $1,000 bonus for a two-hour turn around. Done. Wu had received stolen passport blanks from a government warehouse located somewhere in Maryland. He had a cousin who worked there, and who filched one or two real passport blanks from each box he handled. Those blanks found their way into cousin Wu's hands. It was the authentic blank that cost so much, not the photograph and printing. Two hours later Jack had his document. He was back in existence.

Would the CIA have someone looking for him in New York and Zurich? He didn't know, but he did know that he would have to be more careful and watchful than ever. Traveling coach was not something Jack did gladly. But this time, coach it was. That's a good lad.

From his seat near the rear, Jack could see almost everyone at some time or another during the entire flight. He recognized no one passing him to use the restroom. Had he been spotted just prior to boarding, and therefore, no agent needed to follow on the plane? Would he be picked up at the airport in Zurich? The game was on, and all of a sudden he realized that he had actually missed the acid churning away in his stomach.

Zurich customs could be quite lax, or a real pain in the arse if it wished. Today it was the latter. Endless questions regarding purpose for visiting Zurich. Baggage check and passport examination went on forever. Finally Jack was cleared and welcomed to Zurich. Cabs were abundant, and he got the next one in line. "Take me to a hotel near the Maerki, Baumann Bank, please." The cabby pulled away wordlessly, and within 45 minutes had Jack under the spacious covered entryway to the Hotel Swiss Skete.

Uniformed bellhops quickly snatched Jack's bags and paid his cabby before he could object. In military march mode, they instructed Jack to follow them. He had seen and dealt with their type many times before, and he knew they could be somewhat intimidating to the uninitiated. So, not wanting to call any attention to himself, he meekly did what he was told. At the check-in counter, Jack asked for and received a single, windowless, non-smoking room for three nights. He paid in cash. The inside bellhops were less oppressive than their outside counterparts, but they also conveyed a no-nonsense attitude. Tipping in this Prussian atmosphere was *verboten*.

Jet lag was upon Jack. He undressed quickly, showered, and fell asleep in less than three minutes. When he wakened, hunger was gnawing at him, big time. Jack dressed ultra conservatively, making it possible for him to be more invisible than normal in this tight-ass community. Zurich time was 7:30 p.m., and most of the really good restaurants were already crowded. But he knew from past visits that a single table could be had almost any time anywhere. He was right. He would have loved a double martini with a twist, but he passed. His eyes had to be extra sharp, in case anyone was on his trail.

Real beef was what he ordered. Rare. Bloody. A good vet could have saved it. His waiter's disgusted look meant 'typical American.' Jack wanted to put a dime under his plate as a tip, but that would have been too memorable. Instead he left the exact 23%, as good manners require. All Americans were considered cannibals, so he and his order would be quickly forgotten.

As he left the restaurant, Jack thought he saw a lady watch his departure with too much interest. Maybe she was just a working girl. Maybe not. A bookstore was two establishments down from the restaurant, and Jack ducked in with such rapidity that it appeared he had just vanished from those walking beside him. Jack knew that if anyone were really looking for him, agents would already be in place at every strategic point along his pathway. The bookstore's owner was just closing, and told Jack to come back in the morning. Back on the street, Jack's eyes were everywhere. Everyone was suspect, even children.

Because public drunkenness isn't tolerated in Zurich, the streets are usually free of alcoholic panhandlers. When an older looking, slightly built 'gentleman' staggered in Jack's direction, his hackles were up and he stood combat ready.

When the old guy apparently staggered and reached for Jack for support, Jack had him face-down on the ground in a flash, his foot on the guy's neck. Jack twisted the man's right arm upward, revealing a needle full of what was probably a knockout drug. He broke the agent's arm, shoved the needle into his neck, and depressed the plunger. The man went limp instantly.

Obviously someone was on to Jack, and he thought it just might be his old friend at CIA headquarters, Director Robert Benton. He and Benton went back a long way. They had always been on the same side, and Jack had never contemplated seeing Benton as an enemy. But Jack's realistic mind developed that picture instantly.

He knew an invisible net surrounding Zurich was already cast, and escape via transportation systems was out. But Jack was short on cash, and he needed to get to his bank quickly. Perhaps the CIA didn't yet know in which bank Jack had money stashed. He could hope. What he couldn't do was return to his hotel.

Jack knew other agents were too close for comfort, and he had to move quickly. The bookstore owner had just turned out his lights and had the key in his door when Jack moved him back into the store and locked the door from the inside. The owner was so surprised by the quickness of his transportation back in that he realized he was in grave danger if he resisted at all. Jack told him he would not hurt him if the man would show him a back door, or a second story window to the roof. He needed an escape hatch to avoid his ground hounds. The man pointed to stairs going to the roof. Jack pointed him towards the front door and told him to lock it after himself as he left. He did as directed.

Moments after the bookstore owner locked his door, the woman at the restaurant appeared and asked him if he knew where the intruder went. "Yes, I do. He went up my inside stairs to the roof. From there, I can't say."

Into her wrist she said, "Roof," and stepped into a waiting car directly behind her.

Jack realized flight was impossible. They'd have him in minutes if he played that game. But if he waited for a mere 30 seconds, he could escape in a different direction. Of course the players would realize his move when nothing showed from air surveillance, and realizing their error they would return to the bookstore. But it was enough of a window for Jack.

Swiss door locks are really good, but not good enough. Jack quickly had the front door open, and stepped smartly in the direction of the restaurant he'd left just minutes before. A public parking garage stood two doors down from the restaurant, and Jack sprinted the remaining distance, knowing he was only seconds away from capture. He took the stairs to the third floor two steps at a time, and began looking for the blandest car he could find. The gray, two-door Saab was perfect. He defeated the door lock in two seconds. It was hot-wired in another seven, and Jack was mobile. Fortunately the ticket was tucked in the sun visor above the passenger side. Jack offered it to the attendant with an appropriate tip, and drove away at a normal speed.

The borders would all be watched, and his car was only good for a few miles. He had to do something to throw the dogs off. Years ago, Jack had used a private jet owned by the KBG, hangered outside the little town of Zug, 20 miles south of Zurich, to ship home a critically wounded KBG agent tortured by Russian mobsters. The man had never talked, and when he died several days later at home in the motherland, the KGB had made sure he was given a hero's burial in Red Square. They also remembered who made it possible for their hero to die at home.

Jack decided it was worth a try.

He parked his stolen car outside the train station and hailed a cab. The driver was unwilling, at first, to drive Jack out of the city limits, but the $100 bill changed his mind. "Take me to the train station in Zug. I must catch the first available train to Milan," were the only words spoken for the next 20 miles. Luck was with Jack. They weren't stopped, and he was safely dropped off at the station.

Of course, Jack had no intention of going to Italy. But the cab driver had to think he was, in order to convince Jack's trackers that he'd left Switzerland. Since it was going to be several days before he could enter any bank, Jack was hoping he could at least hide at the old hanger outside of Zug. As he remembered, the hanger was nearly three miles east of the city.

It began to rain quite hard, and although Jack knew he'd have many hours of discomfort, he started walking toward the old hanger, thanking whatever lucky stars were his for the cover. To his dismay, when he finally got there, it was abandoned. Perfect, he sneered to himself. He'd have to forage. But he could do that. Anything was better than capture. Then he realized he was getting too old for this shit. But it was all he knew. Perhaps he'd call his old friend Robert Benton and see if he could still make a deal. Being hunted was no fun. He'd know what to do in a few days. Right now he was cold, tired, and hungry, and he didn't see anyway of satisfying any of those needs.

Chapter 37

Rusty McCaffry had never gotten over his mad at Somolia. But what he wanted to do and what he actually did were two different stories. He wanted to fly to Somolia and begin shooting every leader he could find there. But his white face would have stood out, and his capture would have been certain. Instead, he decided to start popping drug dealers, the way Mrs. Saraf had described in one of her faxes to CNN.

He stayed right in his Washington D. C. apartment on Blakely Avenue NW. Before everything had been destroyed, Rusty had asked for and received one of the six vans used in several of the killings. He thought the 1993 GMC Safari, with no windows on either side panel or at the back door, would be perfect for his new work. Lloyd Evans, the little Welshman who kept the vans in top running order, had done such a good job on this one that Rusty didn't have to do one thing to improve it.

What Rusty didn't and couldn't know, was that Lloyd Evans had wended his way back to Wales after the band dispersed. Cliff Craft, who had worked with Lloyd in the Center, had thrown his $10 million in with Lloyd's, in Cardiff, Wales, and the two began to buy up numerous old industrial buildings through a foundation they established. After cleaning out the buildings and making them fit for human use, Cliff and Lloyd converted many of them into fine mechanic and paint shops for students who wanted to learn a car craft. Several of the buildings became music schools and fine arts buildings. Over the years following the shootings, they drew artists and potters and painters from all over the globe.

The Welsh government would hear nothing from the American FBI about possible links to the Congressional Killings. The English Parliament knew that it neither wanted nor could afford another situation like the one they had in Northern Ireland. And if the world thought the Irish were fanatical, they never wanted to stir up the Welsh. Cal Hunter just wrote these two men off, knowing they had to be connected to the killings, but also knowing he'd never find out anything about them as long as they stayed in Wales.

With his reconditioned van, Rusty had a plan. He had to ruin its paint job, dent its sides, and make it look like the 13-year-old vehicle it was. That accomplished, Rusty assembled the weapons he needed to kill drug dealers. He traveled to nearby Baltimore, where he bought a used SIG SG 550 Sniper rifle, like the one he had used to shoot several lobbyists. Besides ammunition and scopes and silencers, Rusty purchased an arsenal of handguns and knives from various pawnshops. He kept his armory locked in the van.

Next he had to find places where the drugs were being sold, and where he could find maximum cover to do the deeds. It took three weeks of driving by several locations before he focused on his first kill site. Three blocks south of the *Been There, Done That*, drugs flowed openly. Cars pulled up and money was exchanged with great rapidity. An outside ladder had been attached to the backside of the social service building, to service the antennas for T. L. Grimes' communication equipment. And although the antennas were long gone, the service ladder was still in place. One evening Rusty climbed it, and realized he had a perfect cover from which to fire in all four directions. His night scope let him see his targets, whereas the darkness would prevent anyone from seeing him. The muzzle flash from his weapon would be the only problem. It would give away his position, but he was willing to risk that momentary exposure to achieve his kill.

For another week, Rusty practiced his moves. He hid everything he needed in his coat and small backpack, climbed the 28 rungs to the three-foot-high parapet, rolled over its red tile cap, and set up his rifle and scope. He found a drug dealer in his sight and pretended to fire. Then he reversed his steps back to his van that was parked one block away. It took him less than eight minutes for the entire exercise. He decided that when he got it down to under seven, he'd fire for real.

In his apartment, Rusty practiced breaking down and reassembling his weapon. He did it blindfolded. Putting the pieces in their places inside his coat and backpack was the slowest part. But he finally felt comfortable with everything, and decided he was ready.

All went as planned. During his practice runs, Rusty had watched one particular drug dealer do a victory dance after each sale. Rusty's scope let him see the big guy's delight as his fistful of money grew into a wad, and the wad grew into a grotesque icon of worship and adoration. Rusty waited for the dealer's favorite gesture before he fired. The dealer raised the money high in the air, laughing all the while, and then suddenly brought it sharply to his mouth for a kiss. Rusty tightened pressure on the trigger, and the gun bucked silently against his shoulder.

A block away, a homeless man sitting against a building noticed the brief white muzzle blast, high above him. As the pinpoint of light faded from his retina his mind went on to other thoughts. Flickering illumination was not unusual in the city night.

Rusty didn't wait to see if his target fell. He never missed. Instead he ran through his entire escape plan, and was in his van and gone before the police were even called.

The next day he bought a paper to see if the killing was even reported. It was. Reporter Lynn Smolen covered the story.

"Last night, around 11:15 p.m., Mohammed 'Bug Man' Salam was shot in the head and killed while selling drugs on the corner of Wilson and 29th Street, N. W. There were no witnesses. Police received a call shortly after the shooting, and found Salam's headless body where he lay. The unknown shooter used an exploding bullet, something this city has not seen since last year's Congressional Killings. Speculation on Capitol Hill is running toward a copycat theory, but several individual members of Congress have expressed grave doubts over the killer's identity. The ones I talked to believe the signs are too great to write off a rogue member coming back and simply practicing for the real targets, i.e., the remaining members of Congress not killed in the first rounds.

"Mr. Salam's mother, Mattie White, said she couldn't imagine anyone wanting to harm her son. He was a good boy who provided for her and for his three younger sisters. Salam was 18 years old. Funeral services will be handled by the Wolfe,

Stiles, and Guffy Funeral Home on Linden Avenue. Burial will be private."

Rusty had thought he would feel more elated over his kill than he did. Instead he went into his bookkeeper mode, and tallied one dead drug dealer for one American soldier killed in Somolia. He decided to stay in that night, and watch the news.

All the major networks carried the story. Interviews with elementary teachers of the Bug Man made Rusty sick. Didn't these people have anything better to do than to dignify this dead rat with more than a 20-second blip? Several members of Congress were asked if they thought this shooting was something for them to be worried about. Of course they were worried. Who wouldn't be? But were they willing to approve anti ammunition legislation? No Comment.

The next day, Rusty drove past the *Been There, Done That* to see if anything unusual was afoot. Nothing caught his eye. The D.C. cops weren't able to establish a line of fire because the body had been slammed into the curb by the force of the bullet, and twisted from the collision. All they could do was speculate. Cal Hunter called Chief Maben to offer the Bureau's help, but he was told that the D.C. lab was quite capable of handling the case.

Of course nothing developed, and Rusty McCaffry was free to kill again. He'd found another hot spot of drug dealing, on lower 11th Street just off Warrington Avenue. Warrington Avenue crossed 11th Street and curved a horseshoe turn over the intersection, then climbed sharply and headed back toward 10th Street. From a building ledge on Warrington Avenue overlooking lower 11th Street, Rusty could see everything below. And that was the problem. If he shot from this position on Warrington Avenue, he'd be seen, too. He had no cover. If he did a drive by, he'd expose the van. What to do?

For days Rusty walked past the intersection. The drug dealers were brazen. It made his blood boil. But he knew anger was not his friend, and he fought to control it. He was so irritated with himself for letting his anger at the dealers get to him that he didn't see the raised edge of the sewer lid in the middle of the sidewalk in front of him. He tripped, but caught himself before he had a serious accident. Cursing his clumsiness, Rusty soon laughed at his good fortune. That was his answer. He'd hide in the sewer and shoot from there.

The sewer lid was over the storm drain box directly below. The box measured four-feet by six-feet. At curbside, a six-inch high by three-foot long opening received runoff storm water gushing down from Warrington Avenue. Balls from children's games were always running into that opening, and the kids would pry off the heavy sewer lid, lower themselves into the sewer, retrieve the ball, climb out, and replace the lid. Sometimes the lid wasn't seated exactly right, and it left a lip that an unsuspecting walker might trip over. Someone like Rusty McCaffry.

The city had sewer maps in the public works building. The next day Rusty went there and began his search of the maps for the lower 11th Street area. He discovered that five blocks away, at 7th Street, a large rain sewer grate had been built in the 1960s. The grate had been in place since then, and had received little to no attention from authorities. Local kids, however, had opened the grate years ago, and could be seen playing near and around it. Rusty thought that if he could find his way from the 7th Street sewer grate to the 11th Street sewer lid, he could off another drug dealer, and escape without a hitch. He paid his $1.50 and made a copy of the map.

At home he memorized each twist and turn before he ventured into that underworld. He'd have to go through the sewers at night, and he'd have to count his steps so he could do it in total darkness. A flashlight was simply out of the question.

He practiced walking his route for another three nights. On the fourth night, Rusty took his Glock pistol and entered the sewer. His silencer was the best that money could buy. It had to be. The blast from an unsilenced gun fired inside the sewer would have deafened him for life.

His window to the target was the six-inch high by three-foot long opening at curbside. He'd have to wait until the drug dealer was still for at least three seconds before he could take his shot. Then he'd run like hell.

His opportunity came when a particularly beautiful woman drove up in a dark green Jaguar convertible. The drug dealer knew her from past sales, and was running a little chitchat game with her. Enough time for Rusty. He aimed, fired, and ran with everything he had. He heard tires squeal, but he was too busy with his footstep counting to care.

It took him six minutes to cover the five blocks between the 11th and 7th Street sewer openings. His van was parked one block below the opening, at 6th Street. Although Rusty was in a hurry to get out of there, he walked as casually as anyone could at that hour of the night, considering what he had just done. He was more than surprised, and then instantly combat ready, when he saw a lone, would-be car thief trying to hotwire his van.

Rusty came up quickly and silently behind the man, grabbed his full head of hair with a vice-grip left hand, pulled it back to expose the neck, and slit it nearly in two with a razor sharp knife. The thief slumped backwards to the ground while blood spurted everywhere. Rusty tried to keep it off himself and out of the van, but some did make contact. It would take him many hours to rid himself and the van of that evidence. He'd have to burn those spots on the van, and he'd have to dump his clothes in some dumpster. He only hoped the guy didn't have Aids.

Surprisingly, the morning paper carried the story. Again, Lynn Smolen.

"A second drug dealer has been shot and killed by an unknown gunman. Last night around 10 p.m., Alphonse Davis was found dead at 11th Street and Warrington Avenue. There were no witnesses. Police believe Davis was shot from the storm sewer opening on 11th Street, and his killer escaped through the underground maze. District Police Chief Maben has indicated that the sewer system will be searched for clues left by the gunman or gunmen, but for now he thinks police are looking for a lone shooter. Further, Chief Maben believes that the Davis shooter is probably the same one who shot Mohammed Salam, several weeks ago.

"A second victim was discovered in the middle of Sixth Street. Salatiel Morales was found with his throat slashed. He was nearly decapitated by an unknown killer. Police do not believe, at this time, that the two deaths are related. Morales may have been a robbery victim. Family members say he was just returning from work for a good night's sleep.

"Members of Congress who I talked with no longer believe that they are the real targets for what was originally dubbed the 'practice' shooting. Nor do they think that the identity of the shooter is linked in any way to the Congressional Killers. They now believe that whoever is responsible for these killings has done them in response to the suggestions contained in one of the Congressional Killers' faxes, directing others to rid the country of drugs by shooting all of the drug dealers. When asked how they felt about known drug dealers being shot and killed by an unknown assassin, each congressman responded that it was terrible to have vigilante justice administered this way, and they intended to do all they could to prevent further killings. When asked about passing significant legislation regulating the sale of guns and ammunition, each indicated that the matter was being studied by staff in order to draft such laws as were good and necessary. But, clearly, from this reporter's perspective, guns and ammunition are still in abundance, and Congress has yet to pass any significant legislation curtailing the ownership and sale of either one."

Rusty turned on the radio talk shows, and was pleased to hear so many callers hoping that more drug dealers would be shot. Calls ran 20 to 1 in favor of more killings. Rusty was more interested in the 1 caller in 20 who opposed the killings, and why. Their responses were familiar claptrap. Denial of due process and system bullshit was all he heard from them.

He decided right then to give them more of the same.

Chapter 38

Wire services and national news spread the stories about the drug dealer shootings. They became the hottest subjects in America. Talk shows had fodder for weeks on end. They couldn't wait for the next drug dealer to be killed.

Floyd Briggs and Lawrence Craig wondered if just maybe, Sarge Reynolds (Wade Jackson) or Scotty Gerber (Rusty McCaffry) might be shooting the dealers. Before leaving D. C., Floyd and Lawrence had realized how dangerous it would be for them to split up and try to live separate lives. They moved to New Orleans, where they found work tending bar at the world famous Moonlight Lounge on Bourbon Street. Both men were expert marksmen, and both felt the need to continue the work. At least, that was how it seemed to them at the time when the Congressional Killings were terminated. But they decided to lay low, at least for a while.

One night Floyd Briggs was walking to his car after his shift when two black kids began to shoot at him. They were high on drugs and needed money. Briggs was too big to mess with, they reasoned, and so they just shot him to death and took his wallet. It had $73 in it. Lawrence Craig took his friend back to Arlington Cemetery, where he received a proper military funeral.

Then Craig went crazy. He got drunk, and stayed that way for a week. It felt as though he'd lost his shield and his defender. Upon whom could he count now? When he woke up one morning in a bed beside a lady he did not know, nor think he would ever want to know, he realized this was unbecoming behavior, and he had better do something about it. He caught the next flight back to New Orleans.

Neither he nor Floyd Briggs had accessed their money. They had read Max Stroble's story. But each knew where the instructions were for doing so, and so Lawrence Craig now had $20 million at his disposal. Briggs had a younger sister, Arlene, living in Canon City, Colorado. Her daughter Lisa was in the hospital at the time of the funeral, so Arlene wasn't able to attend her brother's burial. After some deliberation, Lawrence

Craig decided that Floyd's money rightly belonged to his sister, and Craig was going to make sure she got it. But first, he had to know if she had a bank account.

Posing as a military benefits officer from the Pentagon, Craig called Arlene and told her that Floyd had a substantial military death benefit, and had named her as beneficiary. Would she please tell him her bank account number in order for the government to wire the money directly to her? Arlene was skeptical at first and did not want to give the information. But when Craig told her that he could not wire $10 million unless and until he had that number, she rattled it right off. He told her that by the end of banking hours that day, the money would be in her account, ready for her use.

Craig committed Briggs' financial package to memory and flew to Wichita, Kansas. There he went to a Kinko's office and wired $10,163,000 to Arlene Whetzel's account in Canon City. That was the sum left after closing costs were deducted, and interest added.

Never having felt so righteous before in his life, Lawrence Craig caught a cab and asked to be driven to the Hilton, downtown. He booked a room for three days, under the name of Ian Lutz, and slept for almost two of them. He got up only to eat and use the bathroom. When he checked out, he paid his bill in cash. Not wanting to leave any trail of people who remembered him calling a cab or renting a car, Craig walked to the first public bus stop he could find. He didn't care where it went, just so it took him away from the hotel. When it passed the Greyhound station, Craig got off two blocks past it and walked back. There he bought a ticket to Oklahoma City. The trip took three hours. In Oklahoma City, he booked the first plane he could back to New Orleans.

When Arlene Whetzel's bank received the wire transfer of $10,163,000, it notified the Treasury Department immediately. Agents had already responded to the wire transfer and swarmed the Wichita Kinko branch, but again found nothing useable. The Credid Foncier de Monaco had been prompted by some user in Witchta fucking Kansas to wire the entire account of Arthur

Habberset (Artie, as Briggs was know to the group) to Arlene Whetzel, in Canon City, Colorado. And it did it!

Arlene knew that her brother could not possibly have a $10 million death benefit naming her as sole beneficiary, so she wondered what she needed to do to protect herself and at the same time keep the money. Arlene was a well-known and popular local weather reporter at KBLG-TV, and she asked her boss if a camera crew could accompany her to her bank around three that afternoon. She assured him that it was a big story, and KBLG would get national attention from it. Tom Pawlowski wanted to know too much for his own good, and nearly nixed the story, but when Arlene pouted, just a little, it drove him crazy and he relented.

Next she called her bank, the Canon City Branch Office of The First National Bank of Colorado. She told the manager, Susan Cowfer, that she'd been contacted by the military regarding a wire transfer with her name on it, which was coming to the bank before closing time that day. Could Arlene possibly be there when it arrived, and could her TV station cover the event? She and Susan had been friends since junior high school, and the answer was, yes, of course.

In front of the bank, Arlene narrated her own story to the TV camera, beginning with the terrible shooting of her brother Floyd in New Orleans several weeks ago. Then she recounted her phone conversation with a military officer from the Pentagon, who had indicated that Floyd had named her as the beneficiary of some policy he'd taken out when he had first entered the service. She was making it up as fast as she could, and the camera loved every moment.

When Arlene and her crew walked through the front door of the bank, Susan met them and directed them to the office where wire transfers were received and logged in. At 3:20 p.m. precisely, the machine came to life. The printout indicated that Arlene Whetzel had just become a wealthy woman indeed.

Praise God!

Cal Hunter had begun to think that the whole country had become enamoured with the sum of $10 million. He saw Congressional Killers every time he saw that sum. But here was a woman in Canon City, Colorado, who filmed her good fortune and ran it on national television. She was a well-known TV personality who had never been in Washington D.C. in her 37 years. What was wrong with this picture, Director Hunter wondered?

Of course agents asked Arlene all kinds of questions regarding the money and the Pentagon phone call. Phone records indicated that no one in the Pentagon had ever called Canon City, Colorado, that day or that week. That Arlene's dead brother had been a Navy Seal years ago only made her belief stronger that he set up an insurance policy through the military, to take care of her if and when he died. The public loved it. Arlene Whetzel was now the darling of the talk shows, and they chewed her up, then spit her out just as soon as the next darling was found.

Because the publicity was so widespread, the FBI decided not to press Arlene too soon. But after a month went by they returned to Carson City to talk to her. She wasn't there. She and Lisa had booked themselves on a world cruise, and wouldn't be back for another three months. The agents could wait, because the pattern of the $10 million wire transfers was crystal clear. The government had watched as seemingly ordinary citizens, some known, some unknown, moved the almost identical amount from some offshore bank to the account of some lucky, unsuspecting recipient or institution, all of them puzzled as to the source of their good fortune. To date, eight such transfers had been counted. Rohan Holiday's task force began to wonder if the Congressional Killers were falling away as did the Indians in the children's jingle; "Ten little, nine little, eight little Indians...." If that were the case, then the nation would never know who killed all of those congresspersons.

The FBI simply had to catch someone in the act of wiring the money.

Lawrence Craig couldn't get the good feeling out of his heart and head. Giving away all that money made him feel clean again. Well, partially clean. He'd done a lot of shit in his time, and giving away that much money somehow paid for much of the clear up costs associated with making accounts come out even.

Time passed. He settled back into his life as a New Orleans bartender. One evening he served a double Martini with a twist to a lady who could not take her eyes off him. She sort of nursed the drink while she swirled the lemon twist round and round. Lawrence began to feel very uncomfortable. He knew such women were usually on the job, and stood out as bait. He wondered if the FBI was on to him. He didn't want to wait until his shift was over to find out, so he asked the lady what she found so interesting in him.

"Your face and hair," she said. "You look just like my daddy, who I adored. He died when I was only nine, but I'll never forget his face and hair."

Not bad, Craig thought. He tried again. "Did your daddy have a name?"

"Of course he did. It was Drew Hubler. He owned this very bar at one time, you know. My name is Lizbeth. Lizbeth Finch."

Craig thought about that for a second, and asked if Lizbeth was visiting, or did she still live in New Orleans? Not only was she from New Orleans, but she still lived in the same house she was born in. Not many can say that these days. How true, he thought. Perhaps, just perhaps, the lady was who she said she was, and he was being paranoid for no reason. Still, he'd have to have more information before he'd feel better. He tried again. "Do you have a career, a profession, a hobby? What brings you here, tonight?"

She answered, "Yes, yes, and yes, and I was thirsty, until I saw your face."

"Care to elaborate?"

"Believe it or not," she said, "I'm a pediatrician. So is my husband, Gregory. We run a small non-profit clinic in the heart of New Orleans. I spoke at one fundraiser on this side of town earlier tonight, and my husband spoke at another one on the other side of town. We try to get some of our wealthier associates to kick in a few hundred thousand dollars each year to help us run the clinic."

Between serving drinks to all the other customers, Lawrence Craig was deeply moved by the stories Lizbeth Finch spun. He'd always been a sucker for kids, anyway, and his interest seemed quite genuine to Dr. Finch. When she tried to pay for her drink, Craig wouldn't accept her money. He said, "Give it to the kids."

The next day Lawrence Craig was drawn to the Finch Pediatric Clinic, on the corner of Tchoupitoulas and Notre Dame Streets. He sat all day long in his car and watched a steady stream of kids and their parents, mostly mothers, stream through the clinic doors. At day's end, Drs. Finch and Finch emerged, each driving separate Volvo 900's. Without a second thought Lawrence Craig decided to give his $10 million to the kids in the Finch Clinic.

Craig thought about how far away he needed to go in order to wire the money to New Orleans. He decided Biloxi, Mississippi, would be just right. He could drive it in a couple of hours. With so many riverboat gambling joints on the water, a fella could get lost there for a couple of days if necessary, and never be seen by the FBI, or anyone else for that matter.

He waited until he had a day off so he didn't call undue attention to himself. Then he acted.

He parked his car in the huge lot behind the Belle Star Floating Casino, tied up at the Forest Avenue Pier. He walked aboard the big boat and bought $100 worth of dollar slot chips. For the next two hours, Lawrence Craig sat glued to his chair as he won and lost, won and lost. He estimated he had $37 left when he cashed them in and left. Enough of that for a while. He'd return here after he wired the money, and before he drove home that night.

As his financial package advised, he found a public fax inside the Kinko's on Main Street, just a block away from the casino. It was crowded, and he had to wait in line to use the fax. He realized that all of these people were gamblers, and they were wiring home for more money.

When it came his turn, Craig fed the machine four one-dollar bills and punched in the code numbers accessing his account. Then he punched in the account numbers of the Finch Clinic, which he had obtained before he left New Orleans. One of the guys he served regularly at the bar worked in the bank where the Finch Clinic had its account. For free drinks for a week, the guy gave Craig the account number. Lastly, he asked the National Commerce Bank of Jamaica to empty his account of its balance, less fees, and send all the money to the Finch Clinic. In less than two minutes, the confirmation sheet came through. Lawrence Craig was again a free man. He exited quickly so the next user could wire home for more funds.

Craig walked back to the Bell Star and asked for another $100 worth of $20 chips. He went straight for the roulette wheel. He plunked them all down on red. The little ball landed on black. He left. His car was right where he parked it, and his bed was only two hours away. All old scores, as far as he was concerned, had just been settled and cancelled.

Life was good.

The news that evening reported another drug dealer had been shot and killed in Washington, D.C. That made a total of 14, to date. Still no shooter was in custody.

By the time the FBI and the Treasury Department watched another $10 million wire transfer jump from Jamaica to New Orleans via Biloxi, Mississippi, they were giddy in much the same way Chief Inspector Dryfus was giddy in the Pink Panther movies. It was senseless to send agents to another Kinko's, but regulations were regulations. At least until they saw the line waiting to use the fax. The agents might start a riot if they shut down that machine. Gamblers were known for their nasty tempers when reason stood between them and their next money fix. Perhaps the agents would have more luck at the other end.

But that was not to be, either. Drs. Finch and Finch were stunned at the anonymous contribution, but they were certainly grateful for it. In 12 years of practice together, they had never received such a donation. It meant that they could endow the clinic and never again have to worry about fundraising. By investing that sum in the stock market, it should double within the next few years.

Bravo!

Lawrence Craig was again tending bar when Drs. Finch and Finch sat down. Both ordered double Martinis with twists. He tried to hide his pride, but his face reddened when he saw Lizbeth.

Before he blushed, Lizbeth Finch had only suspected that Craig was the silent donor. But now she knew. And Craig knew that she knew that he knew she knew.

"Mr. Craig," she said, "I'd like you to meet my husband, Drew."

"Dr. Finch," Craig said, "it's nice to meet you. I had the pleasure of serving your wife one evening last week."

"Yes," he replied, "she told me, and she was absolutely right. You are the spitting image of her father. Uncanny."

Craig began, "Well, I'm told we all have a twin somewhere in the world. I guess if I remind you of your father in some way, that's good."

"It is," Lizbeth agreed. Then she reached over and touched his arm lightly and said, "Thank you."

Lawrence Craig felt as though the earth could part at that moment and swallow him, and he would not care. Thousands of kids were going to be treated by these fine doctors, and he had helped make that happen. He also liked being touched by this woman.

Drew Finch excused himself to go to the men's room. As soon as he was gone, Lizbeth offered that several FBI agents had been at the clinic asking all kinds of questions regarding the identity of the donor of $10 million to the clinic.

Interesting, Craig noted cautiously. "What did you say?" he asked.

"That I didn't know anybody from Biloxi, and could not imagine from whom such a sum could arise," she answered.

"That's good," Craig observed.

All during the conversation Lizbeth's eyes danced, and fire burned at the tips of her fingers as she once again touched Craig's arm. He had to lean forward against the bar to cover his hand going down to pull his expanding dick upward. What was happening here, he wondered?

Lizbeth knew what was happening, though, and her eyes danced all the more because of it.

Just as Drew returned to his seat, his beeper went off. Again he excused himself and went to the phone in the lobby. When he returned, he said he had to go straight to the hospital. Little Amy Kurtz had to be admitted. Sounded like pneumonia. Lizbeth offered to go with him, but he said no. Take a cab home, darling.

Will do.

"Can you get out of here?" Lizbeth asked Craig bluntly, leaning provocatively towards him.

By now he knew exactly what was going on. "Probably, but I'm not sure I should."

She wasn't to be denied. "If you don't, we'll both explode in the next three minutes." Craig pulled one of the waiters back and asked him to take over the bar. Sudden diarrhea.

Dr. Lizbeth Finch was 17 years Dr. Drew Finch's junior. And Lizbeth was 46, if the truth be known. She hadn't had a good lay for more years than she could remember, and she needed one right then. So did Craig. He lived only 12 minutes away from the bar, but it seemed like 12 hours before they got into his apartment. Lizbeth was like a wild animal. Craig loved it. Suddenly she stopped cold in her tracks. She saw his scarred right side, and the doctor in her asked what happened. An old war wound, he replied. Where did it happen? Can't remember, but if you'd like, I'll pull on a T shirt and cover the damn thing. No, she insisted. No. I want to see it and kiss it.

Craig had been with some really passionate women in his lifetime, but none compared to Lizbeth Finch. With hardly any effort on his part, she enjoyed multiple orgasms several times that night. And just when he thought he couldn't move and she couldn't possibly want any more, she attacked him again, as though she were a 16-year-old, full of piss and vinegar.

"No more, Lizbeth, please," he begged. "No more. I can't do this again."

"Bullshit," was her reply, and with a little effort on her part he found himself thinking, what the hell, maybe I can. Not only could he, but did he. Actually, he did she, and vice-versa.

At first light, Craig realized that Lizbeth had left him sometime in the middle of the night.

Unless she called him, he would have no further contact with her. Besides, nothing would or could ever compare to that night. They never saw each other again.

Chapter 39

From time to time, President Huber called FBI Director Cal Hunter, and CIA Director Robert Benton, to the Oval Office for an update on the Congressional Killings. Today it was Cal Hunter's turn to give the report. He began by detailing the list of $10 million wire transfers that had gone to good causes. Women's colleges, a pediatric clinic, the Union of Black Farmers, the sister of an ex-Navy Seal who was murdered by dope addicts in New Orleans, educational programs in Wales, England, countless millions sent to New Zealand to endow the Symphony and hospitals and police pension funds, and Maxon Stroble's suicide and note.

The president was fascinated. But were they any closer to an arrest than they had been several months ago? Not really. What about Hannah Minsk? Dead end there, too. She had been quiet as a mouse. However, she too had moved $10 million from an account at the K.B. Luxembourg Bank of Monaco, and created a trust fund with it for the Washington Symphony Orchestra in Deborah Saraf's Name. She did the same thing out of inherited funds, and made the Israel Symphony the beneficiary.

"What do you think is happening?" the president asked.

It was Benton who answered this one. For the next 25 minutes, the Director of the CIA told the President of the United States exactly what he thought was going on.

It appeared to Benton that the Congressional Killers were exactly what they said they were. Ordinary people, driven by extreme injustice. For example, the unsuccessful prosecution in the death of Max Stroble's daughter had pushed him over the edge and turned him into one of the assassins. When the assassinations were finished, and these people found themselves with a huge glut of money on their hands, they didn't want it. So they found a way to give it away, turning unrighteous mammon into righteous mammon, to use an old ish-ka-bibl saying.

Several of the assassins had died. Benton thought Jan Christianson was the first, in that freak garbage truck accident. Benton also thought that Wade Jackson was murdered by someone inside the Taj Mahal II in Las Vegas, and that Floyd Briggs, the murdered ex-Seal, was also one of the Congressional Killers. Miss Clarissa DeBeau had taken her $10 million and reinvented herself as a French citizen. Benton believed that one of the killers was still in D.C., killing drug dealers. He'd nailed 27, to date. Drug sales in the District had fallen 59% over the last six months. It seemed people were afraid of ending up without their heads if they sold drugs.

Further, Benton thought Congress had become a better place. He still saw a lot of lobbyists on the Hill, but some were seen still carrying their suitcases full of money at the end of the day. Some coalitions were forming between farmers and bankers, that Benton saw as positive. And once these people learned how to form a bill and get it passed, Benton believed the country would be the better for it. As far as he could see, he thought Washington D.C. had received a great gift from the Congressional Killers. New, untainted blood.

Grudgingly, both President Huber and Cal Hunter had to agree. Publicly, of course, they were still outraged, and committed to catching the assassins of so many good public servants, etc., ad nauseam. But short of a miracle, they all knew they'd never catch any of them alive.

Chapter 40

T. L. Grimes caught the first flight out of D.C. for Barbados. That's where his money was, and he figured he could retire there without any difficulties. English was also the principle language spoken there. His plane landed at the Grantley Adams International Airport at 12:30 p.m. He cleared customs quickly because he'd brought no luggage. All he had was his passport. Whatever he needed from now on he'd buy new.

Hunger and his noon Dilantin pill delayed his departure from the airport complex. A quick burger, some fries, and a Coke were all he needed. He caught a cab and asked the driver to take him to the Alamara International Bank in Bridgetown.

T. L. entered the bank and asked the guard inside the main doors where the withdrawal slips were located. He was escorted to the center table in the middle of the cavernous room, and handed the requested item. His hand shook as he identified himself by number 8402-197BL-446K. He marked the sum of $750 in the withdrawal box. Fear seized him like vice grip pliers. All of a sudden he wondered if there really was $10 million in an account with his name on it in this bank.

He stood looking at the slip, then tore it up. He stuffed the pieces in his pocket. What if someone reassembled them after he left and began to withdraw his money? A man with $10 million doesn't withdraw $750, he thought. What was the matter with him? Maybe he should go for twice that, fifteen hundred.

And that's what he did. His teller took the slip, typed the numbers into the computer, waited for the transaction to clear, and handed T. L. $1,500 in cash. It was real. It wasn't a dream. He thanked the teller and folded the cash and the slip and put everything into his pocket. Upon reaching the front doors of the bank, he had another thought. What about a checking account?

The guard pointed him towards the lovely young woman seated three cubicles down, to his left. Her name was Wanda Olnuska. Ms. Olnuska was quite friendly and very helpful, but she was very sorry. She could not help him get a checking account until he had a permanent address. As soon as he had one she would be glad to finish the paperwork for him. Fair enough. What about a credit card? That she could do, so long as it was tied directly to his account in the bank. For a small fee, money would be taken directly out of his account to pay charges, and his card was good anywhere in the Caribbean and South America.

T. L. left the bank with money in his pocket and a credit card that sizzled. He hailed another taxi and asked the driver to take him to the most expensive and most luxurious hotel on the island.

"You want the gold coast area," the driver said. "There are many beautiful hotels there, but I'd recommend the flagship of them all, the Sandy Lane Hotel." T. L. asked for and received all of the information he wanted, and said he'd like to go to the Sandy Lane Hotel.

It was everything the cabby said, and more. It had been completely renovated several years earlier, making it *the* place to visit. But it was the view of the ocean that made his sea-loving heart sing. Unfortunately, there were no rooms available at any price. But he had traveled so far just to get there. Sorry. Where could he go? Not wanting to be turned away to anywhere else, T. L. asked if it was possibly to lease anything for at least a year? The desk clerk picked up the phone and asked the manager to come to the front. Introductions were made, and T. L.'s request was voiced again. Indeed. For a mere $700,000, up front, a year's lease could be arranged immediately. T. L. whipped out his Alamara credit card, and before he knew it, he was being shown to his very own suite. Home for at least one year.

The $700,000, he learned, included everything. All food, drinks, cleaning services, room services, laundry, spa, workout room, and all sundries imaginable. T. L. was in paradise. He would, however, be responsible for renting or buying his own yacht.

Chapter 41

For the first time in months, Melvin Hogan felt like he needed a drink. But he didn't want to get drunk. At the same time, he didn't know how to stay sober on his own, now that the mission was over. Ten friggin' million, and it was all his! He had plenty of money left from his $7000 monthly salary, and didn't really need to touch the big stuff for a long time. He just needed to get through the day without a drink. It occurred to him that maybe he ought to call Alcoholics Anonymous. Several times in the past he had thought about calling AA, but something had always kept him from picking up the phone. But today was different. He really wanted help. That was the difference.

He looked in the phone book, found the listing, and called the number. A friendly voice on the other end asked him if he wanted to stop drinking. Affirmative. Was he drinking today? Negative. Good, good. Did he have transportation? Yes. Can he get to a meeting? Yes. Directions were given, and Melvin caught a cab to his first AA meeting.

It was in the basement of an Episcopal Church on Union at French. He could smell the coffee as soon as he started down the stairs. Someone at the bottom extended his hand and said, "Paul."

"Melvin," he answered, taking the hand.

It had begun.

Melvin got a cup of coffee and sat down at a table full of other men and some women, all talking and laughing and enjoying each other's company. Paul sat next to him and asked if this was his first AA meeting. Melvin didn't remember making a big signboard saying "It's my first AA meeting," but evidently he might just as well have.

When the meeting got under way and the speaker was introduced, Melvin wondered what he had gotten himself into, but then he realized it couldn't be anything worse than he'd just gotten out of, and decided to listen to what this guy had to say. For the next 20 minutes, the room laughed many times and cried several times. Melvin began to think that everyone in the joint was either crazy or just plain rude, laughing at the poor man's misfortunes. But then the speaker said something that got Melvin's attention. He said, "If you don't take the first drink, you can't get drunk." Later, Melvin also remembered him saying something like, "Just don't drink today. Don't worry about tomorrow 'cause it ain't here, yet."

For the next six months, Melvin Hogan lived inside AA. He asked Paul to be his temporary sponsor until he knew enough people to select just the right person for that job. He started to work the 12 steps of recovery. But when he got to the one about listing people he'd harmed, and then the other one about making amends, Melvin began to get real scared. He knew if he didn't do what the program asked him to do, he'd probably end up drunk, but if he did, he'd probably go to jail for the rest of his life. Boy, would a drink taste good right about now! He needed to talk to someone he could trust, and Paul, his present sponsor, wasn't it.

He told Paul how much he appreciated his help, but that he felt the need to get a Vietnam vet to help him the rest of the way. Paul understood and wished him well. His special gift to the program was getting people started. And he loved watching his 'pigeons' fly.

Vernon Bauer was Melvin's man. The two had gone out for coffee several times after meetings, and Melvin felt he could trust Vernon to handle the information he needed to tell him. He asked Vernon to be his sponsor. Yes, of course, was the answer. Melvin then asked if they could go to the Vietnam Vet Center one morning for coffee, and a long talk. Yes, of course, again.

Melvin didn't extract any promises of silence from Vernon. It wasn't necessary. And for the next four hours, Melvin Hogan told his new sponsor everything he knew and did in the Congressional Killings.

Vernon understood Melvin's dilemma. The AA program called for complete honesty, but not to the point of total self-destruction. And then Vernon had an idea. He and Melvin talked about the newspaper speculations regarding other $10 million donations. The money might be Melvin's ticket out of the moral quagmire he found himself in. What if Melvin donated it, anonymously, of course, to the George Washington Hospital wing dedicated to helping other alcoholics who still suffered?

Jackpot! Melvin loved the idea. But how could they get the account number of the GWH, and how could they make sure the money would go to suffering alcoholics trying to get better?

Vernon told Melvin that in AA there were lots of people who were talented and connected beyond belief, and if he'd stick around long enough, he'd discover this for himself. One of the city's eminent cardiologists was a member of their home group. Did he know that? No, he didn't. Who is he? Clyde M.! You're kidding, Clyde, a cardiologist? No way. Clyde is on staff at GWH, and he can get us the account number.

At the next AA meeting, Vernon and Melvin sat on either side of Clyde, and could hardly wait for the meeting to end. When it did, both men grabbed Clyde by the arms and told him they had a medical emergency that required his immediate attention. The good doctor began to protest, but soon realized it was important.

The three men went back to Vernon's apartment. Without giving Clyde any details beyond the fact that they knew someone who wanted to make an anonymous donation, they asked him if he could get the bank account number for his hospital. Also, did the hospital budget have a specific line item designated for the alcoholic ward? Yes, and yes. He could get the account number, he thought, but it would take a few days time. Hush, hush? he asked. Hush, hush they replied. The donor wanted to remain nameless. Clyde nodded. He understood anonymity well.

A week went by, and at the next home group meeting Dr. Clyde M. greeted Melvin and Vernon with a Cheshire cat grin. He handed them a small slip of paper with the two requested numbers on it. Was he going to regret this, he asked them? Only if he ever breathed a word about it to another living soul. He knew they both meant every word.

Next day, Melvin and Vernon met at the club to plan the money transfer. Melvin knew that it had to be done from a public fax, like a Kinko's, and Vernon knew just the one.

Melvin didn't like doing the transfer in D. C., and suggested they go to Baltimore. Agreed. They wanted to do it at rush hour, so they could fit into the crowds and the traffic. No Feds could get to them at rush hour. They waited until two o'clock in the afternoon, and left for Baltimore. An older Kinko's store was located in the heart of downtown Baltimore, on Fourth Street. A public parking garage was on the same street, and Melvin would have no difficulty walking as quickly as he could back to Vernon's waiting car.

Everything worked as planned. The money was transferred, the two men merged into rush hour traffic, and the George Washington Hospital general account number 87-K302 had $10 million, plus accrued interest, that had not been there moments before. The second fax into GWH account number 87-K302 indicated that the $10 million was to be applied to its alcohol rehabilitation unit.

The familiar dance/drill of agents and interviews left the Bureau even more convinced than ever that blood money was being given to worthy causes and institutions. This last donation caught Lynn Smolen's ever-alert eye. When she wrote her article, she asked several shrewd questions. Was Baltimore symbolic, or just convenient? Did it imply that the donor was an alcoholic, or one of the former Congressional Killers turned alcoholic by his actions, and trying to sooth his guilty conscience? Was the donor also the shooter of drug dealers, whose last kill was number forty-three?

The administration of George Washington Hospital had no idea how the money had arrived in the general account from the Banco Central de Bolivia, but they really didn't care. Among other things, they planned to endow a chair of medicine at the university with it, dedicated to finding a cure for alcoholism.

At the next AA meeting, Dr. Clyde wanted to ask Melvin and Vernon if what had happened at GWH was a result of the numbers he had given them. But he thought better of it and simply nodded to each man, who both sat at the opposite end of the room from him. The looks he got back expressed no recognition or acknowledgement, so he just smiled inwardly, knowing that in some way he had 'done good.'

Chapter 42

Although romantic involvement between the operatives had been discouraged while the assassinations were taking place, they were not forbidden, and sure enough, widowed housewife Judy Morton and chemist Wallace Keenan had fallen in love. They had gotten together as soon as the group was disbanded. Like all the other operatives, they soon realized their financial packages created many problems rather than many blessings. Neither Judy nor Wallace wanted to return to their former homes, and each had enough money in current accounts to meet needs for many months, if they were careful. Perhaps they could start over again in Florida. The Salvation Army pickup made it possible for them to rid themselves of nearly everything they owned, except their clothes. They even donated Judy's old 98 Saturn. Wallace had a newer and larger Buick.

Each had kept up with the news, and every time a story surfaced about another mysterious $10 million donation, they realized some of their fellow assassins had figured out what to do with their money. Reason suggested that it had been a problem and curse for the others as well, but of course, they knew nothing about Clarissa DeBeau, T. L. Grimes, or Williams. T. L. and Clarissa were the only ones who had never participated in an actual killing.

Wallace and Judy spent many long hours talking about how they should get rid of their money, and make a fresh start together. Wallace figured out that Willie Batts probably dumped his money in the Union of Black Farmers Association. Wallace had always thought Willie was such a good man, so Wallace decided he'd add his money to Willie's. Judy missed her children and still mourned their deaths. She remembered reading about the Finch Pediatric Clinic in New Orleans, and decided it should get her money. On their way to Florida, they'd stop somewhere in South Carolina and dump their funds.

At Myrtle Beach, along the grand strand, they found a Kinko's, and first Judy, then Wallace, wired away $10 million each. By the time the FBI arrived, Wallace and Judy were safely out of Myrtle Beach and almost to the Georgia border.

Chapter 43

Cal Hunter was almost persuaded to close the books on the Congressional Killers with the last two wire transfers. But hope springs eternal in the heart of a hunter, and he was the most hopeful of them all.

Ken Springfield destroyed his financial package without even looking at it, returned to his family in Iowa, and got a job in the local Wal Mart, working in the garden center. His money would remain forever in the South African Reserve Bank. He never wanted to think about it, ever again. And he didn't.

But Clarence Henry was different from all the others. His hatred of the government was visceral. He had never wanted to stop killing congressmen and women. And he was angry that he only had $10 million to work with. He wondered if he could ever find a way to continue the work.

Nearly a month went by, and Clarence sat on his duff waiting for lightning to strike. He was getting quite bored with himself and his lot in life, when he caught the tail end of a news story about a paramilitary group holding a meeting in Reno, Nevada, in two days. According to the reporter, this particular group planned to analyze what had happened to the country since so many in Congress were assassinated by unknowns. Clarence didn't catch were the meeting was to be held, but he figured if he got to Reno, he could find it.

And find it he did. For two days, Clarence sat in the back of the room listening to this one and that one speculating wildly, and missing the mark each and every time. Because he sat so quietly, he called attention to himself. Two burley types sat either side of him near the end of the last plenary session. They wanted to know if he was a spy from CIA, ATF, or the FBI. Hardly, he responded. Then what, they wanted to know? Clarence asked, was it possible to talk privately with Gerard Kunkel?

Kunkel was the paramilitia leader from Montana, whose members were full-time patriots, not weekenders. They were known as Kunkel's Militia. They thought of themselves as

God's army, whose task it was to defend America against anyone and everyone who threatened to undermine the great principles upon which she was built.

Kunkel himself had a winsome way about him. He could charm the sox, or the pants, off anyone who'd listen to him for as little as two minutes. His sources of money were his best kept secrets, and the FBI had tried unsuccessfully, for years, to cut his supply lines.

Clarence didn't realize how much trouble he'd gotten himself into when he made his request. Only Kundel decided who talked to Kunkel. Anyone making the first move was automatically classified as dangerous, and suspected as being Federal. Clarence's two unknown questioners looked more grim by the minute, and Clarence began to feel genuinely worried about his safety. He realized he was in grave danger.

In a panic and without thinking, Clarence blurted out that he wanted to talk face to face with Kunkel about donating a large sum of money to Kunkel's organization. In fact, he'd like to join up. Also, none of the people attending the meetings knew squat about the Congressional Killers. But he, Clarence, knew everything.

As if on cue, and without a word, both men lifted Clarence Henry out of his seat, patted him down for weapons and/or electronic listening/transmitting devices, and marched him through the door and into a waiting car. A blindfold was applied over his eyes. Clarence sensed that his life was no longer in danger, so long as he was able to produce the money. Obviously, however, these boys were not to be toyed with.

For the next two hours the car droned on and on. Not a word was spoken. Finally the driver turned onto a bumpy gravel road, which brought them to a guarded compound. Once the car stopped, Clarence sat quietly for another half hour, not daring to move. He heard a window open, and felt some fresh air rush in. The order to take him in was given, and Clarence Henry was guided up several steps, across a wooden porch and through a door into a smoke-filled room. His blindfold remained in place.

A pleasant voice said, "Tell us your name." Clarence did. "Well, Clarence Henry," said the same pleasant voice, "you've said a few things to my friends that have gotten our attention. Do you want to tell us your story, or do you prefer the question and answer approach?"

Clarence said he'd like to tell his story in his own way, but could he have some water first, and would they remove his blindfold? He was a friendly. Water was brought, and the pleasant voice ordered the blindfold removed. When Clarence had a few moments for his eyes to adjust, he saw the large form of Gerard Kunkel sitting across the table from him. Surrounding him were the two burly men who had accosted him, plus seven other grim-faced men, who never said a word during the next three hours.

Clarence began with the story of his 18-year fight with the IRS. Kunkel interrupted rarely, but each time he did, Clarence knew he was believed. When he told them that he was one of the Congressional Killers, several around the room murmured "holy shit!" But it was the Center located in the heart of D. C. that fascinated everyone, especially the part about it being underground next to a social service center called the *Been There, Done That*. Clarence didn't know if the Center was still operable, but he speculated that it must have been destroyed.

The seemingly unlimited source of money available to the assassins also fascinated the group. And speaking of money, Clarence indicated his financial package had the name of a bank where $10 million, plus interest, waited his pleasure.

Kunkel had followed the press speculation that the anonymous donations of $10 million had led the FBI to conclude the money had come from some of the Congressional Killers. Maxon Strobel's suicide note had confirmed that speculation. But Kunkel was well aware that any more such transactions would be closely monitored. If Clarence Henry were to wire his funds into Kunkel's accounts, the FBI would swarm all over every facility Kunkel was known to associate with. They'd also confiscate the money. A better way had to be found. That would take some time, and effort.

Did Clarence have any ideas of how the money could be wired to Kunkel? None. But would they let him join Kunkel's army? Affirmative, and welcome. Clarence then asked if he might sit on any intelligence committee within Kunkel's organization. He'd learned many things about warfare from a couple of ex-Seals, and someone else he thought was a CIA spook, and he thought it might prove useful sometime. Agreed. Could he get something to eat, now, and then get some sleep? He was very tired. Affirmative. But first, give us your social security number. Done.

As soon as Clarence Henry left the room, it erupted. Order returned only when Gerard Kunkel raised his huge bulk, slammed his fist on the table, and demanded quiet. "One at a time, please. Norman, you first."

Norman was one of the two men who had first contacted Clarence in the auditorium. A big smile came over Norman's face as he said, "He didn't shit his pants, Ger. And you know, me and Donnie can put the fear of God into a man who's not telling us the truth."

Another voice, "What if he's FBI? I mean, the Feds can put $10 million into any account they want. What if he's a plant, and the money's the bait? We'd all be sucked into the joint in no time, and I for one ain't never going back inside. I say we check out his story. Any way we can get his back tax records?"

Affirmative. Their resident computer nerd was able to hack into anything they needed. Kunkel sent Norman away with Clarence's social security number, and instructions to have the geek print out Clarence's tax records from the last 25 years, if possible.

It took the hacker nearly three hours to get the last seven years back tax records. The rest of Clarence's records were in cold storage, somewhere off line. What interested the group the most was that Clarence had not filed any IRS tax forms for the last two years, and the year before that he had made $18,000 working in a nursing home. Maybe he was genuine. Maybe he hated the government more than any of them. Maybe he had done more for the country as a congressional killer than any of them had ever dreamed they could do. But everything would be clear to them in a couple of days. That's how long it usually took them to find out the truth about any man.

The quietest man in Gerard Kunkel's inner circle was the man they called Donnie. He and Kunkel were first cousins. Both men were born in 1963. They grew up together on family farms in Montana. Donnie's mother and Kunkel's father were brother and sister. Donnie's last name was Quinlan. Donnie Quinlan's parents had been killed by a drunk driver when he was twelve. Gerard Kunkel, Sr., raised Donnie beside his own boy, Gerard Kunkel, Jr. No two men were better brothers to each other than Gerard and Donnie. So when Donnie said something, everyone listened.

Donnie remembered watching several of the gamblers in several of Reno's casinos get chips from an account they had established in house. He also remembered that some of those gamblers wired money from home banks directly into their casino accounts. What if, he speculated aloud, they sent Clarence Henry into one of the casinos with $10,000, and opened a house account with it. Then he could wire his money into his casino account. The casino would be paid a fee for laundering the money, and from its internal counting house, hand over the $10 million to them.

Applause burst out in the room. The element that would help it work was the fact that Clarence wasn't known to the Reno establishment. Everyone knew that for the proper, yet to be negotiated sum of cash, it could be made to happen.

Gerard Kunkel had associates in nearly every walk of life. He was able to tap into their patriotism, and their rage over the Federal government's actions or inactions, to push whatever personal buttons required pushing, to make their cash registers sing and dance and cough up money. For this particular job, Kunkel needed his accountant, Vince Buffolini. Vince knew everyone in Reno and Vegas, and they all knew him. They also knew Kunkel's politics, and tried to stay out of them as much as possible. They'd gladly give him any donations he wanted, within reason, if they didn't have to know any more about where the money was going. That's how scary Gerard Kunkel was.

Vince suggested he talk to his cousin Big Al, head of security at the Taj in Vegas. Vince also knew the manager there, one Billy Jelks. Jelks was known as a reasonable man, who never turned down a reasonable business offer. Go, Kunkel said.

Buffolini's plane landed in Las Vegas the next day. He'd called Big Al as soon as he got the assignment, and asked Al to pick him up at the airport. Done. On the way to the Taj, Big Al told Vince that Billy Jelks was none too keen about this meeting. They had had some Feds sniffing around several months ago, and Jelks didn't want to attract any more attention to the Taj than he absolutely had to.

Buffolini was instantly on guard. What Feds? Big Al told him the entire story of one Wade Jackson, AKA Edmund Sargent Reynolds. Vince immediately called back to Kunkel and asked him to find out if Clarence knew anyone named Wade Jackson or Edmund Sargent Reynolds.

Bingo. Clarence knew 'Sarge.' He had been a crack shot, and Clarence had personally watched him shoot several congressmen.

Big Al was getting a headache. He realized he might have a big problem on his hands. It appeared that all the assassins had been paid $10 million. Wade Jackson had wired $6 million into the Taj on the house fax, which gave the house his account number. What had happened to the other $4 million? Al would have to let his superiors in New York know about this possible problem, or he would be remiss in his duties. He had always liked Billy Jelks, but he liked breathing more.

Big Al's phone call to New York delayed the money exchange by several days. All Vince could tell Kunkel was that there was something wrong at the Taj, and that he didn't want to do anything that might endanger him. Be patient, he advised Kunkel, $10 million was worth a few days' delay.

When Big Al's counterpart walked unannounced into Billy Jelks' office, Billy knew he'd made a terribly big mistake. Paulo Stuarti barely fit through the door. Unlike Big Al, he was brainless. He couldn't tell if a guy was telling the truth or lying. He didn't care. His job was to make the guy shit his pants. Nothing more.

Behind Paulo came the brains. A little guy everyone called Mr. Nice. Paulo and Mr. Nice played the best good cop/bad cop routine anywhere. The difference between Paulo and Mr. Nice was seamless. When Mr. Nice didn't hear the right answer, Paulo got the head nod and did something extremely painful to the liar. Billy had watched them operate in the past, and was quite impressed by their ability to extract truth out of bullshit within one pain session. Rarely had he ever seen it go to three. By then the victim was usually dead.

As if on cue, Billy Jelks shit his pants, literally. Mr. Nice didn't have to ask one question. Billy spilled everything. He opened his file to the day he contacted the Caribbean Bank of Commerce Ltd., on St. Johns Island, and transferred $3 million plus out of Edmund Sargent Reynold's account into his personal account in the Mizrahi Bank on the Cayman Islands. Billy also volunteered that at the time he knew nothing about the $10 million sum. Perhaps Jackson, or Reynolds, did something with $1 million before he ever came to the Taj. That was reasonable, Mr. Nice agreed. They'd send someone to St. John's and find out. In the mean while, Billy needed to clean up, and to write several checks. Maybe it would be enough to mitigate his offense. Probably not. But as of this moment, assistant manager Tommy D'Agilio was in charge of the Taj.

Then Big Al asked Mr. Nice if he could have a few minutes. Of course. Big Al explained the Kunkel deal. It was an opportunity for the casino to make $500,000 in less than 20 minutes. It was dangerous because of the Jackson/Reynolds thing, and Big Al wanted approval to do the deal.

Mr. Nice called New York and got the go-ahead. Big Al was to oversee everything. Tommy D'Agilio wasn't out of the loop, but he didn't need to be in it, either. Gerard Kunkel would have to bring a van to the back of the casino at the precise hour the funds were being wired. Loading all that cash in every denomination imaginable would take at least 10 minutes. The casino would assemble it and have it in boxes, ready to go out the door, just as soon as they got confirmation it was in the casino's account. Kunkel was to get $9.5 million.

Kunkel bitched, but to no avail. "What about the interest?" he demanded. Big Al was to get it as a bonus, on top of the fee for brokering the deal. Even Kunkel had to laugh at the extortion, but he agreed to it. After all, $9.5 million was better than zero, which was what they had before Clarence Henry arrived. And it was all in cold hard cash.

Because Billy Jelks had served the bosses so well for so long, mercy was extended. However, he was stripped of any fortune he had accumulated, and he was sent into exile. They were never to see or hear from him again.

Against such a day and such an event, Billy Jelks had squirreled away $750,000, in a small bank not far from Las Vegas. Just over the Arizona border and nearly 100 miles south is the town of Bullhead City. Over the years Billy had hand-carried his stash there, and now he was in need of it all. He was allowed to keep his car, but jewelry, *objet d'art,* and other valuables were all taken from him. He felt lucky to be alive. And he was.

But not for long. Big Al knew Billy Jelks, and he anticipated that Billy might have something hidden, that he had failed to turn over. Al put a directional finder under Billy's car, and followed him unseen, from a distance. As Billy Jelks walked out of the bank with his suitcase full of money, Big Al escorted him away, took the money, and fed Billy to the blades of his Davy tree machine. He also turned the money in to his bosses. They gave him 20% of it. His stock was rising.

When Big Al returned from his grim disposal of Billy, Vince Buffolini had Clarence Henry in the little fax office just off the office of the late Jelks. The cash had been stacked into empty whisky cartons, and was all ready to be carried out the door moments after Clarence made the transfer.

Deborah Saraf had chosen the Cayman National Bank Ltd., for Clarence Henry's money. He took the next numbered sheet on the pile, which told his bank where to wire the requested funds, then wrote the bank's name at the top, and his account number. The amount he requested was everything in the account. He added, 'Please close the account when this transaction is over.' He pushed send. The machine came to life.

So did local FBI Special Agent in Charge, Howard Chauncey. The Bureau had a court order to monitor this fax machine. It was good for only three more days before it expired.

If that fax machine was ever used again to contact an out-of-country bank and ask it to wire the magic number of $10 million, the FBI was permitted to print out the transaction, for purposes of arrest and possible prosecution.

The clock was ticking. Chauncey had to assemble his fellow agents ASAP, but a glitch that should never have happened slowed him down. The contacts on his cell phone charger were dirty. He was speeding to the Taj alone, figuring he could contact everyone on his way there, but his dead cell phone made it impossible for him to reach any of his agents, who were working other crimes at the time. Some were at lunch, or on break.

All Chauncey knew was that he was the Lone Ranger, minus Tonto, and he didn't like it one bit. He definitely didn't like the idea of entering the casino by himself. Whoever made the wire transfer would by now be out the door. It seemed futile to try, but try he must.

Just as he was pulling up to the front door, Gerard Kunkel's van, loaded with $9.5 million, was speeding away from the back. At the front desk Chauncey identified himself as an FBI agent, and asked to speak to the manager. The manager was out of the building. Could he talk to someone else? How about head of security?

Big Al's pager went off, and he sensed it was trouble. He ushered Clarence and Vince out a side door and walked calmly to the front desk. Agent Howard Chauncey informed Big Al about the evidence he'd just gathered, and asked to be given the in-house record of the wire transaction. Big Al denied that such a wire transfer had taken place in the casino, and asked Mr. Chauncey if he had any court orders giving him the right to enter the Taj for purposes of seizure. Indeed he had, and he waved them under Big Al's nose.

Mistake. Instantly Big Al had the papers, and Mr. Chauncey in a very painful arm lock. There was never any question about Big Al. He would always beat anyone in the physical game, but he'd cream them in the mental one.

To others in the casino, it appeared as though an unruly patron was being escorted away from some problem he was causing. When Chauncey began to scream for help, Big Al upped the level of pain until his victim stopped talking. Big Al always dominated every victim unmercifully. It's what he did.

When he had Chauncey inside his own office, Big Al asked him where his backup was. Coming. Really? Why aren't they here? Don't know.

Big Al hit Howard Chauncey squarely on the left side of his head. Chauncey dropped like a dead man, which he was soon to be. The inside pocket of his suit coat contained the other document Big Al wanted--the copy of the fax Clarence Henry had sent from the Taj just moments ago. With that in hand, Big Al twisted Howard Chauncey's head until the neck snapped, killing him within seconds. Big Al would dispose of the body later. Right now he had to get rid of the car.

Inside Agent Chauncey's left front pants pocket was the key to his government car, which was parked outside the front door. Big Al locked his office door, walked out the front door, and instructed one of the bellhops to take the car around to the garage and put it in the basement. Done. It would be hours before anyone would begin to miss Agent Chauncey. If the Taj was about to be raided, he should be hearing sirens off in the distance. He stood and listened intently. Silence. Just maybe this foolish fellow had acted alone and in haste. He'd know soon. But right now, he had a body to get rid of.

Big Al had a dumb waiter elevator in his office, in which he loaded dead bodies for transport to the basement. He moved the transport van and parked it directly in front of the elevator opening. When Chauncey's body decended, Big Al dumped it in the back of his van and drove the 45 miles into the desert for grinding and burning. He thought, there's got to be a better way of making a living.

Hours later he moved the government car back to its garage. He kept the keys and tossed them into a near by trash container. They'd end up in a landfill in a few days. Too late for anyone to do anything about it.

Chapter 44

When Gerard Kunkel's van entered the militia compound, three men were called out for special recognition. First was Clarence Henry. Talk about manna from heaven! Last week, nobody knew there was a Clarence Henry. Now they sure did. Second was Donnie Quinlan. He had had the brilliant idea of using the casino to get the money into their hands. And lastly, Vince Buffolini, accountant and broker of deals. He had the contacts to put it all together. They were going to party that night.

Kunkel ordered so much food and booze for the night's festivities that Clarence felt he was single handedly throwing the party himself. It was not how he thought his money should be spent. He made the mistake of saying so. Gerard Kunkel's face grew mean and ugly. His grabbed Clarence by the throat and nearly choked the life out of him, before Donnie interrupted and suggested he not do it. When Clarence was breathing properly again, Kunkel was, too, and he admonished Clarence to remember whose money he was talking about. It belonged to the Kunkel Militia now, and Clarence had better never forget that, or the next time Kunkel would not be so gentle.

Although Clarence Henry was only half the size of Gerard Kunkel, Kunkel had made a huge mistake by not killing Clarence right then and there. It was never the size of the dog that mattered in a fight. It was the size of the fight inside the dog that counted. After all, Clarence Henry had fought the IRS for 18 years, and won. He'd help kill 244 congressional representatives, for God's sake, and he was not to be treated this way by anyone, especially by the man to whom he had just given $10 million in cash!

The look Clarence gave Kunkel did not go unnoticed. Norman stored it away for future use. Who knew? What if everyone got drunk enough? Little Clarence might act on his impulse that night. Wouldn't that please the boys back in the Hoover Building! It might be enough for Norman to get out from his deep cover, and return him to normalcy, whatever that was these days. He could hardly wait to let everyone back there in the Bureau know about the Center located next to the *Been There, Done That*. He also needed to recover as much of the money for the Bureau as he could.

By 2:30 a.m., the debauchery was nearly complete. Most people in the compound were either passed out, dead drunk, or screwing their brains out with any number of the women in the group. Kunkel was passed out at the table, with an unfinished beer in one hand and his hunting knife in the other. The only ones still alert were the six guards on point, and Donnie Quinlan. He didn't drink, and he didn't like it when his cousin did. The six guards had been promised their party would be the following night.

It was perfect. Norman made his move. He jumped on line at the geek's computer and e-mailed D. C. "Now! Need 15 choppers full of Marines plus one crane for van full of money. Congressional Killer case SOLVED." Signed, "Ziegler."

Although it seemed like hours to Norman, only 25 minutes expired before he heard the first helicopter arrive. Marines were everywhere in seconds. The six guards were quickly neutralized. The huge aerial crane Norman had requested dropped a sling on top of the van. Marines attached the sling and the van began to lift immediately. It also began to be carried away by the big copter's forward motion.

In less than three minutes, the entire compound was covered with bombs set to explode in five minutes. Gerard Kunkel was in handcuffs, Donnie Quinlan lay dead, Norman "Zeigler" was in handcuffs, and so was Clarence Henry. The choppers lifted off with all personnel on board, plus the three prisoners, before anyone inside could pull on pants.

The explosions lit up the night sky for miles. The next day, local authorities held a news conference detailing the number of bodies found at a bombed-out compound in the Eldorado National Forest, near Kyburz, California. One survivor of the event, Ruthie Lemmon, known as Gum Drop, told reporters, "It was the Marines." Both the Federal government and the Pentagon denied any knowledge of, or participation in, whatever had happened in that remote mountain setting. Pentagon officials further deny that any military activities or exercises had been conducted within 200 miles of the area.

Chapter 45

CIA Director Robert Benton met with President Huber and FBI Director Calvin Hunter in the Oval Office at 6:30 a.m., following the capture of Gerard Kunkel. The president wanted to know what the hell was really going on, and why he had not been briefed before it happened. He was fit to be tied.

Both Benton and Hunter knew they had not really miscued on this one, and that they would soon be squeezing the political sponge, wringing out a win for the good guys. Cal Hunter spoke first, telling the president of the 15-year campaign the Bureau had waged against the country's most notorious militia leader, Gerard Kunkel. The president acknowledged that he knew about Kunkel, and how he had rubbed the Bureau's nose in the dirt all those years. He also knew that the FBI had infiltrated Kunkel's inner circle, although he did not know the details.

Cal Hunter knew it was just dumb luck that the Bureau had been able to score the victory over Kunkel the night before, but he wasn't going to say so. "We received this urgent extraction call last night," he said, "and we had to respond immediately. There was no time to wake you, Mr. President." He handed the president a copy of 'Ziegler's' e-mail.

"My God!" President Huber exclaimed. "The Congressional Killings, solved! Tell me, tell me."

"Well, sir," Hunter said, "we can't quite do that, yet. We haven't been able to talk to either Ziegler or a man named Clarence Henry, who was at the compound. Ziegler pointed him out to the team leader as one of the Congressional Killers. I'll get back to you after I know something for sure. Right now, both men are in custody and sleeping. So is Kunkel. I've given strict orders that no one is to talk to them until they are brought here for questioning. We'll have them flown in this evening, and begin the questioning tomorrow."

"Well done, Cal, well done," was the president's reply. "But what about all the explosions, and the deaths of our ill-informed citizens inside that compound?"

Hunter replied, "We've asked the CIA to help us on that one, sir."

Robert Benton picked up the narrative. "A conference of militia groups took place last week in Reno, Nevada, Mr. President. In one of the sessions, Gerard Kunkel didn't like a particular response to something he said. Jamie Nutting, the responder, and Kunkel, have had nothing but bad blood between their groups for years. Typical of Kunkel, he blasted Nutting, calling him, and I quote, 'an idiot whose head's been so far up his ass for so many years that he's brain dead from lack of oxygen.' Umbrage was taken, harsh threats were shouted back and forth, and both leaders huffed and puffed out of the meeting, leaving everyone else in a lurch. We've already planted the story everywhere that the Kunkel compound was raided and bombed last evening by Kunkel's sworn rival, Jamie Nutting. APB's have been issued for his immediate arrest for questioning regarding last night's destruction and loss of life. Of course Nutting has been long gone from Reno, and with any luck, he'll stay hidden forever. We never want to bring him in. He could prove that it was the government, and not he, that did the dastardly deeds late last night."

The slight smile at the left side of President Huber's mouth assured Hunter and Benton that the cover up was acceptable, and all was well.

The next concern was the capture of Gerard Kunkel. They couldn't just keep him locked away forever, could they?

"Of course, not, Mr. President. We have no intention of keeping that poor man on ice for very long. After we get all the information out of him that we can, we'll simply confuse him before we turn him loose. He'll be found wandering around in San Francisco, not quite sure who he is or how he got there. If any of his former militia members from other states ever find him, he'll not recognize any of them. Nor will he ever remember being in our custody."

"You can do that, Robert?" the president asked unbelievingly.

"Certainly, sir. We've been doing it for many years. We just don't talk about it."

"I should think not," the president said sternly. "Now tell me about the van full of money, and Clarence Henry."

Cal Hunter's turn. "Last evening, at his extraction, FBI Agent Ziegler identified Clarence Henry to Marine Captain Nelson as one of the Congressional Killers, and ordered Nelson to take Henry into custody. Henry apparently wired $10 million from the Cayman National Bank, Ltd., to the Taj Mahal II Casino in Las Vegas, yesterday afternoon. We watched the money fly, and thought we could catch whoever wired it in the act. But something has gone wrong with our Las Vegas Office. The Agent in Charge, Howard Chauncey, has disappeared. He's gone. But Agent Ziegler specifically identified a van full of money in his extraction message. We've been counting the money since we recovered it, and so far we're up to nearly $9 million. The problem is that it's in every denomination printed. Rubber bands hold it all together. It's a mess, to say the least.

"What makes us real excited, however, is that the same casino had $6 million transferred into its in-house bank several weeks before. The Bureau had been unable to establish the identity of the person wiring the money right then, but felt sure he was indeed one of the Congressional Killers. But he simply vanished as soon as we made contact with the casino. We fear he has been killed by the casino people, because within an hour of the time we asked about one Wade Jackson, AKA Edmund Sargent Reynolds, another $3 million was transferred from his account on St. John's Island to another one on the Cayman Islands in the Mizrahi Bank. When we hacked into the computer system at the Taj Mahal II, we discovered a Wade Jackson was registered there, and that he had been the one wiring all the money to himself, over a 10-day period. We're looking into the possibilities of the Mob having funded the Congressional Killers."

Chapter 46

Gerard Kunkel was not a happy man. He, Norman, and Clarence Henry had all been flown to the McClelland Air Force Base in Sacramento. Guards had to separate him from Clarence, because even with hands cuffed and secured at his waist by a chain used to prevent prisoners from using their arms offensively, Kunkel tried to bite and head butt Clarence. He blamed Clarence Henry for the mess he was in. He kept shouting over and over, "I should have wrung your skinny little neck last night!" Kunkel was a big man, and in the state of fury he reached, it took six guards to do anything with him. No, he was not going to behave himself. No, they could not reason with him. Besides, he knew his rights. He wanted to see his fucking lawyer. Guards felt sorry for Agent Norman Ziegler, and they removed him altogether from the unit, and let him get some sleep in the officer's quarters.

Kunkel refused to cooperate with the guards in any way. He soiled and wet himself numerous times. It need not have happened, but he was ready to fight them all to the death if they'd only uncuff him.

But when he saw Clarence Henry with one hand uncuffed, enjoying a cup of coffee, Kunkel began to re-think his position. Henry had showered, and been issued a bright orange jumpsuit with the word 'PRISONER' stenciled prominently front and back. Kunkel was told that they would be leaving for D. C. in about 25 minutes. If he changed his mind about a shower and clean clothes, all he had to do was say so. He said so. Eight guards with Tazer guns stood at the ready. If Kunkel signaled a wrong move, they were going to electrocute him by hand, and they were going to enjoy it.

Kunkel knew he was beat, and gave the guards no trouble. Besides, he was glad to get out of his smelly, wet clothes.

Like Clarence Henry, Kunkel was issued an orange jump suit. He also submitted, without protestation or incident, to being re-shackled hand and foot. He walked with a Tazer gun held at the back of his neck by one guard, and another held to his heart by another guard. "Where's Norman," he asked his other guard, who held the foot tether that would jerk him off his feet if need be. Silence. But as Kunkel was about to be seated for the flight back to D. C., he thought he saw Norman up front talking to the pilot. It couldn't be. Norman was in a real suit, and he didn't have any restraints.

Kunkel went crazy. Tazers flashed and hummed, and Kunkel screamed in pain and humiliation. His feet were unceremoniously jerked out from under him. His head struck an armrest in the aisle, and the lights went out.

When he regained consciousness he was strapped in and down in his seat. He hurt all over. It felt like he'd been beaten with a ball bat. The plane had taken off, and he had no idea were he was, or where he was going. But his rage renewed when Norman appeared, and asked him how he was doing. The string of expletives spewing out of Kunkel's mouth, accompanied with as much spit as he could hock up, made Norman laugh. "You're pathetic, Ger. You know that? If you're not good, and if you don't tell the boys back in D. C. what they want to hear, I'm going to recommend that they sic Clarence Henry on you. He'll get you to talk. You should have seen the look he gave you after you nearly strangled him last night. He's not to be fooled with." More expletives from Kunkle.

Norman received the same type of verbal abuse when he visited Clarence Henry in another section of the plane. Like Kunkel, Clarence was strapped in and down in his seat. But unlike Kunkel, he didn't have a mark on him. Director Calvin Hunter had issued strict orders that no one was to talk to either prisoner until they were in custody in D. C. But Norman felt he had earned the right to ask just a few. And so he asked, "What got you into the killing business, Clarence?" Silence. "Tough guy," Norman responded. "Try this, did you think we'd never catch you?" Silence. Then one of the guards reminded Norman of the Director's order, and Norman backed off.

At two in the afternoon, the plane carrying Agent Norman Ziegler, Militia Leader Gerard Kunkel, and Congressional Killer Clarence Henry, touched down at the Marine Base, in Quantico, Virginia. A sleeve-like contraption was drawn tightly over the door of the aircraft. Absolutely no one was to see these two prisoners emerge from that plane. At the bottom of the steps a windowless prisoner van was waiting to carry them to their cells. The two prisoners were strapped in and whisked off to separate cells in Quantico's Brig. Once inside, the biggest Marine anyone had ever seen uncuffed and unchained Gerard Kunkel. Kunkel responded, "Thank you, sir," and walked meekly into his cell.

Good boy.

A similar scenario played out at Clarence Henry's cell. Both men were on suicide watch. Cameras were on them unceasingly.

Chapter 47

Interrogation specialists are surprisingly laid back. At least that's how they appear to those they face when practicing their craft. Kunkel got a double surprise when he was led into the interrogation room. Seated at the table was a lovely young woman who identified herself as Special Agent Gloria Fitzhugh.

She just wanted to ask a few questions, and was that all right? When she told the guards to uncuff Mr. Kunkel and leave, they didn't know what to do. Clearly, she had the authority to order them out of the room, but they had a duty to protect her. "It'll be okay. Mr. Kunkel needs a smoke, and I need to score a few points with him." Kunkel was on guard, but charmed at the same time. He wondered if Special Agent Gloria Fitzhugh was some kind of Kung Fu expert who didn't require guards to protect her, or was she just crazy?

"That's better," she began after the guards left. "Coffee, Mr. Kunkel?"

"Black," he responded.

She got up from her chair and walked to the coffee maker. When she returned, she smiled at Gerard Kunkel and handed him his coffee. He thanked her warily.

"Mr. Kunkel," she began, "do you have any questions you'd like to ask me?"

Kunkel didn't know what to say. He knew why he was in custody, but for some reason he didn't understand, he wasn't angry at this particular Fed. All he could get out was a much restrained, "Let's just get on with it, shall we?" Before she could reply, he hastily added, "I'd like to have a lawyer, if you don't mind, Ms. Figzhugh. I know my rights."

Agent Fitzhugh just stared at her opponent. "When I was a girl," she began, "I had a younger brother named Dennis, and sure enough, we called him Dennis the Menace. He had an independent streak bordering on the fierce. He never wanted to do anything the family wanted to do. 'I'm not going,' was his standard response to everything from church to parties. My father invoked his two-line litany every time Dennis announced

249

that he was not going. Daddy would say, 'Dennis, there's an easy way, and there's a hard way. Your choice, but you are going.' Invariably, it was the hard way. I used to feel so sorry for them both. Neither one could quit the behavior that pained them."

Surprisingly, Kunkel asked, "Still?"

"Naw," she replied. "Daddy died before Dennis was old enough to have any sense. In case you give a shit, Mr. Kunkel, when you asked for a lawyer, it reminded me of my dad and my younger brother. Asking for a lawyer is telling me you want to do this the hard way. Am I right?"

In spite of himself, this gorilla of a man, used to commanding and getting, laughed out loud. "Well, I'll be damned," he said. "Never thought of it that way. How can I help you, Special Agent Fitzhugh?"

"Just talk to me," was her answer. "I'm well aware of your rights, and I'll not trample them, unless, of course, you insist on doing this the hard way. The sooner we just chat, the sooner you're out of here. As soon as I hear nothing more about a lawyer and your rights, the sooner we'll be finished, here. Clear?" She smiled charmingly.

"Clear," he responded.

"Good," she said. "Now tell me what it is about our government that you hate."

"It looks like I'll never get out of here," he laughed.

Agent Fitzhugh added her hearty laugh to his. "I know, I know," she said. "Mind if I run a tape for posterity?"

"Knock yourself out. Hope you gotta lotta tape." They both laughed again.

Gerard Kunkel was in his element. He wasn't asked anything about himself, his organization, his finances, what he'd been up to for the last 25 years. Nothing. Just tell the nice agent what he hated about the government. It took him two days before he began to repeat himself. Agent Gloria, as he began to call her, was spellbound. The man could really weave a story.

For the first time in his life, Kunkel didn't reach into his standard lines, so familiar to his faithful. Instead he let his mind go free, and his speech followed in an unorganized way, unfamiliar to him. It was nice.

First and foremost, he thought that every American should be required to own at least one gun, and that shooting a gun should be a required subject in every grade from K-12. He thought the only thing the Congressional Killers did wrong was to kill NRA leaders, and to try to make ammunition illegal to buy. But he sure was in favor of killing the Congress. He only wished he'd been a part of it. Maybe he'd take up where that group left off.

When he got to taxes and the government giving billions of our hard earned money to foreign countries, like Columbia, he became so animated and so loud that the guards looked through the window to see if Agent Fitzhugh was okay. She was.

His biggest gripe centered around attitude. "Clearly," he said, "the government thinks it knows best. And it doesn't. It looks down its patrician nose, sniffs, and tries to cover the smell it imagines emanating from all of us below. When natural disasters strike anywhere else in the world, the U. S. of A. sends billions to be given away. The money never gets to the people. We all know that. It goes into some Swiss account with the local politician's name on it. But let the mighty Mississippi flood out hundreds of miles of American families, and the god damn government loans, *loans*, mind you, American tax paying citizens their own confiscated money to rebuild. That's wrong. Why ain't we good enough to get the same free money as some damn earthquake victim in Turkey?

"We can't drink our water anymore. You know that yourself, Agent Gloria. I'll bet you drink some designer water from those little plastic bottles, don't you?" Her smile gave her away, but only encouraged Kunkel to keep on. "I'm surprised anyone still lives in New Orleans. Everyone living along the Mississippi dumps something into it, and long before it reaches New Orleans, the water is toxic. There's more cancer in the population of New Orleans than in any other city in America. That's a fact. Why can't the all knowing, all mighty government spend all of the money it gives away to foreigners, and clean up our water supply? You tell me that. But, no. They say, vital interest, and shit like that. Vital interest, my ass. If we're all poisoned by, or get cancer from, our drinking water because we gave all of our money to foreign vital interest, what good is that? We're all dead, including the government. Some jackass pipsqueak from West Bum-Fuck will walk in and take over. But I'm here to tell you that ain't never going to happen as long as I'm around."

Kunkel's most vitriolic ammunition was aimed at Arabs, (which he pronounced A-rabs), Muslims, and our government's inability or unwillingness to bomb them back into the stone age. Kunkel wondered why no one ever got on the talk shows, and asked why A-rab Muslims never sent any aid to their A-rab Muslim brothers when a disaster hit.

"Where was Saddam's army when Bosnian Muslims were being attacked by non-Muslims? Nowhere, that's where. But the all knowing, all mighty and wise government of the United States of America sends our money and our soldiers to do for the fucking A-rabs what their fucking A-rab brothers don't or won't do. And then the sons of bitches send terrorists into our country because we're the evil ones in the world. Explain that one to me. Make me president, and I'll show those fuckers what would happen if they so much as touched one single American."

When Kunkel's vitriolic wad was shot, Special Agent Gloria Fitzhugh left and was replaced by the second team. They were the hardball players, getting Kunkel's vita and organization information. He gave them nothing. He wanted his lawyer, now. Instead, he got strapped down on a table, an injection of truth serum was administered, and Kunkel answered every question without hesitation.

Then the truth serum drip was replaced by another clear liquid bottle, containing a different solution. By the time it dripped into Kunkel's arm and traveled to his brain, where it began to destroy certain memory cells, Kunkel's expression changed from one of intelligence to benign lunacy. The needle was removed, Kunkel was given new clothes, boarded on a military aircraft, and flown to San Francisco, where he was released in the middle of Chinatown. He had $200 in his pocket, no identification, and no idea where he was or how he got there.

In the year of our Lord 2006, what could a man expect if he went up against the good government of the U. S. of A.?

Chapter 48

Clarence Henry fared the same as Gerard Kunkel. His interrogator, however, was just the opposite of Kunkel's. Special Agent Duk Ki Han was a third generation Korean-American. Han had no accent. English was his only language, although he wished his parents had taught him Korean. But like so many descendents of foreign-born parents, Duk Ki's wanted their son to be a thoroughly languaged American. Korea was the past. The future was 100% American. When other ethnic groups complained about Orientals getting ahead and getting all the breaks, Duk Ki tells them to learn to speak English, clearly and properly. What corporation wants to trust its products into the hands of a spokesperson who can't be understood?

Like Gerard Kunkel, Clarence Henry arrived in handcuffs. But unlike Kunkel, Clarence's handcuffs stayed on. Duk Ki Han didn't know what to make of the man. He had been part of a group that had killed 244 American congressmen and women, and many others who were lobbyists, IRS officials and NRA leaders.

"Mr. Henry, I'm Special Agent Duk Ki Han, and I'm going to ask you many questions. It may take several days, but we'll get through this with or without your co-operation." Duk Ki Han didn't waste any time establishing dominance.

"I want a lawyer," was all Clarence would say after each and every question Agent Han asked.

"Mr. Henry," Duk Ki tried again, "I'm afraid the straightforward question and answer method isn't going to work with you. I'm going to leave for about half an hour. When I return you will be strapped down on a gurney, and a needle will be in your arm. The bag of solution connected to that needle will be full of something we call truth bubbles. Of course, there is no guarantee that you won't have a violent reaction to the chemicals after we're done with you. At least half the people we hook up to the bag commit suicide in less than a week. The other half go mad within six months. But before all of that happens, we get all the information out of you that you now refuse to give me voluntarily."

Henry sneered, "You can't do that. I have rights, you know."

"Not here, Mr. Henry. Not here. Your ass is mine, and I determine what rights you have. Believe me, once I hook you up and turn that drip on, you won't give me any more lip. Clear?"

"Whatever," was Henry's sneered reply.

As soon as Agent Duk Ki Han was out of the room, Clarence Henry's guards opened the door to the interrogation room and wheeled in a gurney. Unceremoniously, they hoisted him up and strapped him down. Next a woman dressed in a white nursing uniform entered, hung a bag of clear liquid on the pole attached to the gurney, cleaned a spot on his arm, and inserted a long needle into a vein. Clarence Henry wet himself, and he began to cry. For the next 28 minutes he lay there wondering how he got himself into this mess.

Han came brusquely through the door and reached for the drip, to turn it on. Clarence found his voice. "Another chance, Agent Han? Please! I'll tell you anything you want. Just don't turn me into a vegetable!"

"Too late, I'm afraid, Mr. Henry. You had your chance," responded Han. With that he reached up to turn on the drip. But the handle broke off. "Damn," Han swore. "I'll have to get another one."

Clarence began to scream and fight his restraints. Of course the broken drip was all theater, designed to get Clarence to volunteer his information. From the hallway, Han shouted, "What do you mean there aren't any more? How do you expect me to do my work?" He stormed back in and ripped the needle out of Clarence's arm. Blood spurted everywhere. Han called for the nurse. She appeared and bandaged Clarence's bleeding arm. "Get him out of those restraints, too," he ordered. "Your lucky day, Mr. Henry. You've taught me a very good lesson, I want you to know. I should be more gentle when I turn one of those damn things on. Now, can we get on with it?"

"Yes, yes, Mr. Han, whatever you say. Thank you, Mr. Han, thank you," Clarence babbled. It was pathetic, Han thought. And so predictable. Amateurs!

"Where and when were you born, Mr. Henry?"

"Detroit, 1950."

"What was your father's name?"

It went like that for half an hour. Agent Han was like a good physician, taking an accurate history of his patient.

"How did you become involved with the Congressional Killers?"

" I was contacted by letter, nearly three years ago. By a gentleman known to me as Williams."

"And who was he?"

"At first I thought he was a nut case. But he wasn't. He was a Welshman capable of anything. I never did find out how he found out about my hatred of the IRS and my 18-year battle with the bastards, but he knew all about it. He sent me a one way ticket to D. C. to talk to him about a job he thought I'd enjoy. Boy was he right. I shot Congressman Martin Koyn, Chairman of the House Ways and Means Committee, on that first day, you know. Of course, you don't. I'm just telling you now."

"How many assassins were there?"

"Close to 20, if I remember correctly. Please don't hold me to an exact number. I'll do my best to name them all for you, but I've never really totaled them. Bear with me."

Han pressed on. "Was Noah Slutski one of the assassins?"

"Yes. I think he was the oldest, but I don't remember exactly. We didn't celebrate our birthdays, or anything like that."

"Was Edmund Sargent Reynolds one of the assassins?"

"Yes. He shot Congressman Quigley, Chairman of the Environment. Sarge lost his ranch in Montana, you know. The fucking government forced him out. He and I especially hated the government for its cruel stupidity and its uncaring, uninformed trouncing of us common folk. But we got a lot of the bastards, didn't we? The country wanted us to kill 'em all, you know."

"Yes," Han responded. "I'd heard that numerous times."

After several hours, Agent Han could see how very tired Clarence Henry was. The gurney routine had been especially taxing, both physically and emotionally. Han ended the session abruptly and told Clarence that they would begin again in the morning. Clarence was grateful and said so. He felt like he'd been pulled through an old fashioned wringer on top of a 1940's washing machine.

But Agent Han had plenty of energy left, and several hours of work to do on his preliminary report. Henry had identified every other assassin he could remember, and Agent Han wanted to get their names into the Director's hands immediately. Han knew the names were all aliases. Henry's own name within the group had been Armstrong. Samuel Armstrong. Everyone had called him Sam.

Bright and early, Clarence Henry was again in the interrogation room, but Agent Han did not keep the cuffs on him. He ordered them removed. Clarence thanked him. He apologized for the bad beginning they had had yesterday. Agent Han was gracious in victory, and waved it off as nothing. Then he began the questions again.

" Tell me about the money. Why $10 million?"

"Originally, our agreement with Williams had been for $5 million, but we were told that $5 million didn't go as far as it used to, and a bonus of another $5 million was added at the very end."

"How were you to get your money?"

"By fax. All we had to do was find a public fax. Since last year, electronic banking has become instantaneous. No more waiting for the banks on either end to clear the prompt, and to credit your account the next day. No, no, no. It was just type in your bank number, type in the number you wanted your money to come to, and push send. It took two minutes, and you had instant confirmation that your money was wherever you directed it to go. But when Max Stroble committed suicide, the game was over for those of us who hadn't gotten our money out before he did his big nasty."

The remainder of day two consisted of questions regarding living arrangements, monthly salaries, and how the assassins had gotten inside the Capitol building and planted 56 deadly cyanide devices.

Day three was the all-important day for Clarence Henry. Agent Han wanted to know where they were all headquartered. He was astonished when told. He interrupted the interview and phoned Director Hunter.

"Sir, you were right from the very beginning. The 'Center,' as Mr. Henry calls it, is in an abandoned underground parking facility next to the *Been There, Done That* building. The assassins went down in the common service elevator that led to the basement showers, and laundry and food storage facility. A specially designed clicker device closed the left side of the elevator car with the first click, and the second click opened the right side of the car into the Center. A third click closed the right side and automatically opened the left side again, leading into the shower and laundry area. Unless you had a clicker, the elevator only gave you access to the basement under the *Been There, Done That*. That's why we could never find any evidence of anything inside the old church."

"Well, I'll be damned," Cal Hunter sighed. "Clarence wouldn't happen to still have his clicker, would he?"

"I'll find out, sir," Han said. "Can you hold the line?" In three minutes Han was back. "Sir, Mr. Henry said that his clicker was on his key ring. It looks like a pen flashlight you might use in the dark, to see your car door lock. He left his key ring in the top drawer beside his bed. Thank you, sir. Yes, sir."

Chapter 49

Cal Hunter was too excited to do anything immediately. Instead, he asked his secretary if she minded getting him a Boston creme donut and a coffee. The case had gone on too long to suit him, but he was unwilling to give it up just yet. Instead of calling the president first, he called his brother in law Phil Ridley, editor of the *New York Times*.

"Phil, it's Cal. Got a minute? I want you to send your best photographer and D. C. stationed reporter to my office in the next 20 minutes. Got that Phil? Talk to you later."

Ridley didn't know what was up, but he knew it must be big. He called his assistants who managed the D. C. beat, and secured the names and numbers of the people Cal Hunter had asked for. Ridley called both immediately, and each answered. They thought it was some kind of a joke, until Ridley gave them his personal number at the *Times* and asked them to call him right back. They did, and both made it in the nick of time, just as the Director of the FBI was about to crack the Congressional Killers case.

Hunter also called WBZZ, and asked for a film crew to meet him at his office immediately. He had something he thought the world would love to see and hear.

Agents were directed to enter Clarence Henry's apartment on Sixth Street between F and G Streets. They were to bring back nothing except the set of keys next to Mr. Henry's bed. With keys in hand, Cal Hunter set off with an excited entourage in tow. He was driven directly to the *Been There, Done That* social service center, and led the group to the service elevator just off College. He took reporters and photographers with him down one floor.

A vast expansive room opened to their left. About seven or eight men were emerging from the showers. They quickly ducked back in when they saw the crowd. Cal Hunter clicked the clicker and nothing happened. His heart sank. Cameras were rolling. He tried the clicker again. Nothing. Then he knew he should have waited, and followed procedure. He reached for his cell phone and called for 50 agents to descend on the place, ASAP.

It was clear to everyone there that the Director of the FBI had anticipated something would happen when he pressed that little device. But whatever was supposed to happen, hadn't. Strike one. They could wait. It seemed like the logical thing to do.

Within 10 minutes of Hunter's distress call, agents were tripping over each other. Hunter took his Deputy Director aside and told him what he knew, and what had happened.

"Jackhammers," was all George Sprong said.

Cal Hunter also directed Rohan Holiday to send someone down to the city building, where building plans were kept, and to bring back all plans of any renovations to the parking garage that used to stand next to the church. He didn't care how old or new they were. Just bring them all. Next he spoke to several other agents, and there was a scramble to leave the premises that was every bit as urgent as the scramble to arrive had been.

Two hours later proper warrants were in hand, as were several workmen with large jack-hammers. By this time, the old plans for the parking garage that had once stood on the site next to the church were in hand. It had been razed in 1983, but the two underground floors were not effected by the blast, according to Clarence Henry. Only a few at the scene knew they were only moments away from entering the lair of the Congressional Killers. All the others just waited, and waited, and waited.

The two men trying to jackhammer through the cement directly behind the elevator wall were cursing and ready to walk off the job. They'd already broken two bits, and there was no ventilation down there. Cal Hunter personally appealed to them to keep at it.

After six hours, the crew called it quits. They had only been able to clear four feet in front of them, and they had no idea how much further they had to go to get to wherever it was the Director wanted them to get. Besides, they were tired and hungry. A replacement crew was called in. According to the plans, the first underground floor of the old garage should be another eight feet away. It was going to be a long night. Cal Hunter went home, feeling defeated and at the same time, hopeful.

He was back at the scene bright and early. He had called the president with the news, but cautioned him not to expect anything for at least another day or two. He also called his brother-in-law and told him the straight scoop.

The story leaked, and television crews from all over the world began to line up everywhere. Yards were overrun. People were screaming at each other. A few fistfights broke out. Reporters droned on and on about what progress the jackhammer crews were making, and just how tense everyone was at the scene.

Near noon, one of the jackhammer men came running up out of the elevator shaft. Reporters shouted at him "Tell us! Tell us!" He'd never faced a camera before, and he didn't know what to do. Even when he tried to talk, reporters kept shouting their questions. A policeman saw the poor guy's problem. He elbowed his way through the crowd, took his gun out of his holster, and fired into the air three times. Everyone ducked, or fell to the ground. When they got up, the cop still held his gun up in the air and yelled, "Quiet! Let the poor man talk!"

A public address system had been set up for this moment, or for any others that were sure to follow. "I can't believe what I saw," the worker began.

The parking lot went nuts all over again. Reporter shouted one question after another. The cop fired again, took the mike from the worker, and said, "Next one who interrupts this guy, I'm going to shoot."

Instant quiet. The man continued. "Me and Louie broke through all the concrete about five minutes ago. And we started to smell something very foul. Each of us thought the other one farted, you know what I mean. Close quarters, and all that." There was general laughter from the crowd. "Anyway, when we got all the concrete out of the way, there was a plywood wall that we started to knock apart with our jackhammers. It started to run through the holes we made in the plywood. The place is full of some kind of shit! I'm outa here!"

Chapter 50

CIA Director Robert Benton was in his office when the call came. He stiffened upright in his seat. The caller didn't identify himself, but there was no need. Benton recognized Jack Sparks' voice instantly.

"Bob," Jack said, "can we talk?"

Benton's head spun as conflicting emotions filled him. Outrage at the killings, anger at Jack's escape from his agents in Zurich; then the quick realization that Jack could be extremely valuable to him. Benton's political savvy won out, and he calmed down.

He depressed the button that turned on the tape recorder, and alerted others to trace the call. "Go ahead, Jack,' he said cordially, his 'old friend' tone only partly faked. "I've been wondering what you've been up to."

I'll bet you have, Jack thought. Thanks for sending the friendly questioning committee to Zurich. "I want to make a deal," he said bluntly.

Jack had been a fugitive too long to suit him. He'd always been a tough guy, but after a few nights in the old hanger he realized this wasn't fun anymore. Driven by serious hunger, and what he had to admit was the simple desire to be warm, dry, and comfortable forced him to break into two homes and three stores for a few bare necessities. And he knew he could no longer touch his money, or establish himself permanently anywhere. He had no desire to spend the rest of his life like this. He was too old. It was time to come in from the cold.

"With what?" Benton replied, just as directly. He had always liked Jack's no-nonsense manner.

"Information," Jack said. "You know I was involved with the Congressional Killers. I see on the news where Hunter cracked the case, and I've got a pretty good idea who his source is." Jack was partially bluffing here. "That source doesn't know a fraction of what I do. I worked closely with the people who planned it, and I know every little detail. Most importantly, I can name the source of the money behind the whole operation."

Benton believed Jack. The man was too good at his trade not to have become an important part of the operation. Benton knew Cal Hunter didn't have all the facts of the case yet, and might not get them all. But he was probably on the verge of finding out who had financed the killings. The fact that Cal Hunter and his men had solved the case first galled Benton. But now this stroke of luck! My God, what an opportunity to upstage the FBI, he thought. What timing! He fought to keep the excitement out of his voice.

"What do you want in return?" he asked.

"My money," Jack said. "And call the hounds off. Leave me alone. Permanently"

Benton weighed the options. Jack was still loose out there, and the resources and incentive to chase him would be much decreased once Cal Hunter went public with enough details of the case. They'd probably never catch Jack anyway. And the chance to one up the FBI with this scoop filled him with glee.

It wasn't a moral issue for the Director of the CIA. "Deal," he said. "The money and total immunity. How do we work it?"

"Ball's in your court. Take all surveillance off all of my accounts. The day I move my money I'll fax you the details, the whole story, including my name and part in it. A real confession. I'll make you look really good, and the information is invaluable for dealing with future groups like this. You'll get the fax, you know my word's good."

Benton did know. They agreed on the time of the transactions. There was a moment's silence, then Jack spoke.

"I'm taping this too, Bob. I know I can trust my old friend. But one sign I'm being followed, just one, and the tape goes public. And you're a dead man, politically speaking. You know you'll never catch me first."

Chapter 51

By now, the odor from the pig shit began to waft into the air, and people began to hold their noses and move back. How did this old underground parking garage collect so much shit? Had a sewer line broken, and the stuff backed up? The FBI must have been given a bum lead on this one, because nobody would ever be able to work in that smell for 20 seconds.

Cal Hunter called Duk Ki Han at Quantico. "Better get your man to tell the truth, Agent Han. We've drilled through 12 feet of concrete to get to a container of shit. Call me right back."

Duk Ki Han looked at Clarence Henry for a full minute, and then asked him if he enjoyed his little game. Clarence was genuinely befuddled. He didn't understand. Agent Han told Clarence what his boss, the Director of the FBI, had just told him. Clarence began to laugh hysterically. Han let it play, then asked what he found to be so funny.

"Don't you get it, Han? Probably some of the others stayed behind and trashed everything. Then they filled the place with some kind of shit. It was their final way of sticking it to official Washington D. C. I'm telling you that there were two floors, at least four or five thousand square feet in size behind that elevator car. Now you're saying that those two rooms are full of shit. Don't you get it?"

Unfortunately, Agent Han did get it. He called Cal Hunter right back and told him what Clarence Henry had just said.

The neighborhood around the *Been there, Done That* began to smell so badly that several of the residents left town to visit family. The stuff was officially identified as pig waste. A full-scale pumping project awaited Cal Hunter and the FBI.

Pumps were brought in, but the liquefied pig shit seeped through regular dump trucks, which dribbled and spread the cargo from the loading spot to the dumping destination. D. C. roads were being covered with the stinky, slippery stuff. The press loved it. So did the American people. Washington D. C. awash in pig shit. How'd they like a taste of their own medicine?

A better way had to be found to transport it to someplace else. Tanker trucks would solve the problem, but who in his right mind would use his tanker to haul away pig shit? Milk or corn oil could never again be carried in it after pig shit.

Or so they thought. Four United States Senators were called. Two were from Iowa, where they knew something about pigs and pig shit. Two from North Carolina were also called, for the same reasons. Could they be of any help to the FBI? Doubtful, was the answer. Neither state needed any more, thank you.

Much to his surprise, Cal Hunter received a phone call from a farmer named Lester Bergemann, in North Carolina. Lester was a pig farmer and a patriotic American citizen. For $35,000 per tanker truckload, he'd take all the pig shit the FBI could send him. He'd just built a new holding pond for the stuff on his farm, and that little bit of content from up north wouldn't even be noticed on his place.

"How soon can you get your trucks up here?" Hunter asked.

"Not so fast," Lester answered. "That's $35,000 *cash*. No names. No records. No fucking taxes."

"But that's illegal. You're asking the nation's top cop to break the law."

Lester replied, "Take it or we leave it."

There was a short silence. Then, "How soon can you have your trucks here, Mr. Bergermann?"

"Tomorrow, best I can do," was the answer. "Just tell me the address." Of course Lester knew exactly where the pig shit was. So did all of his drivers. The last thing he said to Cal Hunter was, "Have $35,000 packed into nice new leather briefcases. My boys will want their money before you load the first quart into their trucks. Understand, Mr. Hunter?"

"Understood," Hunter replied.

Lester could not believe his good fortune. He got on the phone and made several calls. In turn, the called made more calls, and within the hour, Lester Bergermann had another convoy heading to D. C. to pick up the shit they'd delivered there just weeks before. The drivers had all agreed that Lester would get $10,000 per load, and they'd clean up the mess out of their remaining $25,000. Mum was the word. In fact, the drivers were to pretend to understand only every other word anyone said to them up there. They were to use the heaviest and thickest drawl they could muster. Lester wanted every FBI paymaster to think that the dumb driver got the shitty end of this deal, so to speak, and that the Yankees, once again, got over on those North Carolina hicks.

When the first 85 trucks had been loaded and were on their way, the worker loading the next truck shut down his pump. He thought he saw something big out there in the lowering shit, and if it was evidence, he didn't want it to get sucked through his hose and into the waiting tanker.

An FBI agent was asked to go down and take a look. He called for a water hose. It took nearly an hour for a fire station to hook up a supply of water to one of its hoses, and to clean off the mound-shaped object. When the hose was shut off, they all looked in complete disbelief. "Well I'll be!" the firefighter said. Sitting in the middle of all that pig shit was a D. C. police cruiser.

The D. C. cops were called, and Chief Mabon was one of the first to arrive on the scene. Cal Hunter was right behind him. So was Lynn Smolen. Sure enough, it was the missing cruiser. They couldn't see if the missing officers were inside the car, but a tow truck with a long winch would soon tell them what they all feared.

It took an hour and a half for a city tow truck to arrive. It had answered two other calls that came in before this one. No one told the driver that this one was urgent. "Hell, they were all urgent," the driver said gruffly.

The pump filled two other trucks while they waited for the tow to arrive. The cruiser's back bumper was now three inches above the level of shit. Just enough for someone to wade in and attach the hook. Since the firemen were the only ones with big boots, lots were drawn to see who the lucky guy was. "Way to go, Mikey!" could be heard two blocks away.

But Mikey wasn't laughing. He strapped on his oxygen tank and mask, pulled on his gloves, and slogged into the muck. The hook became harder and harder to pull as more and more of its cable sank into the goo behind him. Finally Mikey attached the hook to the back bumper and waded back out. He was greeted with cheers all around, and would be known forever afterwards as "Captain Hook."

The old tow truck winch began to protest the work it was asked to do. The line became tauter and tauter. It seemed to be a contest of wills. If the cable snapped and flew out of the hole, someone would surely be killed by its ferocious backlash. The operator sensed just when he thought that was about to happen, and he backed the cable off to a slack position. He told the pump guy to empty out some more shit.

Another two trucks were filled, and the winch operator tried again. This time the cruiser began to move toward the opening into the elevator car. As the cable wound backwards, it soon showed evidence that it had been somewhere not nice. The tow truck operator asked the firemen to hose off his cable as it emerged from the goo so he didn't have to live with that mess. They accommodated him.

Forensics was on the scene, but to no avail. When the cruiser was finally pulled outside, the firemen were asked to squirt as much of the offal off as they could. They were also asked not to use the highest pressure available, just in case some clue could be harvested.

The car doors were opened, and a flood of product splashed to the ground. The two partly decayed bodies of missing officers Riese and Heslip were slumped in the front seat, completely covered in pig shit. A more degrading way to be buried could not have been imagined. Chief Mabon turned away. He knew both men, and he knew their families.

Although the perimeter and setback lines were clearly drawn, cameras with long lenses were on the tops of film crew trucks, and the indignities suffered by officers Riese and Heslip were unfortunately caught and broadcast instantly. Their remains were gingerly lifted into body bags, and placed in the coroner's van. Autopsies later showed both men had died of broken necks.

They were buried with great pomp and circumstance. The President of the United States spoke at their funerals.

It took two days to pump everything out, and another week to hose down the rooms used by the killers. In sucking out the pig shit, the pumps also unknowingly removed the tiny particles of computers and supplies that Williams and the others had exploded and burned. The rooms were completely empty.

Debate went on for months whether or not to implode the underground structure, or to let the *Been There, Done That* use it for expansion and storage. Laura Isaacson, the new director of the social service agency, formally asked for the facility for future expansion. Her appeal was granted. Besides, it could always be used by the Bureau to show future agents the importance of being persistent and thorough.

PART THREE

Chapter 52

CIA Director Robert Benton looked at the fax from Jack Sparks. It was all there. Immediately he called President Huber, and told him his undercover sources had just sent the information about the Congressional Killers that he'd been expecting. Yes, it far exceeded what Hunter had discovered. Could they call a press conference immediately? Good. Yes, it named the person financing the operation. He'd bring the fax over and let the president read it for himself.

Although Cal Hunter knew that Deborah Saraf was the brains and the financier behind the Congressional Killers, he needed to hear it from Clarence Henry. He asked Special Agent Han if he minded company on what was to be the last day of the questioning of prisoner Henry. Not at all, sir, was the reply.

Even before Clarence was introduced to Director Hunter, Clarence knew who Hunter was from the TV and newspapers. Hunter's immediate impression of Clarence Henry was that he looked so ordinary and incapable of doing what he did. When the introductions were complete, Hunter asked Clarence if he would please tell him the name of the person who was the leader of the Congressional Killers. Clarence Henry smiled and said, "Certainly, sir. Her name was Deborah Sar...

"NO, NOT MY NAME!" Deborah screamed, as she writhed suddenly in her bed. Her husband Isadore was holding her hand, and their butler, Williams, was looking on anxiously. Over and over she repeated in anguish, "Not my name, not my name, please, God, not my name, not my name." Finally she lay trembling, and said she was terribly cold.

Five days before, she and Isadore had been riding horses over their estate when a sudden summer thunderstorm interrupted their outing. They knew they could make it back to the stable before the terrible winds and lightning struck, if they hurried. Isadore's gelding was in the lead, and Deborah's mare was only 20 yards behind when a lightning bolt cracked, splitting a large maple tree. Half of the tree fell and clipped Deborah squarely in the forehead, knocking her monkey over tin cup. Her

275

right collarbone was broken, as were her right arm and leg. Although the horse was untouched, the split tree trunk had nearly crushed Deborah alive. She'd been in the hospital, in a coma, ever since.

Her sudden, explosive awakening astonished her husband and Williams. Isadore held her. "Easy, darling, easy," he murmured. "Nobody is going to hurt your good name."

For the next few days Deborah Saraf fell in and out of consciousness, and upon awakening each and every time she cried out the same words; "No, not my name!" Weeks went by, and then a month had expired. Her waking time was increasing, and her sleeping time grew less disturbed. Her appetite returned, but she spoke to no one except Dr. Thompson. She was getting stronger and better, and would be ready to talk to her husband after they returned to their own home.

That day arrived, and true to her word, Deborah Saraf told her husband and their butler, Williams, the terrible dream she had had while she lay near death in the hospital. It was an incredible dream, they all agreed--detailed and chilling.

They talked of nothing else for days on end. Certainly, they had the money....

About The Author

In 1995, Tom Fairley retired from a scholarly life and moved to a resort community in North Carolina. Seeing a need for a good house cleaning business, he created and ran a company called Dirt Busters. His ordeal as a new business owner was compounded by the tax and re-tax system in our country. After paying state, federal, FICA, county and local taxes, paying workman's compensation, paying for insurance and paying suppliers, he realized everyone else was getting paid except him. He sold the business in 1998 and began to work on ***Absolute Responsibility, Strict Accountability***. Today, he researches real estate titles for his wife's law firm, and on occasion, tries to raise funds for the local sea turtle hospital.

Printed in the United States
17822LVS00001B/52-123